C000044806

The Tippling Philosopher

JEREMY JAMES

With illustrations
by Jonathan Heale

Merlin Unwin Books

First published by Merlin Unwin Books, Ludlow in 2004

Text copyright © Jeremy James 2004
Illustrations copyright © Jonathan Heale 2004

All rights reserved. No part of this book may be reproduced in any form without the prior written permission of Merlin Unwin Books

Merlin Unwin Books
Palmers House
7 Corve Street
Ludlow
Shropshire SY8 1DB

Jeremy James has asserted his right under the Copyright, Designs and Patents Act 1988 to be identified as the author of this work.

ISBN 1 873674 740

Typeset and produced by Merlin Unwin Books, Ludlow.

Printed and bound in Great Britain by Cromwell Press.

Table of Contents

For Keith Morris
The Master

I started jotting stories and comments down in pubs in the 1980s and made no secret of it. I always took a notebook with me. That was a great pleasure and a lot of fun and I still have stacks of pub notes, some of which I can actually read. Those were wonderful days and I shall not forget them: nor shall I forget to state the deep sense of gratitude I hold for the people of the valleys where that fun was to be had, and in which I now live, and in which these stories are set.

The Beguildy and Clun Valley people have embroidered the landscape into a lovely one and that landscape, for me, reflects their character: inter-dependent, strong, smiling, confident, full of warmth and goodwill. In other words: a very healthy community. But get on the wrong side of them and for a while you're on the hill in winter without a coat and it blows shot gaskets up there. I know, I live there.

But on the summery side: it's crusts-off sandwiches, beer on tap and a good anecdote. My profoundest thanks to you all for these acres of happiness.

Jeremy James, 2004

Foreword

If Somerset Maugham can name a book after a pub, then so can I and if that's where the parallel ends, that's tough. At least this book is about pubs, which his wasn't. More correctly, this book is about some of the characters who make up pubs and is the product of several decades of polishing the wood in such places, which I trust is some sort of vindication of that time in my life. At least something came from it.

Writers take notes and I am no exception, so those with whom I shared time over those decades became wittingly and unwittingly, contributors to this book. Reparcelled, rehashed and re-told in this collection, are some of the things they said.

However, even although the stories I was told at the time might have been true, this book remains a work of fiction. The characters are constructs. If someone skimming these pages catches a glimpse of themselves, then I think I do as many other writers do, which is to include fragments of friends, to be seen across a line, fleetingly: it is a salute to them, en passant, as it were, no more.

All these character are composites and do not represent anyone in particular, at all, anywhere. I have thrown events together, jumbled them up, given them a stir, seen what floated to the surface and tried to make something of it.

In order to give cohesion, I have given these stories a single setting, told them in a single voice and lived them out among a single group of characters.

To keep true to tone, I have included, where relevant, complete passages of dialogue that I jotted down shortly after I heard them, wherever that might have been - including some of the most implausible historical allusions, all of which, I have heard someone, somewhere say, and of which I have not made small event.

It's a difficult job trying to find the right voice when you are writing fiction but I hope I hit on one by chance. I found it in the sing-song Shropshire/Radnorshire dialect when I came to live on the Welsh borders in the late 1980s. It was here, working on farms, riding around on horses and staying too late at night in the locals that I made friends. What struck me about them then and still does, is the singular voice that distinguishes them, and which to me at least, is its euphony. Although it's impossible to catch the cadence of their speech on the page, the turns of phrase, the unusual words (see Glossary) are unique to the area and I felt at once, then, that that voice, that idiom of speech alone, was worth recording, if only upon the written page.

Since I first started jotting down these stories in 1987, the cultural landscape of the countryside has changed: the character of the country local has changed – in some areas more swiftly than others.

I think it would be true to say that these days, the visitor to the pub is a lot more widely - if not necessarily better - informed than he was. He or she also demands higher pub standards. Gone are the outside Gents and cellars full of iffy beer. Gone is the sawdust and Nine Men's Morris, and for the greater part, the old makeshift skittle alleys. In their place has entered the fitted carpet, dralon furniture and electronic music. The rose-covered arbour, through which the hobnail-booted local with his plug and roll-ups stumbled in for a few pints of cripple-cock, is already a thing of the past.

A few old pubs still exist, but not in anything like the abundance they were to be found twenty years ago, when pints of mild foamed across grimy bars, where only beer or cider was sold, where no children were allowed, where no music was played, where no food was offered – except pickled eggs – and no spirits – other than gin – and frequently, the beer arrived in dripping enamel jugs drawn from a wooden keg in some damp cellar, deep underground.

All that character has pretty much gone – sadly.

So one is bound to ask if the old country characters are disappearing as well?

I fear that they are.

And the reasons for this, perhaps, are partly economic: they have no place in a modern, go-getting society. Their values were different: in hindsight one wonders if, perhaps, their values were finer, more down-to-earth, kinder and a lot more tolerant of others' mistakes and shortcomings than we find these days. Certainly their vocabulary was generous. In fact I wonder if the politically correct will ever be a match for these people, who added time and understanding to their relationships, and whose general approach to their fellow-beings was far more tollerant and far more forgiving than the swift-to-accuse types one comes across these days.

There were other things about them too: the old country characters never moved far from the valleys or villages in which they lived. They came to know their surroundings very well, field by field, gate by gate, track by track, and because of this intimate knowledge, had a story, or some event to mark the significance of every place, for them, at least.

These people are very much the last of an age, and it has been a great privilege knowing them. Not that they were all rural charm and illumination to encounter: some were truly appalling.

Yet, nevertheless, their loss will be a very sad one because with them will go a sense of integrity that is a profound as the landscape that shaped them. What will also go will be a deep sense of belonging that imbued their whole being: they share cynefin, to use the Welsh term, for which there is no direct English translation. It means a spiritual belonging to a place. When they disappear, a big chunk of living history will disappear with them.

Glossary

Some of the words used in these stories will be unfamiliar to the general reader so it was thought a glossary would be instructive.

Many of the words used in these stories are peculiar to Shropshire and in particular to the Clun and Beguildy valleys.

The cadence of the English language both in Shropshire and Radnorshire lends a particular rhythm to local speech, its idioms and idiosyncrasies.

This particular glossary is adapted, abridged and extended from *Clun Dialect Words*, compiled by Sheilah Hamer and illustrated by Ruth Buckley, which was compiled in 1980 as part of the Women's Institute Domesday Book Project.

I have extended it to include some words omitted from the 1980s compilation. It still remains an an inexhaustive list.

Adland Headland of a field
Askel Newt
Bait Meal between breakfast and lunch
Beethy Limp, like unmade hay or vegetables left too long after picking
Big-sorted Puffed up with self-importance
Bing Alley in a cow house
Blart Animal noise: can be a cow, or sheep or owl, cat or dog
Bleg To tidy up
Boozey Manger
Beezom Broom – as in witch's broom
Bleat Cash, money
Bont Bump on the head
Boondooks Wilderness
Butty Friend
Caggy-handed Left-handed
Caimit Idiot
Cakey Simple minded
Canna Cannot
Castle Bishop's Castle, Shropshire
Cawsed To be cornered, barked at or chased by a dog
Clem To starve or underfeed
Clencher An alarmingly difficult thing to do
Cloff To clog up

Glossary

Comorondo A row, argument
Corks Money
Coutch To crouch close to the ground
Cratch To have a good meal
Crowsty Bad tempered
Dackey Piglet
Dawny Not sufficiently dry (of hay)
Doondering Worrying about something in a distracted way
Dunna Do not
Ellern Elderflower
Eeyore Money
Feg Long, dry grass, as in winter
Fineeg To dodge work
Flitch A side of smoked fat bacon, traditionally eaten in rural areas
Fretchit Irritable, peevish
Gaff Home
Gallous Mischeivous
Gander Glance, look
Glat Gap in a hedge
Gwathel Nasty mess
Keffel Clumsy person
Kimet Daft
Larrup To thrash
Leech Doctor
Long hooking Long period of work
Long acre Roadside grazing.
Lungeous Cruel – ill treatment of animals
Maggoty Fidgety
Manaferni Man on a Fergie (Massey Ferguson tractor), farmer
Midden, mixen Manure heap
Moither To fuss over
Ognel Awkward or contrary person
Oolert Owl
Oont Mole
Oonty-tump Mole hill
Pikel Pitch fork
Pikling Pitchforking
Pishty Sheep dog puppy
Poother To poke about aimlessly
Purdey General expression for a shotgun
Quist Wood pigeon
Ratling Smallest pig in a litter
Ronk To stink
Roozle Hens 'roozle' their young when they gather them close
Sclem A rogue

Scort to shoot off, to speed away
Scrat Skinflint
Scratcher bed
Scrawl To creep
Scrowge To crush, or squeeze
Sebunctious Something very special, very good
Sidleand Steeply sloping ground
Silver Buttons Uniformed police officer
Slang Long, narrow meadow
Sniving Crawling, ie crawling along or crawling with
Starve To feel desperately cold
Surree Familiar way of addressing someone (e.g. How bist 'ee surree?)
Swodgey Big and sway bellied
Tallant, tallet Hay loft
Thother The other
Thrape To thrash.
Tiddling Hand-reared lamb
Tightener An amazing thing or person. Or a miser
Tirbury Peat moor
Trow Trough
Tummock Small hill
Tump Mole Hill
Welsh cuckoo Curlew
Yarb Lout
Yarping Talking in a loud or argumentative way

DIALECT PHRASES

He's got a charley on his back He's in a very bad mood
They're not cousins Not on good terms
I doubt I feel certain
The Lord hanna finished him Mentally sub-normal
Hardy as a ground toad Very strong physical constitution
Crowsty as a ground toad Fixed on a mistaken or jaundiced opinion
Pert as a spoon Bright
In with the bread and out with the cake Simple-minded
Singing out the same book Going out together, going steady
Danker me! Expression of surprise
Incomer Someone from away who has moved into the area
I canna conceit of that! I don't fancy that
Her's a bit heavy behind To be lazy

Chilled to the Bone

A bit over a twelve-month ago, when old Heavy-Behind Horace, a friend of mine, has enough wind in him to suck a stem of briar, he runs a daily routine which begins at ten or elevenish of a morning when he ups and starts himself awake with a good wad of twist.

Then after he's given this a good gnawing, he rolls out of bed, pulls on his pants, laces up his hobnails, smacks on his hat, picks up his stick, and come snow, tempest or shine he's down The White Horse bang on opening time.

So then he sets himself down by the bar, quietly, and orders himself a pint; he orders himself another; then another; and he swigs away at this stuff harking at the general hubub going on around him.

Then, when he's got about six pints down him, old Heavy-Behind looses in with how everyone present is as useless a heap of nobodys as he's ever seen; how what they're all saying is a load of horse-eggs; that there isn't one of them knows anything about anything and the whole lot of them wouldn't add up to a good pile of cold goose-poop, at that.

Then, as he is some halfway through these observations,

Queenie, the landlady, tells him that's enough of that for today, whips his beer away from him and heaves him out on the end of a good beezum so's everyone can get on with whatever they were getting on with before.

Then, after old Heavy-Behind has bawled himself hoarse on thother side of the door he goes staggering off up the hill to Gwatherel Farm, on the top of the mountain, where he lives.

And, but, although people know old Heavy-Behind is in the habit of doing these things, and people are accustomed to it, and though they say he is a bit of an old character and quite a card, what people mean, in actual fact, is that he is nothing but an old skinflint, and a garglehead, and that no idler man ever crossed the Beacon by foot or pony; in fact, people say, that however you look at it, old Heavy-Behind is the miserablist and awkwardist old wuzzuk as ever spat twist.

Anyway up, old Heavy-Behind, in that he is supposed to be some sort of a farmer, apart from these other things, specialises, at The Gwatherel in growing a larraping good crop of docks, thistles and moss.

He hasn't got any cows or sheep, or anything, and they say, people, that when the Big Stockman in the Sky puts His Knackerman on him, his farm will go under the gavel within the week just to pay off half his debts, and his son Squirrel will spend the rest of his life paying off the remainder.

That's what they say: people.

They say this because old Heavy-Behind is always down The White Horse and because all his life he's been that fond of hard work he's parked himself down beside it: which is how he comes by his name.

Anyway up, Squirrel, his son, is not like Heavy-Behind at all.

Not a bit.

Squirrel is a real grafter.

Squirrel slogs away night and day on all the farms round

about and he does not go to The White Horse at all. Never.

So people say that Squirrel is all work and no play.

This, they say, makes him a glum sort of a lad – even if he is steadier than his old man, and knows what hard work is when he clocks it.

But, they say he might as well have spent his time down The White Horse after all because he's only going to be shafted with debts, anyhow.

The years tip by and the day comes when Heavy-Behind does not go down The White Horse.

Nor the next day.

Nor the next.

No-one sees him for a week.

Instead, Squirrel comes in.

And like his dad, he sits down nice and quiet by the bar and when people ask him where his dad is he says how he's got a nasty cold and will be stopping home.

And though they say they are sorry to hear this, and they say they all miss him, in private they are glad the old duffer isn't in there hurling insults about because some of old Heavy-Behind's remarks comes a bit tight to the mark and people don't like to hear these sort of things blarted out all over the place, no they don't.

They say they are sorry to hear he's ill, then turn aside and wipe the froth off their mouths with the back of their hands and think that's a ruddy good job too.

Six months go by and Squirrel comes down The White Horse one night to say the old beggar is chewed the rind off of his last roll of pig-tail.

So they fix up a bit of a funeral, or something, with the vicar, or someone, and half the valley turns up, and they bung old Heavy-Behind in the local boneyard and that's that.

Then these people keep a keen weather-eye out for a piece of land coming on the market, just now, and cheap. And though they nudge one another, and wink and say these things, it does not occur like this.

What occurs is that Squirrel gets in The White Horse more and more, and now he is behaving like a proper slice of the old twist, and he's telling everyone, after he's had a few, that they are no more than a heap of cold goose-poop, as well, just like his dad.

So they toss him out.

Just like his dad.

Then a few days go by, and a few weeks, and not only is The Gwatherel not on the market, but the new owner is Squirrel, who has inherited it, with no debts.

No-one is able to understand this.

Not even the solicitor, from the town, who goes in The White Horse by and by, who says it is a miracle. And he says it is dead lucky, because old Heavy Behind only drew up his will the seven years before and if he'd left it six months later Squirrel would have been clobbered with Death Taxes.

And it happens, while the solicitor is in the bar saying these things, that the local leech is in there too, and he is a man by the name of Shuftiscope Sid, who is named this on account of his habit of messing around with these little hosepipe gadgets, the sort you jam in your ear-holes when you visit someone poorly, if you are a leech, to have a bit of a rootle about, to see if they're still breathing, whatever, which seems a bit of a waste since a good prod with a sharp stick would do the job just as tidy and more quick.

Anyway up, Shuftiscope says, in actual fact, that when he comes to give a cistificate for Heavy-Behind being dead, he thinks he is the coldest sort of a corpse he's even seen.

In fact, he says, he is so cold he is froze solid.

Even though this is bang in the middle of the summer.

But, he says, knowing The Gwatherel and what a poor sort of an old citadel it is, being bunged up in the middle of the mountain with all the wind and the crows, he just scribbles out the cistificate, and that's sorted that.

But then Queenie, the landlady, gets to thinking, and she says: when did old Heavy-Behind make out this will? And the solicitor says, he just said: seven years previous. Queenie says old Heavy-Behind stopped coming to the pub six months before.

So, this solicitor gets to thinking and they all get to thinking and Queenie says that considering old Heavy-Behind was poorly for six months it is strange that Shuftiscope Sid was not asked to visit him.

Then Shuftiscope Sid says that is very peculiar because no-one told him old Heavy-Behind is taken bad, ever, and the first he knows about it is when Squirrel calls in to see Bill the Box who rings him to say Squirrel has asked for a box for a dead man, and Bill the Box needs to have a proper death chart, so that's when Shuftiscope nips up to The Gwatherel to see what's what and finds this very cold corpse sitting in a chair in the kitchen, with his pants and his hat and his stick.

Then as they are discussing these matters in some depth, Squirrel drifts in the bar and plonks himself down on a stool and

rolls himself a smoke and noticing everyone has become suddenly very silent assumes all these customers are giving him the dead-eye because he has trodden in dog muck or his flies are undone or something.

So he checks these things.

Finding no dog muck on his boots and his flies well-buttoned he reckons maybe something else and, being an affable sort of a fellow, asks Shuftiscope what the matter is.

But Shuftiscope shakes his head and says nothing and that they were discussing some medical matter which just happened to finish as he walked in which has nothing to do with him.

So Squirrel orders a pint.

This he gets down him pretty sharpish because it is a boiling hot day and before long everyone is chatting away and getting not a little ratted-up when old Queenie, who has been on a very long gin session, and is a fairly direct kind of lady anyway, asks Squirrel point blank if it is true he stuffed his old man in the freezer for six months just so's he could get away with Death Taxes.

Quick as a jack snipe Squirrel says that's right, he done just that, and wouldn't she have done the same, because a corpse is a corpse is a corpse, and if you can save a shilling, why not, especially after you'd spent all your life slogging your heart out working all the hours God made just to earn enough money to keep the old blighter in booze in order for him not to mortgage the farm to the brewery, so's Squirrel could get to keep it one day. So what with Heavy-Behind signing the will six months short, it seemed to Squirrel not unreasonable to chill his bones for the missing duration until the farm was all legal and proper made over to him, and stuff the Chancellor of the Exchequer and his gang, which was when Queenie says he done right, and no-one argues with Queenie. No-one. And from that from that day to this, if anyone catches a cold in The White Horse, they calls it a Heavy-Behind.

All Hang Together

Kipper Northern is an uncommon kind of commodity it has to be said, a rare specimen, a long, stringy sort of a creature with long, dangly arms and long, dangly hands and he's got these pale blue eyes and pale skin and he always looks half-ate out from the inside, somehow, as if he's got a rat in there, gnawing him away, bit by bit, or maybe it has something to do with him going down the valley for his dinner, all the while, which he absorbs in liquid form, like one or two others I knows about here.

Anyway up, Kipper Northern, he ranches a stretch of moss and sedge and gorse and hummocks over the mountain somewhere, with this heap of Welsh Blacks and hairy cobs, as in fact, resembles, more closely those woolly rhinocerous gadgets they got photos of in the museum in Ludlow. And he runs this dose of Kerry sheep up there and a three-legged Suffolk tup or two up to their eyes in the tirbury.

And, but, like everyone else, Kipper, he has a duffed-up blue Landrover all caked up in mud, all bunged full of sheepdogs, with a sign on the back as says: 'Baby on board', only the baby bit is crossed out and he has scratted 'sheepdog' instead. And in with the sheepdogs, there's cake sacks and string, and wire, and sticks, and drench sacks, and bottles of jollop, and leggings and a few stakes – much the same kind of stuff as everyone else. And, as I says, Kipper, he is prone on occasion, well, every day, in fact, to nip down the valley to The Buffalo, for his dinner.

And so, this January past, of a Thursday, he is in The Buffalo debating with thothers, in there, about this and that, while running the obligatory errand from one end of this place to thother, in order to put one type of liquid in here while getting another type of liquid from there, as he is fond of this habit, like thothers, for some reason, and is apt from time to time to regard this liquid from there as some kind of therapy, and nutriment, which it is as it makes him very glad to be partaking of it, by and by.

And, but, the thing is, he is also much taken up, at the same time, with an advert in The Star about a motor auction on down in Kingsland where there is this Special Four-Wheel Drive motor gadget going on the nod.

And Kipper, being as he is a man prone suddenly to be took-up-with-things, especially if he has been in The Buffalo for a while, and has this took-up-with-things disease quite bad, in fact, for a bloke like him. And also, this disease strikes him extra hard if these things happen to be in auctions, which he could get to, just, and smack a bid on.

So now, on this Thursday, Kipper finds himself hankering very hard for this special Four-Wheel Drive going on the nod in Kingsland.

And even though he puts the paper down, and plays a round of cribbage, and darts, and shove half-penny, and puts on his favourite music and then plays Nine Men's Morris, he cannot stop himself dreaming about this Special Four-Wheel Drive gadget, and him driving it; how he really needs it, why he needs it more than anything else in the world, and how every way he looks at it, he sees this is just what he's been after, even though he only saw the thing advertised about twenty minutes ago.

So he goes back to this newspaper, picks it up and reads about it all over again.

An hour tips by and he says to Knukky Stubbs as he intends to go down to Kingsland to bid on this motor.

But, Knukky Stubbs, being a man not suddenly took-up-with-things, says he should not do this. He should wait until this took-up-with-things spell is burned out.

And, but, also, he should not do this buying of this Special Four-Wheel Drive gadget either on account as no-one else in the valley has a motor like this and if he gets it then everyone will know where he is all the while.

He will not be able to park it outside The Buffalo without everyone knowing he is in there – especially his missus when he told her he was going to be doing a stroke, somewhere, perhaps.

No, Knukky Stubbs says, stick to your blue Landrover like everyone else, specially because when Silver Buttons comes along from Ludlow at night, he cannot tell whose is whose, because he cannot see the number plates through the mud, and being all the same colour does not know which one to chase, which is why everyone is safe with the same muddy blue Landrovers.

But, the thing is, Kipper cannot shift this thing from his mind.

It is stuck in there: fast.

And, but, Kipper, it has to be said, knows himself well enough to reckon as the only way to do this now, is to go to Kingsland and get it. Even though he knows, in fact, as this is a big mistake. And he knows also, that if he stops thinking about it, just for a day, he will forget about it. Even for half a day.

But he doesn't do this, on account of a kind of needing-to-have-the-thing-he-just-saw-immediately disease, which usually people have when they can't afford the needed-to-be-had-thing, as well. It is in fact true to say that quite a lot of people suffer from this disorder, a most financial debilitating terminal disorder and makes them as have it, totally bankrupt all the while, which causes them to be miserable, which makes them do it more and more.

And so Kipper, because he knows this auction is on now, today, he scorts off to Kingsland quick as a jacksnipe.

As soon as he arrives, he jams his Landrover in the Late

Entrants, rushes over to the gaffer for a lot number and bungs a 'No Warranty No Reserve' on it.

So now, he is very deeply committed indeed to proceedings at Kingsland auction, one way and another.

And, but, so now, Kipper is beginning to feel hot, a bit, and although he hears this little voice screaming away inside his head, he ignores it. Even though this voice is bawling at him that he really needs a fresh motor like he needs a bigger bill from the Inland Revenue.

Up comes the bidding on this tool, and Kipper in that he is keen, and everyone knows he wants this car by now as he has been sitting in it for an hour, they run him up something evil and he has to fork out full whack for this thing, which is a lot more eeyore than he would have paid if it was gold-plated in the garage in the village.

But even though he knows this, and this makes him feel sick, he tries not to look at the cheque as he is writing it.

And then he does not wait to see what his Landrover fetches as he has abandoned that and that's that as far as he's concerned. He doesn't care if it fetches nothing.

So he jumps in this new Special Four-Wheel Drive of his, which only just makes it to the petrol station. In the petrol station, Kipper, he fills it up and this is when he has a near cardiacal stoppage, when he is forced to part with the bleat for a tankful of juice on this thing and Kipper, when he jumps back inside, notices he is sweating somewhat, on account of this and that, and Kipper, although he knows he ought to do a little mental arithmetic, does not do any.

Instead, he turns this thing's CD player on only there is no CD in it.

So he turns the radio on and tries to hark at this instead, only he cannot understand how the thing works.

So he goes off down the road at full bore, without any radio, or music but he thinks to himself as this does not matter. This is one posh outfit, there is no mistaking this.

He is back in The Buffalo at nine-ish.

Inside The Buffalo, Knukky Stubbs asks him if he gets this motor.

He says yes.

So Knukky goes and inspects it and says as this is a evil tool, and costly in every respect. It is not, he says, a wise thing to do to have a motor like this. If he sticks this new white motor in the ditch he will not be able to haul it out with chains and lumps of wood and tractors and stuff because it is too expensive to mend.

If you bend your Landrover, nobody minds.

If you bend a Special Four-Wheel Drive gadget, everybody minds.

And, but, the thing is, motors like that are only properly owned by people who live on the M25.

But this advice is of no interest to Kipper.

No, he says, he likes this new Special Four-Wheel Drive.

So Knukky says, well, that's up to him then and since he can afford to buy a motor like that it's his turn to buy the next round.

Anyway up, a few months slip by and Kipper is running round in this thing extra cautious not to put a mark on it, and people notice he seems to be spending a lot of his time in the petrol station in the village, nowadays.

When Knukky Stubbs asks him if this is true, he does not deny this.

He says, actually, this motor is making him extra stressed and debilitated and doing things to his bank account as he dares not find out what.

And, but, also, his missus knows where he is all the time, just like everyone said.

And he says it is expensive in every respect, just as Knukky Stubbs says.

And you cannot fill it with sheep.

Then he says, actually, he feels very ultra conspicuous driving around in this thing anyway, and is pretty certain Silver Buttons from Ludlow has got his evil eye on him. But, he says, he reckons he might just hang on to it a bit longer to see what it's like in snow, because he's heard that these motors are good in snow.

Well, then the snow comes and Kipper is skimming up across the mountain to The Buffalo one evening, and on the way back, slams this Special Four-Wheel Drive into a good dyke, and though he gives it plenty of juice, and spins the wheels, and then tries to do it all again only more slower this time, he cannot get it out.

It will not go forward and it will not go back.

So he begins, very seriously, to dislike this motor.

In fact, there is not much about it that he likes anymore, at all. Not even the wood on the dashboard, or the leather seats or the tinted windscreen or the big tyres – which don't seem to do much for getting this car out of this hole.

And even though he punches the wood on the dashboard, and bites the steering wheel, still it will not crawl out.

He tries everything.

He even gives it a good kick in the radiator and in the wheels.

But it will not climb out of this hole.

Then he scrawls back in out the snow and considers the fact that maybe he might have to kip in this motor.

He tries this.

But he cannot.

It is not designed for kipping in, even for him as he is a dead ringer for kipping anywhere at any time, anyhow, as is how he comes by his name.

Now he becomes very anxious and desperate to divest this thing out of his ownership and possession altogether.

He thinks maybe a match down the petrol tank will do the trick.

But, being a responsible ratepayer, decides not to do this. So he is forced to walk home, in the snow, and arrives back half-perished in daylight, drinks the rest of the cupboard contents and zeds off in a armchair.

Somewhere round late morning-ish, he comes to in a very muddled state, which is when he recalls the fact that his motor is jammed in a hole on the mountain.

So he thinks to hoy it out with his tractor.

So Kipper he sticks his Barbour and woolly hat on, and leans out in the blizzard as is whipping up well, clambers in his tractor, and grinds up over the hill.

But, feeling a shade dispeptic in the stomach, and migraine-ish, he thinks, half way, to cure himself by a quick visit down The Buffalo beer clinic for some therapy, then fetch the motor out on the way back – with a bit of help, maybe, from Knukky Stubbs.

But it does not happen like this.

Instead, there is a very strong representation of cow-chasers, pony-breakers and sheep-hurdlers from the valley, in The Buffalo. And they have all come on their tractors. And they are involved in some very serious debating, and whatnot, indeed.

So Kipper gets some of this stuff for himself and assists in these debates, some of which are about his new Special Four-Wheel Drive gadget, which everyone has seen is in a hole on the mountain, but he does not like to talk about this vehicle anymore. Even if it is in a hole on the mountain. On its own, with the keys in.

At booting-out time, Kipper clambers back in his tractor and fires her up having discussed with Knukky Stubbs to forget the motor-in-the-hole business, until tomorrow.

Then he trundles off the way he normally trundles over the

mountain, home to his place.

By this time the snow is whipping over the hills horizontal and there are very big drifts, which is when he goes clumping over some lump all stuck up in the ground and hears this crashing and shattering glass, which is why there is now a very creased Special Four-Wheel Drive gadget in Tranders the Scrap and why Kipper has got a muddy blue Landrover again, like everyone else, and no-one knows where he is again, like everyone else, and he is happy again, like everyone else, only a little less well off.

But I did hear thother day as his missus has had something to do with him not having a cheque book these days and has had a small word with him about dinner in The Buffalo, with the aid of a big, cast frying pan, which is why, probably, no-one has seen him of late, except for Knukky Stubbs, who crep up there to lug some heifers to the Castle market, and says, in fact, as he is looking a little fatter these days and is, in fact, since his cheque book is took off him and his bank account is took off him, a happier and wiser man.

A Little Understanding

It is a strange thing as if a animal, say a dog, does harm to a kiddy say, like bite it, or something, as people will never forget.

And, but, because they will never forget, people, they will always hold the opinion that that dog is forever to be regarded with the narrow eye, as it is a mischiefer. They say, people, as this dog is apt to be wayward, and dangerous, particularly to kiddies, even though the kiddy was busy trying to rip its ears or pull its tail or rowzle it up or something, at the time.

And so it is come about, the expression as everyone knows, to give a dog a bad name: this means that dog is forever in trouble, and suspiciousified and if someone's sheep get chased say, or something, then the blame will fall to that dog. Doesn't matter if it was another mortal being entirely as committed the offence, even if that old mutt was fast asleep in his kennel when this crime took place. They will say, people, that this dozy old article, now scratting hisself and yawning in the sun, is definitely the guilty party and needs a rare hiding for what he done. And they will say, people, that his owner has to pay damages to assist them to get over the wicked hurt and injury and shock as this creature has created.

And they will become moody and sullen and awkward for

ever more, just because they hold this opinion, whether it is true or not.

And this old flea-bit article will not be able to change their view of him, not even if he rolls over on his back and stops like that for the rest of his natural. It is that people get a fixed idea as is how the saying comes about: that once a dog has got a bad name, that is that: final.

And as I recall, as just this did happen down our way, in our parish, one day, in The Crown Inn, to Ivor the Wellies' dog, Tyke.

And this Tyke, he's only a scrit of a gadget, being some sort of diesel hound or other, or Bristol street dog or something, with a dash of Jack Russell in him and this and that. And, but, Tyke, even though he's a scruffy looking sort of a mongrel altogether, and always itching hisself, and making smells, he never does nobody no harm. Never. All old Tyke likes to do, is to go chasing after rats or mouses or coneys or sets about chewing up dead Welsh cuckoos or half-rotted old quists or something, or fetching mankey bits of old oont into the house, as he pegged out in the grass somewhere, and give him a good gnawing on the mat, in front of the fire. In fact, he is as like many old mutts as you might meet about the place, if you wanders about a bit, as we do round here.

Anyway up, this old Tyke, he is laid down quiet as a grating spider, in The Crown dinner time four Fridays back, snoozing, with his head in his paws, as we all is discussing politics or the weather or something, when this kiddy creeps up.

And this kiddy, he goes sliding up to Tyke on his belly.

And old Tyke, he opens one eye and spies this. But he does not stir, being a nice-natured old mutt, even though you can see him saying to hisself, 'Oh no, here comes a kiddy'.

Then this kiddy, he sets about to molest old Tyke and to twast up his tail in some sort of a knot, and pull his legs and stick his fingers down his ears and poke him in his belly and try to twiddle his feets inside out.

And old Tyke, being as he is a nice old dog, he takes this in his stride.

For a while.

But then, as this kiddy does not desist from doing this, old Tykes gets up and drags himself off a distance, then flops down a few yards away and closes his eyes.

But this kiddy, instead of leaving him alone, goes up to him and does this again.

So now old Tyke, he gets up and sets down quietly, as far away from this kiddy as he can.

But this kiddy seems slow on getting the message this old dog is giving him and he commences all this ear tugging and tail knotting malarky all over again.

So old Tyke gives this kiddy a bit of a warning.

He looses off with this growl.

And this growl as Tyke gives is definitely the sort of noise as is very clear to understand. What it says is: pack it in.

But this kiddy, he does not take a scrap of notice of this. He does not pack it in.

So old Tyke does it again, only a bit louder, then gets up and slinks under Ivor's chair.

So then Ivor, as is Tyke's dad, and is in fact very like him, as he is a bit of a diesel hound as well, come to that, if you look at him close enough for a minute or two, he says to this kiddy: 'Little kiddy, leave the doggy alone as he is not accustomed to kiddies and if you go annoying him, he is apt to give you a bit of a nip.'

And even though Ivor says this, this kiddy goes on.

And even though Ivor says it again, this kiddy, he goes right on until Tyke, he is had just about enough of this and gives this kiddy a good sharp nip, quick as a adder.

And the thing is, Tyke, being as he is getting on a bit, he's still as quick as a adder, and this nip he gives this kiddy happens so fast as the kiddy isn't sure it is occurred for a second or two. But then, when he twigs as he has been given one very hard bite by this scruffy looking diesel hound, who is now regarding him very close, dead-smack in the beezer and the look in his eye is very clear to read, even to a little kiddy, and the look says: if you do not clear off right now, you are going to get another one – and now the sting is beginning to smart, this kiddy, he fairly hollers out like he has got all his arms and legs ripped off.

Then this kiddy's mam, as has even been watching this performance, she goes bull-mad, even though Tyke is not in the wrong, as everyone knows, and gave this kiddy plenty of warning, and was only defending hisself, poor old devil, what else could he do? But this woman, she is out to get him.

And this kiddy's mam, she says as she is going to report Tyke to the Constabulary to have him put down for biting this little urchin of hers, and she goes on and on and on with all this kind of caper.

But, because we all know as Tyke is a soft old mutt, even though he eats sheep's daggings and chews up the parings of Ivor's horses' feets, Nonsuch and Melilot, as stinks to high heaven, and even though he sits on Ivor's knee in The Crown or The Buffalo or The Six Bells in The Castle, in fact, he is placid. Even if he does stink, we likes him, even if he does give kiddies as is annoying him a good hard nip.

And so when this woman, as is from a town as is plain to see, is trying to pin the blame on Tyke, we is quick to defend him and say it is not his fault – yet still this woman says it is.

And now, because she's a woman from a town and this is a kiddy, there's no getting around this.

So all this business is soon running up to a pretty good head and soon enough Ivor and her is screaming at one another, and here is old Tyke, slinking about guilty as a chicken coop thief, under the chairs and tables while this kiddy is bawling his eyes out and everyone is shouting as has an opinion and soon, Spud, the landlord, he steps in to prevent a big nuclear fallout here.

And so, just to keep the peace and to avoid having Silver Buttons from Ludlow actually being invited to the valley – as is a mighty periculous thing to do – Spud, the landlord, he says to Ivor as to take Tyke home and not to bring him again, even though Spud, he likes old Tyke and is always giving him lumps of bacon fat and pheasants' legs and bits of half-chewed sandwich and that as these tourists are apt to leave lying about.

And so Spud, he tells this woman to clear off, as well, with her kiddy and not to come back and though she goes off ranting and raving none of us is much concerned about her, nor her kiddy come to that as we prefers Tyke any day – but it's best not to say things like that these days on account these political correct nutters is apt to have a crack at you for it.

And so it is anyway, and perhaps you catches my drift by and by, as a dog gets a bad name. As it is not commodious or fair or anywhere near the truth.

And the thing is, it happened once a similar thing in our valley, only sort of different.

And this is a story about how country people deals with this kind of to-do, without getting all fretchit about it, and without going to the law and trying to get money from people for nothing, all because of their animals doing what animals do and it cannot be helped and no-one is rightly to blame.

It happens there is this man lives down our way called Jacob the Sheep.

And this Jacob the Sheep, he has this little bunch of these goose jobs, and Jacob, he loves these gadgets.

And these gooses of Jacob the Sheep's are a rare commodity in that they are white and have bright blue eyes and hard yellow beaks and big pink web feet and they go strutting about the place waggling their tails and hissing and spitting at every mortal as ever picked a daisy.

And these gooses of Jacob the Sheep's, he calls them by name: one is Matilda, the same name as his tortoise.

Now this tortoise job, what it does, is to go creeping about the place, cropping up buttercups and nothing else. It does not answer to its name nor do anything at all as makes a scrap of sense. And this tortoise job is likely to strike out sudden-like for some distant part of his farm and Jacob, he has to get his kiddies to go and round it up else it'll bung up his forage harvester good and tight as this tortoise gadget, Matilda, is more less like a walking rock and in every respect is unsociable and prone to keep its own council on every matter as there is. And this tortoise dunna give a twaddle if you bawls its name out or yells at it or picks it up and turns it round or anything at all, and why it is alive I do not know, nor have I any idea what it is for at all. But there it is, the Almighty made it, so I suppose there must be more of them somewhere and there must be some good purpose to them but what it is is a mystery to me.

Anyway up, the thing is, one of these gooses is also called

Matilda, and thother is called Gertrude and thother one, Bingo.

It is not certain as to why Jacob anoints them with these names, because they are just like this tortoise gadget – they dunna give a twaddle if you bawls their names out at them or yells at them or anything at them for that matter. They dunna take a scrap of notice of Jacob blarting at them anyway, even if all the veins in his neck is stood out and his face is gone purple from the effort.

These gooses, all they do is scort about the place hissing. And Jacob, he says as if he turns his back on them they attacks him, even though he is their dad, and gives them their daily bread and is every way patient with them. They still bite him. And Jacob says that without a doubt it is true to say as they are indeed the miserablist, sourest, rudest, rowdiest, commonest bunch of poultry as ever cracked wheat.

And also, these gooses, they stands outside Jacob's back door and bangs on it with their beaks and gives off this honking and blarting fit to wake the boneyard skelingtons.

And they goes on and on and on doing this until Jacob he comes out the house and gives them bits of bread or bacon rinds or anything as a goose will eat if it is hammering down your back door and leaving a heap of cold poop there for anyone as is not in the know to break their necks on, first off.

And, the thing is, if you ask Jacob as to why he keeps these creatures, he will say he does not know. He will say they are the muckiest bunch of heathens as ever honked in a valley, and that they are violent and untrustworthy and disrespectful in every respect and as far as mortal creatures go they are the worst.

And if you try to catch them, he says, you canna.

They are that canny as to make off immediate you have it in your heart to grab one. It is as if they seem to know before you have even thought it as you are intending to give them any grief. And these gooses of Jacob's if you say to him perhaps he has got them because he plans on roast potatoes and carrots and parsnips and gravy with stuffing and one of these big birds sizzling away quietly in the oven, he says he couldn't do that.

Even though, he says, these birds are terrible gadgets, he couldn't bring himself to knife one or to pounce out and throttle one, or something, to roast it up with potatoes. No, says Jacob, if he does this he will choke on it for certain.

And if you ask him if they are good guard dogs, he will tell you they are the most useless guard dogs there is.

In fact Jacob says, if anyone – say a burglar – was to come to his gaff in the midst of the night to steal his spanners or quad bike or to nick hay or pinch his cows, these geese, they would not say a thing. They would sit in their house silent as moths.

But when he, Jacob that is, comes back from The Crown of a night, walking up his track, these birds come flying out at him hissing and spitting and biting and attacking his legs and hands so as he always has to fight the last few yards to his back door.

And Jacob, he admits at times like this as he plans to murder them, but when he comes back out with his Purdey, to give them a good dose of lead in the livers, these gooses of his, they are gone.

In every way you look at it, Jacob says, these things are a very, very rare commodity indeed, but, you have to admit, that the one and only thing these gooses have got going for them is that they have a lot of style, even though that style has to be about the worst in the county.

Anyway up, two weeks last Monday night past, as Jacob is quietly stretched out in his snoring overalls, slumbering away, dead past midnight somewhen, and he is dreaming of a land where there is no gooses, he harks in his dream the sound of gooses being chased about by old Mr Renard. And as he is lying there, thinking as this is a very good thing too, Jacob, he stirs in his sleep, thinking that these noises are, in fact, outside and not inside his sleep.

And this has the effect of waking him up somewhat, so that

he harks with his awake ear to the commotion as is being wreaked beyond his back door.

And what he hears is this: he harks his gooses shrieking and screaming and creating and honking and flapping and taking off and landing and crashing against their shed.

So, Jacob, he jumps out his bed and he grabs his Purdey.

Jacob, he goes thumping down the stairs.

Jacob, he jams on his wellies.

Jacob, he dashes out into the dark with his lamping lamp. And he shines this lamping lamp out into the dark, and though he canna make out for a minute what is happening here, he suddenly spies this.

He spies one goose, Bingo, on the ground flapping, feathers flying. Thother goose, Gertrude, hobbling about with a broken leg and thother as is in the goose house but is so stirred up as it is sat in total shock and fright, rigid as a chestnut post.

And running down the track is a pair of Golden Labrador dogs.

Jacob, he looses a shot after these two dogs as he is so wild as this thing happens in his yard. As it is not on for dogs to go savaging people's poultry even if they are the most worst poultry in the neighbourhood.

And Jacob, being as he is so upset at what is happened to his gooses, even though he says he plans to murder them every day, the truth is he loves these old birds, as they have character and side and plenty of vim and besides, he has had them about his gaff for a long while, as they are part of it and of him and his home.

And, but, so Jacob, he drops his Purdey and runs to these old gooses and picks them up and is near as in tears as a man can be about a bunch of filthy old gooses who have been biting him every day for the past fifteen years.

Then one by one, he garners them tender in his arms and

lugs them back to his house, to mend them.

And although he is up all night, with his Mrs and their kiddies, bandaging them and whispering to them and soothing them and making them goose broth and keeping them warm, by the morning two is died and thother is as near to dead by fright andJacob, he knows it will not last the day.

So now, the thing is, Jacob, he knows whose these dogs are as has done this to his gooses.

But, the thing is, they belong to his friend Charlie Jones, who is his mucker and ally, and his friend and he likes him and does not have no axle to grind with him at all.

And, but so, Jacob, he doesn't know what to do.

Only he knows that he must do something.

And so Jacob, he buries two of his old gooses in his garden under his cherry tree on Tuesday morning, when he is feeling that upset and sad as he can hardly speak. Even his kiddies are sad, and his Mrs, Mrs Jacob the Sheep: even she (although she has been saying for fifteen years as these filthy old gooses is got to go – even though she is being saying this for five thousand four hundred and seventy nine days!) she is distressed and sad and wrings her pinny in her hands and bursts into tears and says the place will never be the same without them.

By dinner time, the other goose, Matilda, she is died and all, so they boneyards her up along with thothers under the cherry, with a little cross on her grave as the kiddies make and a slate as says:

Here lies
Matilda and Gertrude and Bingo
Pongiest, Filthiest, Poohiest, Hissiest, Bitiest
Best loved goosers
In the whole world.

And they all stand over this little grave and they hold hands as this is for them, especially for Jacob the Sheep, a very sad moment.

Come Wednesday night, Jacob he nips down The Crown.

And in The Pendagon, is his old mate Charlie Jones.

Jacob, he buys Charlie Jones a pint of Bowel Vowel and sets down with him.

He says: 'Charlie, what do you make of this weather then?'

Charlie Jones, he replies: 'It is just a cracking job for mixing muck in.'

Jacob says: 'And who is it as you are mixing muck for then?'

'It is that old kiddy Judge Grimshaw. And you know something?' Charlie carries on saying straight away as Charlie Jones is a bit of a talker: 'That old Judge Grimshaw is a rare commodity, I can tell you. Not only is he a judge and has innocent and guilty citizens tossed in pokey every day, but also he is apt to give his Mrs a good cuffing every now and then.'

'Oh this is a terrible thing for a man to do even if he is a judge,' Jacob says.

Then Charlie says: 'And this is not all he does. I seen him one day chewing up bits of paper and flicking them at her.'

Jacob says: 'that is an atrocious thing to be doing, and a little weird. How do you know this?'

'It is well known as he does this every time he starts hitting the old Scottish distillery products.'

'That is a poor old show. People who go around glugging these Scottish Distillery products then lambasting their Mrs should not be allowed. In fact they ought to be thrown in pokey. So maybe we should get a decree to have this Judge stuck behind bars along with all these others as he keeps committing to them regular.'

'Not before he pays my bill,' Charlie says.

'This is true. And how are you Charlie, my old mucker?'

'My arms ache and my head aches and I am flat broke, my Mrs is having a funny old turn all the while these days and I am fed up with everything.'

'It is the same with me,' Jacob says: 'on top my old Mrs is not in bad order though, considering her vintage, given as she is a bit shot in the gaskets these days.'

'Well, there we are then. We aren't none of us getting much younger.'

'This is true,' says Jacob. And then he says: 'Charlie, I am sorry to have to inform you of a sad thing.'

'Oh no, is your old motor's chimney fell off?'

'No,' Jacob says.

'Is your quad bike been nicked?'

'No.'

'Them gooses of yours – are they done a mischief to Jim the Post?'

'No. But it is on that matter as I am much saddened,' says Jacob. 'You see,' he says: 'Yesterday I buried my old gooses under the cherry in my garden on account as they are died.'

'Oh, poor old gooses: I hope you gave them a worthy send off.'

'We do. The kiddies of mine given them a proper old funereal, with hymns and flowers and graves with a slate on saying as there are old gooses buried under there.'

'This is a proper job. Why are your gooses died then Jacob, was they sick?'

'No,' says Jacob: 'They was murdered.'

'Hellfire!' says Charlie: 'murdered? Your gooses murdered? This is terrible news. Who is this culprit as we shall send a possee out to get him.'

'It's not a him, it's a them.'

'Never mind. We shall send out a possee and hang the blighters from yonder withy stump.'

So Jacob nods and says: 'Well, I don't think we want to that.'

'Why not? People as goes about the shire murdering other people's goosers needs harsh laws applying else they will do it in thother shires.'

'The thing is,' Jacob says, 'I don't think you want to go shouting this out loud too much, my old mucker.'

'I think I should shout it loud and tell all and sundry as your goosers is murdered by a murderer and we are going to go and get him.'

'Them.'

'Them.'

So now Jacob, he keeps crossing and uncrossing his legs and saying: 'Well, look, it doesn't matter,' and then he starts polishing the table top and saying things like: 'Hang on, hang on,' and clearing his throat and saying: 'Well, they was only a heap of old goosers,' and that it is not worth dangling the culprits out the withy stump for this. But then Charlie, he jumps out and shouts in The Crown: 'Here! Everyone – murder most foul has been done! We have to avenge this deed! We must go out and seek out these perishing criminals as has murdered Jacob the Sheep's goosers and apprehend them – and bring them to justice so help we God. I shall tell Mr Judge Justice Grimshaw of this felony and

crime and mayhem and torture and he will pass sentence immediately on these culprits and see as they are dealt with according to the law and given a good stretching or put in the stocks or dangled out the withy stump.'

And so now everyone agrees with this pronouncement. But, Jacob, he says: 'I don't think we needs to be so hasty, as they was only a bunch of three goosers as gave everyone in the county the gip from day one fifteen years ago til last Monday night.'

'No! No!' they all says: 'Charlie Jones is right. Bring the culprits to justice. Who is it as has done this wicked deed, Jacob old matey: say, and we shall apprehend them this instant!'

And then old Dennis the Pigs, he looses in and says: 'Jacob, who is it as has done this to your goosers? Did you see the murderers doing this murder with your own eyes?'

So now Jacob, he sets down very quiet and he knows now as the moment of truth is arrived. But he doesn't say anything.

So now you can hear as it is gone very quiet in The Crown as these people they knows Jacob the Sheep is not a man to make big of things or tell tall stories and draw the longbow in any way. And Jacob, he says nothing. And this makes matters worse. So Dennis: he says again: 'Jacob, did you see who done this murder?'

And so Jacob he looks off through the smoke in the bar at the old bottles and optics lined up on the shelves and he shakes his head, but says nothing.

So now Dennis the Pigs and Charlie Jones and George Gunter the F and Blast and Trouser Jabez and Knukky Stubbs and Ivor the Wellies are all thinking as he knows who done this but is not going to say.

So now this is having an effect on these people as they now all begin to shuffle their feet and cough and wriggle their shoulders as though they are expecting Jacob to put the finger on one of them and say: 'It was you, you done it!' So Ivor the Wellies, he says: 'We'll it wasna me,' and George Gunter the F and Blast says: 'F and Blast, it wasn't me neither.' And so in a minute everyone in The Crown says it was not them. Then Jacob the Sheep he says: 'I know, it was none of you. It was a animal as done it.'

'I knew it!' George Gunter the F and Blast says: 'It is that old Mr Renard from over the tops. He is a canny old devil. I seen him only last week murdering a mallard down by the river.'

'It wasn't him,' Jacob says.

'It was that old Mr Brock!' Dennis the Pigs cries thumping the bar: 'I seen him on the road last Monday night, going up to you place Jacob: he must have had it eviling away in his dark old mind there and then!'

'It wasn't old Mr Brock.' Jacob says.

'Who was it then?' asks Dennis the Pigs.

So then Jacob, he says as although he goes out in the night, he does not actually see it happen but what he finds he knows as his goosers is attacked by a animal or two.

Then old Knukky Stubbs he says: 'Here, it wasn't that old cougar or lion or jaguar or leopard or sabre tooth tiger and his mate as been on telly, is it?'

And so then everyone says, ah yes, that might be the type of animals as had committed this crime.

Then Jacob he says: in any rate, whatever it was, 'I loosed a shot off, more to scare them off I should say as anything.'

So then Charlie Jones, he is being very quiet all of a sudden. Then he says: 'When was all this murdering done then?'

So Jacob, he says: 'Two nights ago: Monday night.'

So now then Charlie Jones is getting to thinking. But he doesn't say what he is thinking.

But what everyone knows is that a while ago, Charlie Jones's two Labradors, as is big and very energetic dogs, he keeps these creatures locked up, as is a very tricky thing to do with a mutt, because he will always try to break loose, and if he breaks loose, he will come to no good. But everyone knows, as Charlie Jones knows, that if he doesna keep his mutts locked up, they will come to no good anyway, as it was a year before as they ripped up the seat on Sid's Quad bike and Charlie Jones had to pay for a new one.

Only Charlie Jones says: 'Well I must be going off home now as it is getting late and past my bedtime.'

So Charlie Jones goes.

In The Crown, no-one says a thing.

They just get on with drinking their liver worm, or Bowel Vowel or whatever it was they was drinking.

It's only old Knukky Stubbs, canny as a dray of squirrels, who comes over to Jacob the Sheep and says: 'That's one of them things, Jacob.'

And Jacob says: 'It is. And he is also my friend.'

And Knukky Stubbs says: 'Yes, he is a good man. We all knows this. It is not his fault.'

So then Dennis the Pigs and George Gunter the F and Blast and Trouser Jabez and thothers, they all say nothing. Only they scrat their arms and say: 'Well, there we are then,' or 'Oh ar,' or something like that, as is what you say when everyone knows but no-one says.

It is three days later and Jacob is up in his place, fiddling around with his cows, jamming some dinner down them, when up his track comes Charlie Jones in his old Landrover.

And so Jacob, he 'How bist 'ee surree' to him, as you do, and Charlie he 'How bist 'ee surrees' back.

So Charlie he says: 'How is this weather suiting you then Jacob, my old mucker?' And Jacob, he says: 'I shouldna mind a touch more rain for March as it has been a long old spell to go dry on.'

And so Charlie says, that is true; only it is fair and clement weather for mixing muck. So then he says to Jacob: 'Is your kiddies in?'

So Jacob says as he will go fetch them just now.

And in the minute there is Jacob's two little kiddies: Henry and Hanna, a filthy little pair of hobbledoys but as pretty a pair of urchins as ever made dams in a brook. So Charlie says to these little kiddies: 'You come here you little kiddies as I have something for you.'

So these little kiddies, they go to Jacob's old Landrover.

David, he opens the back door.

He reaches in.

And he brings out three fluffy little goslings, still a bit yellow and downy and only a month or two old. And they have got bright blue eyes and yellow beaks and the first thing they doos is to set up this hissing malarkey. And these little kiddies, they loves them straight off, and they says thank you Mr Jones, and Charlie he turns to old Jacob and he says: 'I am sorry my old mucker.'

And Jacob he says to Charlie: 'Charlie, you are my friend, and always will be, but as soon as these goosers are big enough, I'm going to bring them down the village to duff up your dogs.'

Safety First

Frank the Plank, a friend of mine, owns a bit of a lumber yard down the valley and this is where he planks up timber. And Frank the Plank, he has been here planking up this stuff for as long as old Typhoon Ted's been gnawing plug, and that is a fair old while now as Typhoon's pegs is as black as pitch piles.

Mostly, Frank planks up big old oaks and he does this through a six-foot circular saw what he runs off an old Perkins diesel he winkled out of a bus from Trenters the Scrap, in 1957. The timber he gets from felling jobs he's called out on and when he comes across a goodish tree, he'll set an offer for her there and then, sned her out, cord off the limbs and cart the lumber home on his old Foden flat-bed. Then he unloads her in his yard with an old forklift he got off Trenters the Scrap, and drags the trunk over to the saw bench with a Fordson Major, he also got off Trenters the Scrap, and in fact, if you think all Frank's kit he got off Trenters the Scrap you would be right, because even his Foden flat-bed he got off them as well, which is what people without much bleat in the bank are forced to do.

Anyway up, all this clobber hangs together with grease and wire and a bit of weld here and a dab of weld there, a lot of sump-oil and plenty of string.

Frank himself lives in a sort of a caravan effort he knocked up on his place, in amongst a heap of timber, and this is where he keeps his Alsatian mutt, who goes by the name of Hoppus Foot, and Hoppus Foot spends all day yapping on the end of his chain.

He does this because Frank keeps his radio going full blast playing Radio One, and it is this which has driven Hoppus Foot insane.

Consequently Hoppus Foot is not a very friendly dog, that is to say, not at least to anyone except Frank, and Frank has a very especial regard for Hoppus Foot because he is a very effective deterrent against strangers poking about in his place when he is out fetching wood.

And if a stranger comes into the yard when Frank is in, he can tell by the change in tone of Hoppus Foot's bark, even if he is busy screaming a few ton of oak through his saw, with the old diesel slogging its rings out, and Radio One blarting.

Any rate, one day, Frank is struggling about in a blizzard of sawdust with all this rattle going on, when he hears Hoppus Foot's pitch change.

Being a Border man, and very polite, Frank cuts the motor and looks up.

Across the yard he spies a fellow dressed up in a posh suit clutching a bunch of papers.

Now Frank has a good mind to fire up the motor again and get buried under a pile more sawdust because he can tell that this is a Ministry bloke and probably something to do with regulations, and Frank, being a bachelor, and having his own business to run, and Hoppus Foot to feed, and all this kit to maintain, and keep himself cleanish, and buy all his grub, and all this sort of thing, has never had much to do with regulations.

And he recalls hearing clients in The Buffalo bad mouth these blokes.

So he feels antagonism towards this man.

Anyway, he's stopped the tackle running now and goes over

33

to hear what he has to say, and this bloke starts tut-tutting away about this and that and no safety, and so Frank tells him, politely, that he's the only bloke that works there, except for sometimes, and that he has never had any accidents in his place, not counting the time he shaved a couple of fingers off in the saw.

He doesn't need safety stuff, he says.

Then this bloke says he has to stick a roll bar on his Fordson, on account of the times he does engage other timber merchants to graft on his place because it is definitely illegal not to have one.

Frank replies that his yard does not hang on the side of a mountain, but is, in reality, flat as a skittle alley. No-one could turn a tractor turtle there, not even for money.

The safety bloke then says that if he does not stick a roll bar on his Fordson he will get Silver Buttons along from Ludlow, together with the rest of the beef from the Ministry, and the judge, and the jury, and turn the screws on him in some very stern order indeed.

So Frank flings his oil rag down in the dust and says, right, he'll weld one on then.

Two days later he has accomplished this.

He has fixed up a big roll-bar of three-inch iron piping over his tractor and thinks that's a pretty fine job, even if it was a waste of time.

So then he gets back to work and goes over to a pile of lumber with his tractor and new roll-bar and lashes the chain and grips round a seven-ton stump and hauls her across the yard to the saw, and drives straight under the shed and the next thing he knows is a tremendous crash and he is in a strange place with girls all dressed up in blue with little white hats and silvery belts on all peering into his eyes.

He is kept in this hospital for three months.

How he gets there remains a mystery to him. Only he's got to wear this anti-neck breaking gadget now all the while because this is more or less what he's got.

When they loose him out he goes straight back to his place and finds Hoppus Foot is gone, his caravan is all grown over with mildew and filled with flies, and none of his kit is running anymore.

So he wanders over to the saw shed, where he lasts remembers being, and there he finds the roof all buckled up and his Fordson underneath with the roll-bar stuck well into the purlins and a big oak beam straddling the seat and the last anybody hears of Frank is him singeing the roll-bar off with his oxy' lamp and is last seen boring round the Borders in his flat-bed trying to find the safety bloke so he can shove this 3-inch metal piping, in its entirety, up where it rightly belongs.

Painted Impostor

Back awhile, sometime ago, perhaps eighteen, nineteen years ago, one small beetle pitches up here, in this country, from America or somewhere; Africa perhaps; or France; Spain. Maybe Iceland. Anyway up, abroad somewhere – probably Wales – wherever, and this small beetle, he is black mostly, with yellow stripes down his back and wiggly eye things and he tootles about munching all the spud-tops and scoffing up very big fields of these, almost entirely.

And, people, farmers mostly, get with this beetle, not a little provoked, what with him putting holes in all their potatoes and their livelihoods. So they decide to give him a good big blast of this yellow spray stuff, which does for small beetles, for ever. And so the boffins in The Ministry, where they magic this yellow spray up, see that this is an opportunity for a very big bonanza indeed, and commence to make mountains of it, and sell it off to everyone everywhere for them to squirt all over these little beetles whenever they see them.

So very soon, everyone of these little beetles is finished and there is no more of them left, at all.

Then, these boffins, being as they are cottoned as these beetles are over and that there must be a lot of this yellow stuff lying about in peoples' sheds, they get the kiddies in the newspa-

36

pers to write as to how this yellow commodity is more lethally periculous than the beetles and as it is necessary to be rid of it, or else.

So people ask where.

So, these Ministry types, they build these depository efforts for people to take their excess yellow gunk to, and so now, these Ministry people, they have clawed back half of what they flogged, for free.

Then, these blokes, they bulldoze all this free yellow gunk into one big heap and dye it orange and then get some other kiddies in the Farmers' Weekly to proclaim as there is some other kind of a sort of a bug which is very deadly to beans or sprouts or something and that the only way to nail these, is with this orange stuff.

So they start all over again and flog the orange stuff. Then, when they've killed all these, they get people to bring back what they haven't used – about half – because they let on as how this agent orange kit is miles worser than the yellow stuff. Then they bulldoze this agent orange into another heap and dye it purple or mauve or something, then get the kiddies on the telly to say as there is another kind of bug, then flog the purple stuff and make even more money and murder even the good beetles as never did no-one no harm, never – not that these boffins give a cowpat anyway – and all I knows is as how they have been going on doing this now, oh, ever so many years and as I sits here I swear that I am probably the only bloke has twigged this.

Anyway up, never mind about that.

This story begins here: there is a very hot day one day and my friend Knuckky Stubbs is poothering about Clun not doing a lot.

He has just been to market in The Castle – Bishop's Castle – and passed off a few head of stock and this and that, and made a bit of luck here and there, bought a heifer maybe, or a pony perhaps and was just thinking it was time to have a bit of bait, in

The Buffalo say, and a jaw with Trouser Jabez and Willie the Pooh and Bill the Box, and them, and play a domino or two, whatever, just for fun.

So he jams his Landrover up under the hedge down by the river, under a big old bush to keep her coolish and then strolls up the lane to The Buffalo and as he is going he is thinking what a hot day it is and that any minute now there is likely to be a very serious pelting thundering storm so he puts some sort of a spurt on so as not to get wet.

Then, just as he is walking to The Buffalo he sees these two little kiddies playing away outside the pub, on a stone, and these little kiddies are painting white paper with watercolours, with small brushes such as you get when you are a kiddy, and they are in a pretty good mess, what with being plastered in this paint all over their faces and hands and in their eyes and ears and hair and everywhere. And, but, Knukky, he likes to see kiddies mucking about having a high old time even if they are covered in paint.

So he bends down to see what they are making on the paper with their paint and as he bends down a big fat beetle comes down from the sky with a good plop, smack onto their paper.

Now, these little kiddies, they jump.

But Knukky, he just picks this beetle up and he sees he is a big old black one much as you get under a good stone, or in your wellies, or see scuttling down the isle in church of a Sunday morning, when the vicar is droning on in his pulpit.

Personally, I like these beetles.

I love to see them scorting down the isle in church full tilt of a Sunday.

I keep wondering where it is they are going in such a hurry? But I suppose it is to go and see their wives or something, sniving about down the grating, with a gang of other beetles, or something, and probably a spider or two and some of them amber colour gadgets with all them legs and big nippers on their backends as goes wriggling about in compost and heaps of leaves and stuff as gives old wuzzuks cardiacal stoppages.

Anyway up, Knukky, he collars this old beetle and says to the kiddies like this: 'Give me your paintbrush little kiddy, for one moment, and I will jam it in a good dollop of this here yellow paint what you have got there, and do stripes upon this beetle, down his back, which I don't think he will mind very much as he is probably bored of just having the same colour jacket to wear every day and would perhaps fancy a brand new outfit for the ladies, who I am sure he was probably busy chasing, by himself.'

So one of the kiddies hands Knukky a paintbrush and he does as he says and jams it in a good dollop of yellow and then very careful, because Knukky has a very steady hand, he paints across this beetle and down his back these very fine yellow stripes and on account of it being a boiling hot summer's day, these stripes dry very quick and so, right now, Knukky has a very genuine potato-top scoffing looking Colorado beetle and so he hands back the paint brush to this little kiddy.

Very pleased with his achievement, Knukky thanks this kiddy, gives them twenty pence each and steps into The Buffalo.

Inside he puts this beetle down on the bar.

He orders a pint.

And he watches this little beetle tootle about.

Now the landlord in The Buffalo at this time is a different landlord from the one as is there now, and he, this different landlord, on seeing this yellow stripes beetle exclaims: 'Where do you find this one, Knukky?' And Knukky, he just shrugs his shoulders, and says he finds him sitting on the doorstep outside.

Which is true, as Knukky is not a liar.

Then the landlord says: 'These ones, these yellow stripey beetles are illegal. They are not allowed in this land. Do you know this?' And Knukky says: 'I do not know this. I just find him outside and being as it is about to thunder, I bring him in out of the wet, so he may be happy in the bar, with us, getting on with his business of being a yellow stripey beetle.'

And then, immediately, this landlord of The Buffalo, he gets hold of a telephone and he makes a call to someone, but Knukky, he is no longer listening as he has been invited to play dominoes, with Willie the Pooh and Trouser Jabez and Ivor the Wellies. So, the next thing happens is that the landlord, he pops this beetle into a matchbox and not five minutes pass before the whole of Clun is alerted by the sound of sirens, and cars, and people running around outside, just before the thunder is about to thunder, and Knukky, he looks up and asks what all this commotion is about.

Then suddenly, in through the door come two very big Silver Buttonses from Ludlow. They barge up to the bar and their presence makes all the customers in there try to be invisible.

So, then the landlord he says: 'Good morning Silver Buttons. Thank you for coming from Ludlow nickery to The Buffalo in order to prevent a very great catastrophe overtaking this land.'

'I have in this matchbox a substance of great illegality, which was brought here by my friend Knukky Stubbs, which is very responsible of him, and thoughtful, and considerate of potatoes.'

And then, the landlord, he opens up this matchbox so that Silver Buttons can have a peek inside, and sure enough, they see this beetle hiding in a corner of the matchbox trying not to be seen.

Then one of these Silver Buttonses, he says: 'Good gracious: this is one of those illegal immigrants who comes from another place, abroad somewhere, probably Wales, and is definitely not allowed here. But we have no beetley type handcuffs for him so we must get hold of the gaffers from the Ministry who make the yellow gunk to come and give him one good squirt.'

But the other Silver Buttons, he says: 'No: we must get hold of the gaffers from the Ministry and tell them we have found, in The Buffalo Inn, in Clun, a very periculous beetle with yellow stripes who is about to infest our land with a plague of eating and when they come they will take him away and work out on their machines, and computers, and graph papers and statistics and stuff, how to overcome this, because, I am sure, these gaffers have a special way of extracting information from this beetle, and this is what we must do.'

So then, this Silver Buttons, he rings up someone somewhere, and there is a lot of ringing up now, all over the place, to Ministries and whatnot.

And, but, sitting down playing dominoes, is my friend Knukky and he is staying pretty quiet. In fact, he is hoping very hard, the two kiddies who were doodling with watercolours on the stone outside, have gone, and are no longer there, and not likely to come in and ask for Knukky to paint another beetle, if he lands nearby.

So he sits tight.

He does not wish to spend time down in the nickery trying to explain this.

Anyway up, then the thunder comes with a big wallop, and down comes the rain, and everyone is running in from outside, and Knukky is hoping now, fairly hard, that these two little kiddies will not make for The Buffalo to shelter in, from the rain.

But then, suddenly, there is another great commotion as a very large white van of maybe two tons, even three, perhaps more, comes splashing into Clun with his sirens blarting and windscreen wipers smacking and he drives straight up to The Buffalo and two gaffers from The Ministry, all dressed in white coats and rubber gloves, and gas masks and white wellies and everything, they come jumping into the bar.

So now, in the bar there is Knukky, very quiet, and Trouser Jabez, and Willie the Pooh, and Ivor the Wellies, and the landlord, and these two Silver Buttonses, and now these other two Ministry gaffers all dressed up like spacemen and this little beetle in his matchbox, who is the cause of all this excitement.

So now one of these Ministry gaffers, he opens this matchbox and looks at this small beetle and he frowns and says: 'Where does this small beetle come from? Who finds him?' And then everyone in the bar, including Trouser Jabez, they all say: 'Knukky finds him: outside.'

So now Knukky is called upon by this Ministry bloke to give a very precise account of how he comes across this beetle. And, but, the thing is, having sunk a pint or two of Buffalo juice, Knukky cannot remember exacly what it was he said before, so he says, as simple as he can, he found him: bang: just like that.

Then the Ministry bloke asks him if anyone saw him find it.

And now this is a very difficult moment for Knukky because he is not a liar.

He is a truthful man.

And so he says, he couldn't really say: maybe they did, maybe they didn't.

And so now this Ministry bloke he looks out through the window and sees a number of people standing in doorways, sheltering from the rain, and it is in his mind to question these people as to whether they saw Knukky find this beetle, or what.

And Knukky now, he is wiping his forehead with his spotted hankerchief.

Then this Ministry bloke, he goes out and asks people how long they have been there, and Knukky, he goes out too, and sees, standing in the doorway, in the butchers opposite, these two kiddies, who are very interested in the Ministry bloke all dressed up like someone from Dr Who, asking everyone questions, and then, when they see Knukky, they wave.

So now Knukky, he does not wave back.

He looks away, which pains him, because he likes little kiddies, but he thinks these two, they will put the finger on him and he will probably be blasted with the yellow gunk, along with this beetle and that will be that, excepting he will have to spend the rest of the month down at the Nickery. And most probably the month after, as well.

So this Ministry bloke, he asks Knukky to step back inside The Buffalo, and everyone else to step inside The Buffalo, which they all do, assuming, which is reasonable, that he is about to buy them all a drink being as he is in a generous mood.

But, of coursing, these people, they become very disappointed when this man makes no attempt to even offer them drinks never mind buy any and they become restive, and disenchanted, especially when they discover these spacemen characters wish to ask them questions about some beetle Knukky finds.

So then one of these people, a fellow by the name of Norris the Spade, he asks what is so special about this beetle Knukky collars, what is it worth? Because if it's worth money he can go out and fetch any amount of beetles for these Ministry gaffers, in their spacesuits, if they want.

So then this Minstry bloke, he explains as this is the most deadliest beetle as ever crep around an English meadow, and is worth more dead than alive. It is, he says, the Colorado, the one as got yellow stripes on him and just when he says this, Knukky, who is a shy man by nature, and not one to seek notoriety, finding himself not enjoying being the centre of attention here especially as people keep asking him if he's got any more, he gazes across the bar to the door and finds himself looking deep into the eyes of one small boy, very wet, covered in paint, and one small girl, very wet, covered in paint, which is mostly of a yellow colour, round their mouths, and on their faces.

Now it is immediately in Knukky's inclination to bundle these two little blighters straight back out, quick, and send them home to their mam, but it is not, it seems to him, most likely a politic thing to be doing.

So he sits tight, and smiles, and sort of holds up his pint, like as if you might say cheers, and takes a sip and the little boy, he makes as if to say to Knukky as he would like a drink too, in that he copies him, and as he makes this motion, he looks up at the Ministry bloke in his spacesuit, who then looks down at him and asks him if he saw where Knukky finds this beetle.

This is, as anyone might imagine, for Knukky a very swallowing hard moment.

This little boy, he looks over to Knukky, and Knukky, being as he is a bit of a dealer and has to be on his toes, and knows this little boy's dad is also a dealer and is pretty quick on his toes, he can see what is going on here, and quick as a flash, he calls up to the landlord as to give these little kiddies a glass of pop apiece. Then this little boy, he asks this Ministry bloke if he can see what he's got hiding in his matchbox, and so the ministry bloke, he lets these kiddies have a peep, which they do, which causes them to do much giggling, but they don't let on.

So now then, Knukky he calls these little kiddies over to him with offers of bags of crisps and bars of chocolates and stuff. But by now, Trouser Jabez, and Ivor the Wellies and them they have got wind as to something funny is going on here, and when they notices as these kiddies are covered in paint, they gets to thinking, and now all of a sudden they gets to chuckling as well, and so Trouser, he turns to Knukky and he says as that his is a pint.

So now Knukky has to buy him a pint, and Ivor the Wellies who is twigged, and Willie the Pooh. In fact everyone in the place gets to twig excepting, that is, the Ministry blokes who do not know what kind of kiddies they are dealing with here, or what kind of a fellow Knukky is.

Now these two kiddies are standing in front of Knukky when the little boy, he puts his hand in his pocket and he pulls out a small pot, an old ink pot, and he takes the lid off this and pours out onto the table in front of Knukky, one small grasshopper, given a good dose of red paint, one woodlouse, covered in a thick coat of green, an earthworm, purple with black stripes, a slug, orange with squiggly white lines, and a couple of pebbles mostly blue.

As luck would have it, the Ministry bloke does not see these things being as his back is turned and he is telephoning the chief of the beetle murdering department or something, and has left the matchbox with the yellow stripey beetle on the bar.

So now then Knukky tips the wink to these two kiddies and he slants his eyes across to this matchbox and then from his pocket he takes another like it, tips all the matches out and inserts into it the squiggly lined slug and an earthworm, purple with black stripes, a couple of pebbles and a red woodlouse.

It is Trouser Jabez who by sleight of hand exchanges the matchboxes on the bar, and who hands this other matchbox to the Ministry bloke, who puts it in a little box, which he locks and this little box he slams in a bigger box which he locks, and this goes in a bigger box with a padlock, and then he takes this out to his white van, where he seals it in an even bigger box, then slams the door, mortice locks them with three separate keys and goes hurtling out of Clun as quick as he'd come.

And if ever he came back to find his Colorado Big Duley beetle, neither Knukky Stubbs, nor Trouser Jabez, Willie the Pooh nor Ivor the Wellies could say as they changed their destination for playing dominoes and drinking Buffalo juice for a while after that, till things died down a bit. Which was wise of them, considering.

Lady of the North

My chum Moreton Morton is known, locally, as The Bishop, but, in fact, he is not a bishop at all. He is, in fact, a manaferni. And, but, the thing is, I don't know why Moreton Morton gets called The Bishop. Anyone else less like a bishop you would never meet. Then again, I do not know many bishops so perhaps he is called The Bishop on account of bishops being like Moreton Morton, I do not know.

Any rate, The Bishop, Moreton Morton, that is, in that he is a manaferni and messes with tractors and corn drills, ploughs and lime spreaders and that kind of tack, you can hear swearing in the next parish when he gets going, and The Bishop, my friend, lets rip with a yard of comorondo as would blow the oil seals out the hydraulics of a D8.

The Bishop, he is exactly the same age as me, being a forty niner, only he is a nice-looking fellow, and well-built, with a clipped moustache, and strong, and well-mannered. But The Bishop, unlike a proper bishop, gets down The White Horse, and The Buffalo and The Hundred House or The Radnorshire or The Lion or somewhere, by and by, and gets himself well ratted up on the local viper wine, as they swills in these parts, whatever.

And, but, for all that he gets ratted up, or taps a domino, or cues at pool, or flings a dart or something, everyone likes him. And they like him because even though he swears, and gets in the liquid therapy shops, and belts his machinery with sledge hammers and lets them have a good hiding with couple of yards of lead pipe, or something, he is a very reliable sort of fellow, and good to deal with, in that when he says he will do something, he does it.

And Moreton Morton, The Bishop, he lives in a big windy old stone hangar of a place called Bentpenny Castle.

And this Bentpenny Castle place, is not like a castle with towers and moats and stuff, but in reality is like a big old stone house, with thick stone mullion windows and great thick walls and huge old barns and a big courtyard and Moreton's people have been abiding in it as long as cows been poaching mud.

And there is a kind of sort of tale about Bentpenny as says no-one ever but a Morton will ever live there. And that it has got a spell on it and it will never fall out of a Morton's hands – which is how it is kept in them all these years past, I suppose. But then, that might have been alright for them in those days when they didn't have to find the eeyore you have the call for these days to keep things going, and living in Bentpenny is different these days.

Living in Bentpenny is both a blessing and a curse, as one day it is a rare old place full of years and age and stories and all that caper, but on the next it is dark and damp and if you sets a trap to catch a mole you are as like to catch an eel, straight off.

Anyway up, the thing is, Bentpenny Castle used to be, so they say, people, at some time, when it wasn't a fort, some sort of an old toffs' hunting gaff or something, being all bunged full of beams, and oak panelling, flag floors and huge great big ceilings with big old plastery carvings on.

And Bentpenny Castle, it has in it one big beam in partic-ular, in the dining room, an eight-foot wide job over an inglenook fire, which is carved, of a scene, very artful, of a pair of wild boar, face to face, only the lady boar, she is shot through the heart with a arrow. And the boar, he is almost touching her nose with his, and behind both of them is a couple of packs of hounds.

To me, I would say it tells a love story, as the lady is lost her heart to a man, but somehow, they are trapped and there is nowhere for them to go: as if they are being chased from all directions and canna do nothing about it. The arrow means more than the lady is in love: it means that she is dead to him – I would say – not because she doesn't love him, but because she does but can't do nothing about it. It's what they calls an allegory.

But my friend Moreton Morton, The Bishop, he says no: it's nothing like that. It was to do with when the place used to some sort of a antique knocking shop, in some king's reign, or somewhen, in the olden days, and the pair of pigs in the middle is just a bit of a diversion, as what it's really about is all the dirty old dogs as used to creep in there.

And, but, the thing is, whatever it is, it's a grand style of work, being well-crafted and detailed, and the museum man from Ludlow, when he sees it, says it is an ancient lump of oak hacked out the woods and tarted up with this picture, back in King Henry's reign – which is a rare old while back now as King Henry is the kiddy as marries Queen Mary after she beats the Spanish in the Battle of Bakerloo, near London – where the trains runs these days – if you are lucky – which is what begins the Wars of the Roses with the Spanish and the Armada and that.

And, to go about this for a minute, this Armada effort, this is what Sir Francis Chichester drives off in his little boat the Golden Hound, and he is able to do this as these Spanish tugs is great big jobs, sailboats, tall as trees; but Sir Francis, his little craft, the Golden Hound, is only a squit of a gadget and he goes ripping in and out these big old Spanish jobs as they keeps on trying to lambast him with their lambasters and grapple him with their grapplers but keeps on smacking into each other so they all sinks in a big heap in the Bay of Bengal out in the ocean somewhere and that's how the English wins the Wars of the

Roses. All that is hundreds and hundreds of years back, which is a fair indication of how old Bentpenny is.

Anyway up, living in Bentpenny Castle with The Bishop, is his lie-by, Laura, and Laura, she keeps this old gaff together with nails and araldite and pollyfiller and string because the windows, they keeps falling out. And plaster, it keeps flopping down, and the wood-worm, he has had a good gnaw at half of it, and at night the death watch tap-tap taps in the beams and the joists, in amongst the floor boards.

And just to go back for a minute, the King Henry the museum man from Ludlow was on about is a different one from the other King Henry with the wives – he came after all this business. The King Henry with the wives was in London, not in Ludlow – that was the other one. But never mind about that.

So, anyway up, the things is, about Bentpenny, in actuality, it is a uncommon pile of stones and the old place could do with a bargeful of corks chucking at it, and Laura, she knows this, and so does The Bishop, but they do not have this kind of scratch, although it is Laura's wish as they did.

And, but, the thing is, what with rummaging around with his tractors and running his business, and whatnot, and everything else, there is never enough bleat to fix the whole place up, so they patch up as best they can, and make do. And Laura, she is very good at this, as is The Bishop at keeping all his kit hanging together, but times come as they seem to be fighting for nothing.

This old gaff, it's a honey-sucker for eeyore.

First, The Bishop, he has to shove in new pipes as the old lead jobs is illegal all of a sudden according to the law. So he whangs these in, with plenty of solder and pipe grease, and U bends and that and never mind about how much half a mile of copper piping costs, it's the time it takes on top. So no sooner as he is done this as the old tank in the roof gives a grunt and splits down the middle as clean as a split cheddar and a ton of water comes thundering down the staircase on Valentine's Day last year and washes half the kitchen out, and Moreton and Laura with it.

So then Moreton has to get a new tank.

So while's he's struggling to get this new effort upstairs, the big ceiling in the hall flops down. And now, because this old gaff is registered as an old gaff in the County Hall, Moreton has to get the ceiling put back just the same as the old one, which cost about a hundred million times more as a bloke with a bucket of Artex could have smacked up in an afternoon, but that's regulations for you these days.

And then, as they are doing this, the floorboards give in, and Moreton goes thumping through them straight up to his armpits, which he does with a lot of language, so help him God. So now he has to get has to get Frank the Plank to slice up a couple of giant oaks and lay new boards and at twenty foot a room, never mind the joists, this swallows up eight tons of lumber one way and another and sticks Moreton half-an-inch away from a County Court summons for being broke, as is the law these days.

So no matter how you looks at it, by and by, Bentpenny is a serious cash shortage liability affair, never mind how old it is or which family's house it is.

This problem, it weighs heavy on Moreton, The Bishops', mind.

One night, The Bishop he comes rattling back to Bentpenny on his Fergi after a day's graft, and Laura, she can see it has been one long hooking.

The Bishop, he is run right down to the wire.

The tractor, it is belching black; the engine, it is knocking, with steam snorting out.

The Bishop: he is as near to snapping as a gutter icicle.

So what happens is this: The Bishop, he comes chugging in the yard – it's a big old courtyard with cobbles and this old leet belting a few tons of water straight into a big old stone trow that The Bishop duffed with the bucket of a JCB a ten month ago so now the water all calumbers straight across the yard and it's now become more or less part of the river as hurtles off down to Big Duley at fifty mile an hour.

So The Bishop, he's about sick of this river in his courtyard as well, on top of everything. So he runs the tractor up against the barn doors and he cuts the motor.

He drops out the cab, straight into this torrent, swears at it and the tractor and everything else, tosses a duff filter in the shed, stomps in the house and he says to Laura: 'I am fed up with all this. I am sick a being a manaferni. And I am sick of all the corks we make being tossed into this old dump as well. I am fed up with it.'

And he says, he wishes he'd never heard of manaferning.

Or ploughing.

Or harrowing.

Or muck carting.

Or driving up and down banks at angles as defies gravity.

And risking his neck every day of his natural.

Or liming.

Or wrapping bales.

Or lugging hay.

Or mowing.

Or baling.

Or chasing other people's cows.

Or catching pigs.

Or this river in his courtyard.

And the bloke he was scorting for today, didn't like nothing The Bishop did: first he wanted this, then he wanted that, then he couldn't decide what he wanted, then he said he didn't want The Bishop there at all; then the tractor it bogged in the mud, then the diesel pump blocked, then air got in, then it rained, then it hailed, then the sun come out and half roasted him, then this tourist jammed his motor in the gateway and went for a ramble with some old wuzzuk who took two hours to creep back, then there was a pile of cows in the lane, then he got a puncture and this pump – and he collapses in a chair with a pile of the black dismals as would fell a flight of black swans.

This manaferni tractor business, he says is best fixed with a few sticks of that stuff Bill the Wallop blows up mountains with down the quarry. And he can stick a heap more of it in the dung cart and the mower and the tedder and the baler and the combine and the ploughs and the barn and the sheds and the sitting room of this old midden as well, proved he lets them know when he's about to do it.

The Bishop, he says, wants out.

Out of Bentpenny.

Out the Valley.

Out of being a manaferni.

Out of grafting, altogether.

And now he has to sit down and do his VAT; and has bills to pay for this and that, tax, and whatnot. Everyone is screaming for money from him.

But no-one has pulled so much as a rusty washer out his pants pockets on his invoices.

This job, he says, is like sticking your head in the septic.

Only worse.

There are better things in life.

This racket, The Bishop says: it has to end.

There's got to be a more better way.

So now, Laura, she knows as to leave him be when he is as flakey as this, and say not a lot.

Laura, she cottons the best is to lug a big dinner down him, park him in front of the telly, bung him with a fresh bottle of Scotch and a ounce of baccy, and keep out the light.

So she acts on this impulse, what she has.

Quick as a jenny wren, she fetches out some kilt wearers' venom, duffs him a tumbler, sits him down at the table, hoys out his dinner, which is steak and kidney pie with mashed spuds and peas and carrots and treacle tart and custard.

Then she winkles him out the kitchen and wops him in his favourite chair in front of the telly with the Scotch, his pipe, his slippers and baccy.

Laura, she clears out.

So, The Bishop, he sits there, as the night goes on, sucking away at his old pipe, tipping back this Scottish snake oil, and Laura, she can see as he's plotting to market old Bentpenny, which is a howling shame as his family been living in it since Noah took to boating.

And Laura, she gets to thinking about this old spell and how it is that nobody but a Morton can ever live there.

And, but Laura, she hopes in her heart as Moreton isn't thinking of doing something, like burning it down or something, for the insurance, as this will rowzle up the old spirits of the place and there's no telling as what will happen as someone does that to a place like Bentpenny.

And she reckons as if he is thinking this, as some old spook is going to come flying out the woodwork and scare them all to death and smack a curse on them for ever, for flogging the gaff off; or worser, some terrible calamity is about to befell them because of Moreton thinking these things.

Laura, she does the washing up very slow this night and with a big worry furrows on her forehead. What they need to keep this place Laura thinks is some kind of a miracle or something. Otherwise for sure, being that pushed for corks, and time and people not paying up on their invoices, in all common sense, The Bishop he will be rid of it.

Anyway up, come ten or elevenish, The Bishop, he shouts from his chair as he's had enough and he's off to his scratcher.

So Laura says fine.

Laura, she hears this: she hears a lot of grunting coming from the sitting room, and a lot of crashing around, and thumping about noises. Then she hears this big wallop, then another, and then a huge crash.

And, but so Laura, she stops running the taps and clanging about with the saucepans and knives and forks and stuff, keeps her hands still, stares into the soap suds, and waits: 'You alright?' she hollers.

But there is no reply.

So Laura, she waits. Then she says again: 'Moreton – you alright?'

Still, there is silence.

Laura goes out and she sees this: she sees The Bishop stretched out under the grandaddy clock, which has taken a pearler off to the left. Moreton, The Bishop, is flatted out on the flagstones with his chin on his chest and rolling his eyes.

'Where am I?' he groans.

So Laura, she bends down, and says: 'Poor old duffer: you're just a bit ratted up, that's all,' and hoiks him to his feet and drags him upstairs, which is more worse as carting two hundredweight of King Edward's up a tallet loft of a winter's morning.

And, so, but, Laura, she winkles him out of his kit.

She jams him in his snoring overalls.

She heaves him across the old brass shaker, and, as he hits the feather, on account of this and that, he is zedding in two seconds.

Presently, Laura, she nips back downstairs, pulls the old grandfather back onto his pins, slips the slate under to steady him, dangles the weights back, flicks the pendulum and away he goes again because he is used to this by now.

She dowses all the downstairs lights, and creeps up.

She gets her snoring costume on.

She slants into the sheets alongside The Bishop, and outs the lamp.

The night goes quiet. There is no sound, except maybe a oolert blarting, or a cow blarting, a sheep maybe, bats twittering.

Downstairs the old grandad clock, he tocks away.

The old floor boards and walls: they creaks and groans.

These two, The Bishop and Laura, they are fell into the land of dreams.

The old night: she slides by, soft and gentle.

The stars: they twinkle bright up in heaven shining on the valley.

The river: she runs quiet over her stones.

The leet in the yard, it burbles across the cobbles.

The mist: it hangs in the withies down the dingle and all round the old stone bridge, that marks the way to Big Duley.

All is quiet.

Bentpenny: the old place itself is fell fast asleep.

Suddenly, bursting apart like a piston shot through a engine, The Bishop, he bawls out: 'I'm going north!'

Laura, she leps out her skin.

But she twigs The Bishop he is sleep talking, on account he does this.

Then The Bishop, he bawls again: 'I'm going north!'

Laura, she thinks he's dreaming and leaves him to get on with it and settles herself down to go back to sleep. But then she gets to sort of doodling in her mind and begins to deliberate as to why it is The Bishop plans to go north. She think as maybe it has something to do with him plotting on getting rid of Bentpenny. So she turns round and asks him.

'Why?' asks Laura. 'Why do you want to go north?'

A minute goes by, and then The Bishop he shouts: 'I'm going north!'

And Laura, she says again: 'Yes, but why? Why north?'

The Bishop he is sleeping sound as a pound. So Laura she

sighs and thinks poor old dab: he's had a bad day. The viper wine has got him. So she gives him a kiss in his cheek, lies back down, closes her eyes and commences to go back to kip.

Bentpenny, it reverts to its slumbers.

Suddenly, The Bishop he blarts right out loud: 'I'm going north to see my woman!'

So Laura, now she is startled by this sudden admission, but then she thinks: silly old wuzzuk, he's addled, and closes her eyes.

But, in about less than a forty second, her eyes smack open and she thinks: hang on a minute, what's all this?

So she sits up in bed, folds her arms and says: 'What's all this?'

The Bishop, he is fast asleep.

So she says: 'Who is this woman?'

The Bishop, he just mumbles and snores on.

But Laura, this idea naggles at her; she needs to know how it is he's saying these things, and what is going on in his mind. What has he been up to? So she asks him again: 'Who is this woman in the north?'

And The Bishop, he blarts out: 'She is the woman I love!'

Now Laura, she is in the pillows, and Laura, she thinks as this is, in fact, a very serious statement to admit to, right out loud, in the midst of the night, even if he is fast asleep.

Laura, she gets to thinking about The Bishop.

And Laura, she wonders exactly what it is he has been scheming at downstairs all evening, while she's been slogging over his dinner, creeping about the place like an oont; fetching him his drink, delivering his pipe, and his baccy, and his matches, and his slippers, and dragging his ratted-up old self upstairs, ripping his filthy old kit off him, packing him in his dozing livery, and assigning him to the old brass rattler.

Laura, she feels provoked, somewhat.

Laura, she's beginning to feel a mite waspish with this new woman malarkey all of a sudden, harking at him snoring his head off, conjuring up images of this fancy bit he's got hibernating up in Greenland somewhere.

Very soon, Laura, she is just about as throttled off as if she's lost the winning lottery ticket.

Laura, she gets to reckoning as maybe The Bishop is not such a good bloke after all.

In fact, Laura, she gets to reckoning as maybe The Bishop is a dirty old gander, altogether.

And, but the thing is, hanging on the wall, above the bed, there is this old big copper bed warmer gismo.

This is a fair size old gadget with a long, turned ashwood handle and the pan itself is a old copper job, as they used to shovel red hot embers into in the olden days and whang down the sheets before they crept in of a frosty winter's night – if they didn't have a lie-by to hot it up first.

Anyway up, this antique warming pan gismo tool dangles on a rusty old five-inch nail banged in the wall above Moreton and Laura's old brass rattler.

And as Laura thinks what she thinks and who The Bishop is running his big dieselly mitts over, Laura, she stands up on the bed, in the darkness, and wobbles about a bit, and fumbles about for this gismo, unhooks it from the nail and she swings this gadget up in the air – as there is plenty of room in this old gaff to take a good swing with a vintage copper bed gadget – and Laura, she brings this down on The Bishop's napper and she gives him the fairest donging on the bonce as any fellow ever had as when he was fast a-doing whatever he was, in the land of Nod.

And, but, even though The Bishop, even as he is a deadweight snorer, this clonk on the noggin with a warming pan full blast, this wakes him, more or less, up.

The Bishop, in a somewhat confused state, thinks as he is being attacked, and because he's quick by nature, he lashes out and grabs this thing as delivers him a good blast on the noggin, and gives it a heave, and this heave it pulls Laura down on him, so now, because he is still not altogether awake in that he is still clipped from the distillery product and the other half is still in the land of nod, is he wrestles with this lot as if it was a monster from the telly.

'It's alright!' he shouts: 'I got him!' and he battles all this heap on him, and the bed pan and the pillows and Laura, then rolls out of bed taking the blankets and sheets and spinning Laura of the other direction and he lands with a mighty crash on the floor.

There, The Bishop, he fights for his life with this tangle, puffing and huffing and thumping at this thing.

Laura, she harks at the terrible fight as is taking place now on the floor as The Bishop he is hammering six parts of the Marquis of Queensbury into this gadget and four parts of the other. And this bed warmer gismo, Moreton, he gives it the larrupping of its life and he is more lungeous at this gadget as ever man could be to a evil beast.

And then Laura sees him get to his feet with all the sheets and blankets wrapped round his head and he swings this lot and the bed warmer with one huge swing and it all goes crashing against the wall and he goes flying after it.

Then comes the huge sound of collapsing masonry and plaster and breaking timber and snapping laths.

And then silence.

Laura, she is kneeling on the bed with her hands over her mouth.

Laura, she hardly dares to breathe.

Laura, she gets to thinking as the calamity she was thinking downstairs is come and The Bishop, he is killed because he was having a dream and she duffed him on the noggin with a bed warmer.

And now she will have to go to the nickery.

And they will have to bury The Bishop.

Laura, tears spring to her eyes. Laura, she daredn't turn on the light.

No sound comes from where all the noise has been.

Dust, it rises into the room.

'Moreton?' Laura calls, wormy quiet.

Only silence replies.

'Moreton?' she calls again.

A stone moves, something scrapes acrost the floor.

'Moreton?' she calls again then smacks on her bedside light.

She dives over thother side of the bed and sees this: she sees a pair of legs sticking out of a pile of stones and plaster.

'Moreton!' she calls and jumps down beside him, pulls the plaster and stones off and grabs his face and commences to start blubbing.

'Urghghghghhhh,' Moreton groans.

Laura, she's that happy as he is not a corpse she begins again to do water-break-its-neck all over him.

'Where am I? What happened? How did I get here?' Moreton asks, rubbing his head.

So now Laura is not about to tell him as she whanged him good and hard on his napper with a copper bed pan for having some dirty dream just now so she says: 'You was sleep walking.'

Sitting in his dirty snoring-overalls on the floor and still rubbing his head, Moreton slowly gazes around at havoc everywhere: the smashed up wall, masonry on the floor, busted bed warmer, sheets and blankets all in a thraggle in amongst the lath and plaster and says: 'Ruddy 'ell. Sleep walking? Looks like sleep-bulldozing to me. Do I do this often?'

'No,' says Laura, 'Fortunately.'

Then Moreton gazes into the hole in the wall behind him, where all the masonry and plaster has fell out and starts rootling around in there.

'Get us a torch Laura,' he says, 'there's something in here.'

'Go on, Laura,' he says, so Laura nips off for a torch and comes back with the lamping lamp.

So now The Bishop, he's digging in this hole in the wall

with this lamping lamp as throws about as much light out as the sun, which is good for this kind of job, and presently, Moreton draws out an old cobwebby box.

And this old box is a very worm-ridden and rusty old commodity with cankered hinges on and Moreton, he gives it a good rattle.

'Anything in there?' Laura asks.

'Dunno,' says Moreton putting it down and clearing the dust and cobwebs from off of it.

'This could be the answer to our problems,' he says, looking for a way to open this box.

'Don't speak too soon,' says Laura.

But he and her are thinking, hoping, praying as there's gold and diamonds in there, or emeralds or sapparites or something.

'It's locked tight,' he says and though he looks for a key in the hole in the wall he can't find one so he gives the box a good hard smack, busts the hinges and wrenches off the lid.

Inside, is nothing but a letter, folded over, wrote on very old and very brittle paper.

'Dammit,' says The Bishop.

But Laura says: 'No, hang on a minute: let's take it downstairs into the light and see what it says: it could be important.'

On the dining room table, very careful, Laura spreads it out and reads. Only it takes her a while as it is in fact, wrote in old English and is very faint.

The letter is addressed to Sir John Morton of Bentpennny Castle and is signed, with a seal, from Eleanor Kielder, York and is dated June 17th, 1545. Laura can only make out: '......in these troubled days...... thou canst not breach the walls nor chance the posterns... suffice it, for you to know, My Lord, that My Heart is pierced, there is none other, yet am I a prisoner in a cage of gold, yet dost Thou set me free.... embrace... my dreams... a gift from me, a token... Our destiny... entwined...Fate obscureth all.'

'And look,' says Laura: 'the crest – the seal – the wax seal –

it's the head of a boar!'

And this letter, and the seal so amazes The Bishop and Laura as they cannot speak. It is as though this lady has cried out to them across the centuries.

And then Laura and Moreton, they looks up at the big old carved beam over the inglenook, in their dining room, at the pair of wild boar, in the middle of the carving, their faces close together and the lady boar is shot through the heart with a arrow.

They looks at this for a long while, and then Moreton, he says: 'I was going to ring up McCartneys in the morning to stick this old gaff on the market.'

And then Moreton, my friend, The Bishop, says: 'We're going to have the day off tomorrow, you and me, and we're going to get on the phone to all the people as owes us money, and round up our invoices, that's what we're going to do. We're going to get back the money we are owed: we're fretting for nothing. Then we're going to make plans for a big restoration job for this old place, get all the grants, English Heritage, Welsh Heritage, Scots Heritage, The EU and ESA, USA and everything else and get on with it.'

And he folds this letter back up and sticks it back in the box, and says: 'For the next generation of Mortons.'

Heaven Sent Bunny

Down in the valley, there's a river runs, and this river, it is a not a very wide one, but it is pretty, with small spratlings in and a trout maybe, a grayling, whatever, damsel-flies, and frogs; a heron sometimes; dippers – kingfishers even – of a summer, by the old stone bridge, underneath the withy trees.

Anyway up, hardish by the water, somewhere down the other side the bridge, that is, away from the withies, is a bit of a rare old shack, being as it is, of some age now, with its walls all flaked over, the windows rusted shut, moss growed up over the slates, and lichens and stuff stuck to the walls.

And this old shack, it is well cluttered up with bits of tackle, half-sawed tree trunks, chains, old tractors and whatnot.

And, but, the thing is, this place was probably an old knacker's yard in some king's reign, or a mill; a wool wharf, maybe. I don't know what it was.

Maybe it was a pub.

Or some sort of a antique Roman effort.

Any rate, whatever it was, this place now, is where The Barbary Chopper, a friend of mine lives, with his lie-by, Jennie, along with a heap of dogs, and a ruck of cats, ducks, rabbits; a few geese, ponies, and this little daughter affair, they call Jemima.

Anyway up, The Barbary Chopper, in that he is a friend of

mine, is, you might say, almost like some sort of a gorilla, in reality, in that Barbary, he is an extremely hairy kind of a bloke altogether, with woolly arms and woolly legs and a woolly back and woolly chest and he is probably the most hairiest bloke in the valley.

And Barbary, in that he is the most hairiest bloke in the valley, and a bit like a gorilla, he is also prone to go skiddley-do up trees all day, with his chainsaw, because Barbary, he is a some sort of a tree smith, and gathers up his scratch in this way.

Also, Barbary, in that he goes skiddley-do up trees with chainsaws, he's forever fiddling on engines, or sharpening blades, or honing up axes or mattocks or billhooks or froes, all these kind of things, because this is his trade.

And usually he is kitted up in a filthy old boiler suit, which stinks of petrol, and oil, and sawdust or bark sap, or something, and sweat.

Also, he wears these big old Dunlops with metal toes, and on his head he wears this safety gismo, with ear muffs. His hands are always black, and he has spanners and screwdrivers stuffed in his pockets, and when he is not up a tree being a tree smith, whatever, he is down rootling about in the back of this old van, digging out engine bits, or grinding axes and whatnot, with this angle-grinder gadget.

Anyway up, one hot summer's morning, Barbary, he is dressed up in all this outfit, sweating through his boiler-suit like a footplate didicoy, screaming through all these axe-heads and mattocks with his angle-grinder as he is in something of a scort on account of as he is supposed to be up the valley doing some tree job for this toff. And while he is doing this he catches a glimpse behind him of this little tiny girl, who is a very pretty little thing, with long blonde hair and big blue eyes and she is dressed in a pretty little frock with lacy collars and she has white socks on, and she, this little girl, she is bawling her eyes out.

And so Barbary, he stops grinding away with his angle-grinder and he turns around to this little girl, who also happens to be this little daughter affair of his, and he says, like this, he says: 'What is the matter with you, my little shushty? Why are you bawling your eyes out?'

But she does not answer.

Instead, she runs over to him and jumps in his lap, bang on top of all his filthy overalls, and she snuggles up to his chops which he has not shaved, and really he must be like snuggling up to an old hedgepig as been kipping in the axle of a Drott, being as he is very prickly, and smelly, and oily.

And this little girl, she is very clean and soft and her hands are very small, and Barbary, he's got hands big as King Kong, and hairier, probably, and he throws these about this little Jemima, which is when he is even more gorillary, and his hands, which are big, like I said, cover up this little girl, almost entirely.

So Barbary, he says to this little girl again: 'What is the matter, little shushty?' and at the same time, he sneaks a quick gander at his watch, as he is in a very big hurry, and here is this engine slamming away and he is sitting in the back of his old van with this little girl in his filthy old lap, and she is sobbing her heart out.

So now, Barbary, he is also a very gentle bloke, even though he is hairy, and big, and strong, and very like a gorilla, he picks this little girl up, and carries her into the house, inside.

Inside there is Barbary's lie-by, Jennie.

And Jennie, she has got the radio blarting, and the washing-machine blarting, and the dishwasher pounding, and the place ronks of soap and onions, and the table is all covered in marmalade; bills; newspapers; socks; dirty plates; tomato ketchup and stuff. And Jennie, she is in a big scort too, as she is trying to get everything done as she has to take this little kiddy to school.

So now, Barbary, he says to Jennie: 'What is the matter with our little shushty what is bawling her eyes out just as I am trying to get off with my chain saw so as to get to work in order for us to be able to buy grub and stuff and pay our taxes and bills and school clothes for this little kiddy, and all the other things which trouble us, even VAT.'

And Jennie, she says: 'What do you think I do, all day, feeding you, and the ponies, and the rabbits, and the geese, and mending clothes, and cleaning the house, and washing your clothes, and scrubbing the bath, and unplugging the drains with all the hairs you keep moulting?'

So then Barbary, on being a touch kanky, he dumps this little kiddy down as he is about to give Jennie a piece of comorondo straight and get this whole thing running up to a pretty good head, when this little kiddy, she runs out the kitchen.

So now Barbary and Jennie, they set to as to who does most work and for what, and pretty soon they are having one good nuclear here, with plenty of slamming doors and shouting, divorce, leaving home, and quitting altogether, the valley, entirely.

Anyway up, Barbary, he glares through the kitchen window and sees, outside, his little kiddy kneeling down beside her bunny hutch and she is holding something in her hands. Barbary, when he sees this he says 'Hang on a mo' and he nips out.

And Jennie nips out.

And now they are standing beside this little girl who is holding in her hands one very dead bunny.

And this little kiddy, she is bawling: 'What is the matter with him?' And so Barbary, with all his anger gone, and Jennie with all her anger gone, they look at one another waiting for the other, and so Jennie, she holds back as Barbary he is about to say: 'This bunny is kicked the bucket.'

But he does not say this on account of Jennie who gets in quick with: 'Poor little bunny. He is died.'

So the little girl, she asks, why is he died? So Jennie, she says, 'Jesus: he calls him.'

So this little daughter, she asks why? How come Jesus gets to calling her bunny, and not somebody else's?

So Barbary, he is looking at his tick-tock again, he says, 'I must go.'

Then Jennie, she says: 'No, you must bury this bunny first.'

So Barbary, he says: 'Later'.

But Jennie she says: 'Now'.

So then, this little kiddy, she says: 'Why must we bury this bunny. What for?'

So Jennie, she says: 'So's he can go to heaven.'

So this little daughter, she is very mystified by this. But she does not say anything. Only she agrees to burying this bunny, now. So then Barbary, he is collecting all his anger back because he can see no point to burying this bunny now, and he says so: again.

But this little kiddy she says she wants to bury him now.

So Barbary, he says he cannot, because he is late. He says he'll come back and bung this bunny in a hole, later.

But the little girl says, no she wants to do it now.

So Barbary, he says he can't.

So Jennie, she tells the little kiddy she has to go to school.

So this little kiddy, she turns on the waterworks again.

And now Barbary he is fed up with this dead bunny, and Jennie, she is fed up with this dead bunny, and so Barbary he says to Jennie: 'You do it; I am in one big rush'.

But Jennie, she says: 'No, you do it; I am also in one big rush'.

So they commence this whole new engagement about burying this bunny, and this little girl, she starts to do Niagara and so Barbary, he says: 'Alright, I will do it.

So off he goes and rootles about in the back of his van for a good digging graft and so now they have to decide where to bury this bunny.

And this little kiddy, she cannot decide.

First it is here, then it is there, and then it is somewhere else.

So then, Barbary, he decides, then Jennie says no that is definitely the wrong place, and now Barbary, he is holding this dead bunny by the ears, and this little kiddy bawls at him about that, and whips it off of him, and then Barbary, he tells Jennie to decide where to bury this bunny, and this little kiddy she is in flood again and so they ask her, and she decides to bury him under the tree.

But Barbary says this is where all the roots are. He is not going to spend all day digging roots.

So Barbary, he goes to slap bang in the middle of the lawn and he starts to dig. And this makes Jennie blow 3-phase because she says about sticking this turf down only six months previous and how much this stung, and here is Barbary tearing into it with his graft and has he got no brains?

But Barbary, he just goes on and on – in his blue dungarees and chainsaw boots and plastic hat and with his screwdrivers falling out his pockets, and everything.

Then this little girl, she sits beside Barbary as he is digging this hole and when Barbary takes this dead bunny from her and is about to flop him in it and boot the soil over him, this little kiddy, she wants to wrap him up in something.

So Barbary he pulls an oil rag out his pocket and tries to wind this dead bunny up in this. But this little girl, she snatches this bunny back.

This starts this thing up about what to wrap him up in so he can go to heaven fairly clean. So then Jennie has to run to the house and rummage through the cupboards looking for an old handkerchief maybe or something, and then she finds one white linen napkin, and so this bunny, he winds up inside this (which is one of Jennie's best).

And then he has to have some bunny food put in with him, and a little flower or two, and some hay, and a bit of lettuce, and daisies all round and a plastic ear-ring, and a few coppers, and picture of Jesus. So now Barbary he has had enough of all this and he leaves: he does the bunk: he is gone.

Anyway up, Barbary he goes off and he does his day's graft.

He goes skiddley-do up this ginormous oak.

As he is up in the crown of this oak he spies, creeping across the sky, a evil black cloud.

And this cloud, he creeps right over where Barbary is grafting.

The sky, it goes black.

And down comes the biggest thundering pelting as ever shook timber.

Barbary, he gets soakeder than brook moss.

Barbary, he gets froze.

Barbary, he has about the bitchiest day as any mortal ever cracked nuts. His chainsaw bungs up; the petrol is full of water. The wind, it turns the job to mariner. He nearly falls out the tree. He squashes a thumb. Sawdust, it is always in his eyes. The chainsaw, she conks more oftener than she fires.

This is one long hooking.

By five o'clock, Barbary, he is kanked.

Duffed from skiddley-dooing up trees; wrunged out from heaving big branches, he slumps in his van, stonko.

He is too pooped even to drive this van.

He shuts his eyes.

He dreams of doing some other job: any sort of other job.

So long as it's something else.

He sits up, sighs, smudges wood gunk out his eyes, leans forward, turns the key and – this van, it will not start.

Then, the toff who he works for comes out and says will he get this van out the way.

Barbary says he is trying to do this.

Then this toff, he looks at the tree Barbary has just done, and he stays schtum.

This makes Barbary think he does not like what he has done; which makes Barbary fretchit.

And, but, so, Barbary he struggles with this van, extra kanky. Soon, Barbary, he is fit to kill this van.

Two hours pass, and he's sucked most the petrol out and blown the fuel lines through, and undone every nut and bolt and given her a good booting, in the radiator-grill even, and in the doors.

At last she fires.

Barbary; he bangs this old heap into gear and goes scorting off down the lane.

If anyone meets him to ask him a favour, say, this would not be a good time.

Anyway up: no-one does.

Barbary, he gets home a touch after seven.

When he gets home, because of this van, and one thing and another, he is not the easiest bloke as is to get on with.

And Jennie; the washing machine: it broke and puddled the kitchen; and she was late for school. And she forgot the dinner money. So she is not the easiest kind of girl either, come to that, to get on with.

When Barbary and Jennie, they meet, the air: well; the air, it is fallout. Barbary steams to a window, slams his fists on the sill and glowers out.

Outside, on the lawn he sees this: he sees his little kiddy, she is standing in the middle of the lawn and she is digging up this place where Barbary, he buried this bunny.

So he shouts. 'Oi!' So Jennie, wants to know why he is shouting 'Oi'. Then she sees this little girl digging up this dead bunny. So Barbary and Jennie, they both rushes out to the lawn to this little kiddy and they shouts: 'What do you think you are doing?' – very crowsty. This little kiddy, she looks up. She is very innocent in her reply: with her big round eyes, and little red lips, and dimply cheeks. She says, very quiet – she says she is just seeing if this bunny is gone to heaven yet.

Barbary, he picks this little kiddy up.

When he smiles, Barbary, he gets these big dimples: as is where, I suppose the girl comes by hers.

He gives this little girl a kiss. Which is probable as like as you can get to having a wet coconut mat rubbed in your face.

This little girl, she throws her arms about Barbary.

Barbary, he grabs a holt of Jennie with his other arm.

Barbary, he turns to look across the meadows behind his place to where a big old rainbow has sprang up. And now the sun, it is smarting upon the river, very pretty. And the bushes, they are full of little birdies playing hide and seek. And the air, it is bluer and clearer as a gosling's eye. In the trees, some old quist is cooing away, and you can even hear the grasshoppers rattling about in the meadow.

And Barbary, he says to this little kiddy: 'Never you mind about digging up this bunny, my little shusty,' he says, Barbary, looking around him at the river and the fields and where the rainbow is: 'This little bunny, you don't want to fretchit about him, as he is been in heaven now, a fair old while.'

The Patriots

'I have little doubt,' Kipper Northern is stating out loud down The Crown two weeks last Tuesday dinner time, round about fetching-out time, 'that the National Flag of this and one or two other shires I knows is in fact, identical. It is exactly the same in every respect. So, being as it is, I believe we ought not to pay our rates and council tax.'

'What these County Hall people in these shires keeps on making their big-sorted claims about is how they is unique, how they does most for everyone: what they do is better and less costly and gooder for the community as the next shire.'

'But everyone knows,' Kipper says, as no-one is opposing him, 'they do as little as possible for as much money as possible and there isn't hardly any point in most of them doing anything anyway, particularly if you happen to be an old wuzzuk jammed in a good snowdrift out in a bothy on the beacon at the time.'

Then, Kipper Northern goes on, as still no-one is opposing him, 'Since the National Flag of these shires is, in fact, nothing but an old silage bag flapping from a fence post, and on account of the numbers of these as you see everywhere, you have to admit that it is a very common sight indeed in these parts, it would seem as everyone round here is very nationalistic and patriotic about their shire and big supporters of the County Hall, that they

71

should be about ready for a rebate on their taxes for showing such undivided loyalty. Do you not agree?'

So then Trouser ups and says: 'Only this morning,' assisting in this argument and helping to firm up this line of thinking, 'as I was steeping into The Anchor Inn up on the tops, I had the opportunity to admire loads of these flags all being fluttered at the same time in the hedge up and down along the road.

The reason I went in The Anchor was to congratulate the farmers that go there for their loyalty and, when I was on my way here, from there, it near enough brought a lump to my throat to see with what vigour the farmers in these parts is given to their shire in such strong shows of nationalistic and patriotic pride as you never saw so many flags in your life flying from here to the Beacon and all the way to Llandrindod Wells, if you go there now, which was the way I came, it being a bright sunny sort of a morning and ripe for a bit of a tootle about.'

And so, we all – that's Knukky Stubbs and Ivor the Wellies, George Gunter the F and Blast, Kipper Northern, Willie the Pooh, Trouser Jabez, The Bishop and me – we all agrees heartily on this and goes to the window to see how many we see flying right at that moment and although it has to be said as George Gunter the F and Blast in fact springs a bit of a cheater on us by stepping out into the road and having a good gander up and down, he does, in fact, collar the prize by spotting no less than fifteen, even though the ones he sees are not as big as some of the ones you find a bit further away from the village, where the farmers are more nationalistisic than those right beside them.

'The thing is,' he says: 'is that, in fact, it has to be said farmers are more nationalistic in wintertime as they are in summertime as is when they loose go of more of these flags by and by and I have been across the tops on The Anchor road one winter time and had to stop and have a little cry in the hedge as there was so much patriotism and nationalism being shown as the fence was nothing but flags for the four miles from here to there and that's without a word of a exaggerated lie.'

And so now we are getting to grips with what it is about our shire as the most unique thing and we are all come to agree that it is without a doubt as it is, in fact, not only the place, but also it is the farmers and them as abides in these parts, in that they are a rare old crew and apt to do some strange things and think some strange thoughts as well.

'I knows a gaffer round here,' says The Bishop, 'as firmly believes that his sheep dog is the living reincarnation of a Tibetan honey bear.

What a Tibetan honey bear is, I do not know, how big it is, what colour it is or what it does but anyway this farmer's dog is the living re-incarnation of one, so who am I to say it isn't? For all I know it is able to get up any amount of tricks. Not only can it understand everything everyone says all the while but also he can speak this Tibetan language, which, is, as far as I know, not that common round here, but then neither is common sense, so what can we do about all this kind of thing then?'

'This is true,' says George Gunter the F and Blast, 'F and Blast, the way this man knows he is able to speak this language is because one day this old Tibetan holy priest bloke, as is called some weird name like a Lada or wildebeeste some such animal as does not inhabit round here, comes on telly and this dog, he leps up to the telly and licks it and starts to howl.

And then as this holy priest is yakking on, this old dog harks like he understands every word he says, which is why this bloke thinks his dog is a reincarnation of a Tibetan honey bear because he probably is.'

'There are many things in life as is strange and we cannot none of us tell what it is and whether this person or that person has done this or that for real or been took away by little green men in flying saucers, but there has been one or two moments when I think it might have happened to me,' says Knocker Morsel, and this is easy enough to credit on account of the state of him, half the while. It is even said, as old Pinzer used to reckon, Knocker Morsel was a little green man hisself the way he flies about in his wagon as you would need to have some kind of a special arrangement with other beings to be able to do it.

'It is the same with some people,' Knocker says, 'as sometimes you wonder if they are giving you the run around or not. You take old Jervey William's Mrs – the strangest apparition as ever climbed out the back of a Landrover. Now well, if she hadn't come creeping straight out of Mars, I dunno what. And she never spoke no language no-one ever could get within half-a-mile of and we all knows what happened to her. Or do we? And there's been those mysterious moments round here when things have just vanished out of sight just like that bang, gone. Like my quad bike for example: there it was in the shed in the morning sitting quietly, minding its own business in the corner and by dinner time it was gone. In broad daylight. What is that if that's not magic? But could I get the insurance man to see it that way? Could I, horse-feathers. He gives me the run around something rotten. And he's not the only one neither. I got a old horse as does this. I canna make head nor tail of it as I wonder he is giving me the run around for a long old while now.'

And so we gets to asking Knocker about this horse of his and this is what he tells us.

Knocker Morsel says he has a very well-wintered black horse called The Cakehole. And The Cakehole, he stands maybe 15 hands high, about the same wide, and has a long black mane and a tangly tail and The Cakehole is a very amicable horse, indeed.

In fact, The Cakehole is so amicable he hangs about Knocker all day.

He hangs about him groaning and snorting and blowing and snoozing and waiting for him to knock the flies off. And he gazes at Knocker with his big eyes, which makes Knocker feel guilty for not giving him apples or mints or chunks of cake or swigs of beer, or really anything that might happen to be in his hand. Knocker says he is, actually, not a very fussy eater. Knocker says he has even known him to eat bananas and bacon sandwiches and sausages and once he even shared bag of fish and chips with him, Daily Mirror and all. Knocker says, not only is this horse not a very fussy eater, but in actual fact, this horse is a very serious gannet. But Knocker cannot work him out. He does not know if he is really a very serious gannet, and very stupid, or is just pretending to be a very serious gannet, and is very clever.

'I doubt that old horse hasn't been giving me the run around for fifteen years now. But then, I do not know: in fact, I gets to thinking all the while as this old nag has got no brains at all.'

This, Knocker says, is on account of his not seeming to be able to learn anything, especially when it comes to riding: he will not steer, or stop, or start, or stand still, and when Knocker tries to put a saddle on him, he pushes off: even if he ties him.

The only way to ride The Cakehole is to find out what he wants to do, then let him do it; so maybe he'll give him a bit of a shuffle around his farm, if he's lucky. But still, Knocker doesn't mind. As he says, The Cakehole is a very amicable horse.

But the other day, Knocker thinks maybe he is giving him the run-around, after all.

He finds out by way of an incident, and on this occasion Knocker is poothering about in his garden doing a bit of this and a bit of that, shaking a few apples out of a tree and one apple, he notices, drops onto a stone wall beside the house and The Cakehole spies this apple.

But Knocker sees also it is a whisker beyond The Cakehole's reach.

So Knocker watches as The Cakehole stretches out his neck and pokes out his top lip as far as it will go. But this apple is not going to go down The Cakehole's gullet. One final big stretch and this apple goes tootling off the wall onto the lawn opposite where it rolls a short distance but stays within The Cakehole's sight. For one minute The Cakehole stands gazing. He is the most disappointed old long-face as my friend Knocker ever saw, Knocker says. But then with a swish of his tail The Cakehole shoves off down the drive as if he doesn't give a pip, anyway.

Ten minutes later he is back.

For another long moment he gazes at this apple. Then he looks along the back of Knocker's house and disappears. Knocker hears him clumping past, hears the garden gate creak, watches as this black head comes peeking round the corner, followed by the rest of The Cakehole, who tippy-toes past the back door (where Knocker is standing), and crosses the lawn, goes straight to his apple and sinks his chompers round it. Then, on his way out he takes a goodish swipe of Knocker's sweet peas, shambles back across the lawn, stops for Knocker to swat a few flies off, then turns out through the garden gate and goes swinging off down the drive.

'Is that it?' George Gunter the F and Blast blasts.

'Yes,' says Knocker.

'Well I dunna credit that's much of a story. Old horses eating or not eating apples is about as newsworthy as getting the old honeysucker up from Leominster. Excepting the time old Wilf went through the top of Elizabeth Beddow's tank as says it's the only time in life he's been pleased to find out as someone is a vegetarian, only not quite in a way as he expected.'

'But I can tell you a story as is historical and true and worthy of a diary or a Chronicle as is about patriotism and animals and flags and everything else as will amaze and astonish you,' says George Gunter the F and Blast, 'as is about a pair of old shire horses in Hancock's Brewery in Swansea as is gone now, but was there once, above the docks, not far from Wind Street, around the corner a touch.'

'These two old horses – I forgets their names now – was pulling the Hancock's dray from Monday til Saturday everyday, been working in harness together all the while when up come the remount man from that army place one fine day in 1915 and grabs a holt of these two and sends them off to the war as artillery horses, right up in the front line in Ypres.'

'And you can imagine how long them old horses used to last up there in those days. Two weeks was about the time for a young officer. Three days for a heavy horse. And, but, the thing is, a lad goes along with them and it's the lad as drives them for the brewery and he signs up to the army as well at the same time as these old horses, and he goes along just to be with them, as he is that fond of them.'

'And this lad, even though he's just a squit of a gadget, he hoys ups these old horses along to this Ypres place when they arrives in France, and straight away, he is told to cart shells up to the artillery along this track as is in range of the enemy guns. But this lad, he does what he's told, only he's very canny to watch where these shells is landing and he weaves these horses in and out along this track in amongst all them bombs and grenades and gas. And this lad, he keeps doing this, day after day and everyone is amazed how he manges to keep not only alive himself, but keep these old horses without a mark on them, when thothers is being blown apart. Any rate, he says nothing, only lugs plenty of dinner down these horses even though he goes hungry hisself. He grooms them and talks to them, carts water for them and even when he sleeps he's got one eye on them. And this lad, he won't let no-one else handle these horses as he knows as long as he's with them, they'll act

sensible and clever as they are a canny pair of yarbs so they are, but only if he's there, with them, even in amongst all the bombs. When he's not there they rears and plunges and acts all frit to death but as long as he's with them, they're sound.'

'Then one day, one of them gets injured, so he packs him off with a mate of his as in the veterinary as he's clever to make friends with. But he goes on working thother on his own, telling him all the while as his mate will be alright.'

' And these bombs keeps falling and shells exploding and he keeps dodging them and then one winter's day, he fetches thother back and so they're working together again and that brings new life to the old horse as had got pretty run down working on his own, even though this lad kept talking to him all the while, night and day. So now he gives him a bit of a rest even though he's not supposed to and then they're in harness again, lugging these shells up to the cannons and he works with these two horses right up to the end of that war: four years straight. In that time they sees terrible things; horses blown up in front of their eyes, horses with their limbs blown straight off, others galloping off across minefields.'

'But the thing is, when that war is over, the army gets shipped back to Blighty in a hell of a state, but the horses – they leaves them and most of them goes straight for slaughter in Belgium and in France, as they eats them out there.'

'This lad though, he wasn't going to let that happen to his horses, because he loves these two old dray shires, and somehow or other he gets them back to Dover by bribery and jiggery pokery and sends a telegram off to Hancock's to tell them he's still got them. So they bungs them on a train and sends them back to Swansea.'

'And when they arrives on the train there is all these flags waving and people comes to meet them and cheer them as they steps out the carriage. These two old horses must have been mighty surprised to find this reception for them since they'd only know kindness or recognition from this one lad in all the years of horror they'd been through: no-one had so much as given them a glance otherwise. But now here they are, with everybody waving and screaming and flapping flags at them.'

'So then this lad, he takes these horses back to their own stables and settles them in and feeds and looks after them til they are fit enough for proper work again. The first round he puts them on is the last one they was on four and half years before, when they was bought up by the remount man and sent off to war. So this lad he hoys ups the horses and sends them off and then drops the reins to see if they remember and the first place they goes is the No Sign Bar, in Wind Street, just round the corner from the brewery and stops there, just as they had done five years before.'

'Well that's more or less the end of that story except to say as these two old horses got the Dicken Medal apiece for bravery but the young lad as looked after them all the while stood back and wouldn't take any acclaim.

'No,' he says, 'it was them as was the brave ones, they are the ones as did the work: they are the ones as deserve it,' and he let them have all the glory all on their own. And now no-one remembers his name, that lad, except I doubt, for a pair of old shire horses and the proud mother that bore him.'

Man of Straw

Islwyn the Invention is also called Islwyn the Invisible and he is called Islwyn the Invisible because when any work is about to commence, this is what he becomes.

He is nowhere to be seen.

He is gone.

He is nowhere.

Not even God can find him.

But when work is ending he becomes visible again and works with all his heart, so that when everyone is tired and worn out, and exhausted, and hot, and thinking about the Speckledy Hen in The White Horse, this fresh pair of hands makes them very grateful to him, and they are happy he has come to help, and make these last few strokes light.

But no-one knows how he achieves this: no-one knows how he manages to go from farm to farm in order to help everyone finish their work, whether it is mucking out calf pens, or cleaning out the hen house, or lugging the last bales or wrapping the last fleeces.

And they do not know how he makes them feel as if he has been there all day and needs his bait just as much as they do, which they give him.

Then at night, when all the sheep herders and the cow chasers and the pony breakers and the muckers out of pigs and chickens and the luggers of bales and pleachers of hedges and the shearers of sheep go down to The White Horse for their entertainment and talk about their day's work, Islwyn joins in, and has a very great knack of making everyone feel he has worked alongside them, so they then buy him plenty of Speckledy Hen and he tells them big stories of when he used to work in Africa and Saudi Arabia or somewhere, then did a few years with the Secret Service in the army then fought in some war or other then rode a motorbike round Brazil or somewhere, then worked on a sailboat, then took the train from London to China – all these kinds of things.

But he does not admit to these exploits until he has had a great many jugs of Speckledy Hen. So whereas no-one doubts what he has to say is true, nobody believes him either. And this is why they also call him Islwyn the Invention.

In fact, they really think he is nothing but a big romancer, getting carried away with himself, and cannot distinguish between the truth and an untruth: that very little of what he says, actually, holds much substance.

Yet they do not dislike him.

He is a very difficult fellow to dislike.

He is always happy, and is always in good spirits and makes good jokes and when he has any bleat, which is not often, he will buy Speckledy Hen for everyone until all his bleat is gone and he is thoroughly bleatless.

Then next day, when the work is beginning, he will become invisible again.

So the sum of what the people in the valley think is that Islwyn is, in fact, a bit of a sponger, and that, in reality, most of what he says is rubbish.

In truth, they think he is a man of straw.

81

Anyway up, one day, when work is not long started and he has become invisible again, he arrives suddenly at Richard the Top's place at one o'clock, dinnertime, on his tin donkey, which is in fact not a tin donkey, but a moped, which is what he calls it, and it is clear to Richard the Top that Islwyn the Invisible has been in The White Horse for the best part of the morning and has become Islwyn the Invention and is about to tell him an untruth.

And Richard the Top feels this because he believes that Islwyn only does these things to attract attention to himself on account of his being a man of straw.

So when Islwyn tells him a fire has broken out in his big stock barn on the other side of the mountain, and Richard glances over and says he doesn't see any smoke, and says that if he does see any smoke he will go and put it out, and that maybe Islwyn ought to go back to The White Horse again and have a bit more Speckledy Hen, that Islwyn spins his tin donkey round and rides away in a very big huff and Richard the Top chuckles and thinks that he is a very weak-headed boy, indeed.

It is three hours later Richard looks over the mountain and sees the smoke.

Then he rings the fire brigade and gets in his Landrover and roars over the mountain and when he gets there the barn is storming.

But well away from the barn is his machinery that has been in a big lean-to beside it, and his horses that have been inside it, and his cows that have been inside it, and all but one of his calves that have been inside it. But there is no sign of Islwyn. So Richard thinks, and everyone thinks, that Islwyn will turn up just as the fire is being put out. But they cannot make out who has driven the animals to safety, and who dragged out the machinery. Nor can they make out why the fire has begun – or who, perhaps, has started it.

And though they wait for Islwyn to turn up, he does not.

And so they become suspicious, and think, maybe, he is

hiding, or is in The White Horse and in a very muddled state.

But when they go there that night, no-one has seen him since morning.

Then they become very suspicious, and they tell the police of their suspicions.

It is the next day when the firemen are going through the embers to find the cause of the blaze they find the electrical fault that has started it. And as they comb the burned out ruin they find beneath collapsed iron sheeting, Islwyn's tin donkey and on the other side of the barn, where the calf pens have been, they uncover the charred remains of a man with a charred calf in his arms that has been wrapped in what they reckon must have been wet sacking.

It is a year to the day that Richard puts up a big new shed on the same spot, and calls it Man of Iron's Barn.

Sign of the Times

It is this last bank holiday past as I am loitering in a gateway, in the valley, of a late summer's evening.

And the reason I am loitering in this gateway is on account of a grand work of art.

In this gateway, there is this gate as is an ordinary, old, oak gate, hung on old iron hinges on an old chestnut post and belongs to none other than Tom Windridge and his brother Ben.

And, but, Tom and Ben Windridge's gates are in fair order for a couple of old wuzzuks, considering, because most old wuzzuks' gates is usually all fell apart and lashed up with plenty of wire and string and if you want to open them you have to cart them acrost their arc on account their hinges is shot and the wood's rotted to pieces and the only thing as is holding them there is the will of the maker and the sticks in the hedge.

But, the Windridges gates, are in fairish order, it has to be said.

But thother thing about them, is that most of them, they are all decorated up most artistical with the copperplate signs.

And these copperplate signs, they are a pleasure to look upon since they are painted with skill, and care, and pride, with scrollwork in the corners and they are wrote on good hardwood, with a shellack glaze: very professional.

And the old kiddy as does these signs is Old Ashe Able.

And, but, Old Ashe Able, he is a moithering old brock as holes up on his own in a small cottage hereby. And Old Ashe Able, he is as mean as a turnip spider and won't address two words to nobody, if he can possibly help it, and is in every way the tightest and hardest old toad as ever crawled out the lid of a Radnor bothy.

And, but, the thing is, Old Ashe, he has got this woodshed and it is in there as he cuts the wood to shape the signs he does these artistical copperplate writings on, although he never usened to do them, when he was working for the Windridges.

But, that was a while back now and the thing about Old Ashe Able grafting for the Windridges is that he usened to suffer from a terrible affliction all his life, and this affliction has cost him dear, as I will explain in a minute, as there are others in this valley as I know as has been struck with the same affliction as Old Ashe Able.

Anyway up, when he was grafting for them, old man Windridge usened to say as Ashe worked more or less a one day week, he was that took up with this affliction all the while and even then was as like to turn up as the sun is to scorch in December. But, even if he did turn up, he was as awkward as a briar in your pants, moithering on, cussing this and that and wouldn't speak to no-one nor do what he was told nor asked, and wouldn't let no-one in the tractor shed nor let them use any tools. And then he'd go off on this afflication again. Why they kep him on no-one knows, he wasna no good for milking nor feeding stock nor running the mill, so they usened to let him do a bit of bodging about the place, which is how he come by writing these signs.

But, the thing is now, as Old Ashe is got that crocked up, he is even more bitterer than he was and there's no point knocking on his door to say hello or pass the time of day as you is as like to get a mouthful, so he's best kep away from by and by, even though he has come to be took up with more Godlier things, these days, and makes these signs as he writes out in copperplate.

And these signs you will find all over the place, on gateways and on footpath stiles and sometimes, nailed to the door of The Anchor, or The White Horse or somewhere, depending.

And it happens this evening, as I am loitering in this gateway on Tom Windridge's land, and looking at the sign as is nailed to the wood, with the nails cleated over so as to make it impossible to shift without smashing it up and even then this would be a struggle as this is wrote on a piece of King Henry's oak, two inches thick and is as hard as a church slab.

Anyway, this sign says: Repent Ye, Vipers, for the Hour of Desolation Cometh.

Sometimes, it is hard trying to get hold of what Old Ashe Able is trying to get across, whether it be to we or to the snakes hereabouts, but whatever it is, these signs has the knack of making you concentrate on something more than the air as was swilling about in your head before you comes across one. Another one, across the meadows says: Look to the Ant, Thou Sluggard, and Learn Her Ways – which had the effect of putting me off nipping into The White Horse a while ago – so I goes to give old Jarvey a hand bottling his dandelion wine, instead.

Anyway up, it happens then, on this lovely late August evening, as I leaves this gateway and its sign and am sauntering along the lane, picking hardheads and gazing over the hedges at the free-flying kites swirling around Tom Windridge's yard and meadows.

I see there's blue ones there and white ones and these are the ones as are advertising something I would say, as they all says Rumavite on them. And if you are a collector of these free-flying kites you can wander about any meadow round here and pick up plenty, as they usually gets jammed in the hedges after a few days flying about, or gets snagged up on fence posts.

They are a pleasure to the eye to see farmers so happy in their work as they expresses it through the flying of these kites advertising this Rumavite stuff, which, I do believe, is a sort of Marmite for cows, and they loves it, these cows, as is why these farmers keeps loosing these free-flying kites all over their land, advertising it.

Anyway up, on this evening, as I am sauntering off to The Crown, to check if the dominoes has been shoved back in their right boxes, I pass another one of the Windridges gateways and finds this new sign as has been nailed to it. Looking at this sign, I realise that Old Ashe Able has been moved by The Spirit again, to pen another, on a black background this time and wrote in gold copperplate, for we sinners to read and learn.

But then, as I am ˈgazing upon this, who should come knocking along the lane in his old diesel estate but my old friend Barney Dawes.

This for me, is a very great surprise, so I turns round and 'how bist 'ee surrees' him and Barney, he slows down, cuts the motor and I can see at once as this is a man in dire distress.

But before I can say anything Barney, he puts his arm on the door rest and with his head weighing heavy in his right hand, he say like this. He says: 'Burt, you are not thinking of going down The Crown to see if the dominoes has been shoved back in their right boxes, are you?'

So I says as in fact, I was just standing here admiring this new piece of art as has just been exhibited for we passers-by to stand and take in, and that, in fact, the thought of going into one of these public house places, especially The Crown, just then, was a mile away from my intentions.

'But,' says I: 'if, Barney, you would like someone to talk to you as you drives there, then I would willingly hop in your motor and go along with you, for company. And, then, if you needs some help to see if the dominies has been shoved in the right boxes, I could come in and verify this.'

Barney says: 'Hop in.'

So I hops in. Barney starts his motor and off we smokes to

The Crown. 'This day I have come as close to being struck off the register of life,' says Barney as we are trundling along, 'as a mortal can be. I have had the most worst shock as anyone as carries the same afflication as me carries, and is as close to a cardiacal stoppage as is possible to be.'

'Oh,' says I, 'Barney, this is a terrible thing. What has took place to inspire such a miserable experience?'

Barney says, as we are drawing up in the car park of The Crown: 'I shall explain in there, since, in fact, it was on account of one of these kind of places as I was near enough brought low, this day and made to suffer in purgatory, for the next year or eighteen months or so.'

When we are arrived in The Crown, we finds in there these customers as are very lit up and excited and are very much delighted in particular to see Barney Dawes, and are hailing him as Champion and Wonder Maker and stuff like this, and are amazed to see him, especially, they are amazed to see him here in his motor.

So now, instead of checking the dominoes, Barney, he seems to forget about this all of a sudden, as indeed I do and we finds ourselves involved in some very intense debating about the events of this day as seems to have distressed my friend Barney Dawes, but brought life and energy to thothers and brings the beer to we.

So by and by, I gets to hear what happens and the story of what happens to Barney today is that close to some of us as to make us shudder to think it could happen to us – those of us who might find ourselves in his position, anyway. And this story goes along a bit like this.

Barney Dawes, in these long years of his being, is, by way of a trade, some sort of a stone mason.

And being some sort of a stone mason, Barney Dawes spends much of his time up ladders and such, on roofs, or beside walls, in barns or something, grafting for toffs, or farmers, or estate agents: such people as can afford to have a stone mason nowadays, grafting for them, about their place.

Anyway up, being as he is a stone mason – and no finer fellow ever mixed muck – Barney Dawes has suffered from birth from a great handicap, and this handicap has cost him dear.

Barney Dawes says whereas everyone else with a handicap gets money from the SS, and is sent cards, for sympathy, and receives benefits, and handouts every week, he receives nothing.

He says other people get dispensations, and allowances, and are given proper places to go, and sit in, and have special places to park their motors, or have seats left vacant for them, in buses and cinemas; but he – he is not offered any of these.

Even though his handicap is a serious one.

He has, Barney says, to struggle on all alone: even though there are many days when he cannot work, on account of this afflication, and the pain it brings him.

And, but, the thing is, if you ask Barney what his handicap is, he is slow to say, being a modest man, and shy, and polite, and unaccustomed to seeking pity. It is only when you gets to know him, that you finds out he do suffer from a terrible handicap indeed: Barney Dawes is afflicated from a scourge which, for some reason, the Government and the SS are not inclined to give help, or assistance or aid.

Which is unfair.

Yet he is not alone.

There are others who I know, like Old Ashe Able, and others, what lives in Big Duley and the hills round about and are pained in the same way, being born as they are of the same disability, as Barney, being as they all share the one thing in common as they all inherited from their great grandads, by and by.

And in order to remedy this, they try, all of them, without

the assistance of the SS or the Government or the church or charities, to help theirselves to overcome their difficulties, and spend, whenever they can, at least five hours of a day in The Anchor, or in The Buffalo, or The Crown, or The White Horse, or The Hundred House or The Lion, whatever.

And in The Crown or The Buffalo, wherever, they discusses their common ailment, and try to put it right, with many, many pints of Bowel Vowel, or Liver Worm, or Noggin Splitter or Black Cat or other such remedial medicines as are available there.

But, the thing is, this, in fact, has nothing whatever to do with this story – excepting to say that it is political incorrect of the Government or the SS not to help these people and so I thought I should advertise this.

Anyway up, this story begins here: on this bank holiday dinner time, the sun is high, and the sky is blue, and the little birdies are playing hide and seek in the bushes, and my friend Barney is up a ladder, just outside Big Duley. Why he's up this ladder of a bank holiday is hard to say. Just that Barney says he works for hisself so he works when he wants to, or has to and that's why he chose today to do this work, rather than tomorrow.

Anyway up, as he is up this ladder being a stone mason, suddenly, his afflication strikes him.

And, but, the thing is, in this moment, he knows he must go from the place he is in, up his ladder, to Big Duley, to The Buffalo, or The White Horse, or The Crown or somewhere, to relieve himself of his handicap, so that he might, in a couple of day's time or so, finish off the job he is asked to do.

So he descends his ladder and bungs it on top of his diesel estate, along with his other ladders, and planks and stuff, and ties them on very tight with rope, and string and them stretchy spidery gismos, and he drives, quick as he can, to The Buffalo – it being the right time to do this.

On arriving in the village, he jams his car on the side of the street somewhere, and dives into this rural gentleman's afflication therapy beer clinic job place.

And, in this rural afflication therapy beer clinic job place are other gentlemen, like him, who have gone there for the same reason, to seek remedy for their ills on this hot summer's day.

And, as is fitting for their complaints, they spend many hours in The Buffalo, playing dominoes, and cards, and reading papers and talking, and making jokes and doing all the things as one is supposed to do, should one be similarly afflicated.

Anyway up, come round about two thirty, just as they have all got very interested in discussion of their ailments and afflications, and are looking for some other venue to sample some remedies, Barney states as they ought to make haste to The Hundred House, in his motor, for one or two more, to make up for the shortage.

Agreeing to this idea, they downs their medicine, and troops out.

But, just as Barney is approaching his motor – he recognises it's his on account of it being where he left it and by the ladders as is tied on the top – but, as he draws near, he spies a slip of paper has been stuffed under the windscreen wiper, and, he thinks, hello, this is interesting. So then as all thothers are piling in his motor, he takes the slip of paper out to read it and sees this slip of paper is not wrote out by Old Ashe Able as it is not wrote in copperplate, but in a more stern hand and it says:

NOTICE:
WOULD THE OWNER OF THIS VEHICLE
CALL IN AT THE CONSTABULARY
AS SOON AS POSSIBLE.

Now this sign causes Barney anxiety.
Very sudden.
And upset.

His heart commences this heavy thumping.

And it causes him anxiety and upset and heavy heart thumping not only on account of the seven pints of afflication-easer as he has in him, but also on account of not being allowed to go to The Hundred House, all of a sudden, because of this officious invitation to visit the local nickery, whose occupants might also object to the taxless position of Barney's estate, its four Yul Brynners, the absence of insurance and MOT and such mundane matters as occupy the minds of people who dream up these tricks, in order to make other peoples' lives as miserable as possible.

So Barney, instead of going to The Hundred House, he has to go to the nickery and let his friends down, all of whom was looking forward to a little outing.

And because they are all fired up to go, and waiting in his motor, they says: 'Forget about this notice. Throw it away: do not go to the nickery. Let us go to The Hundred House, instead, and see if we can overcome our handicaps, there.'

But, being a man of integrity, and sound, Barney firms himself up to face the nickery, even though this is an arduous task, and periculous, for a man with seven pints of afflication-mending-gear down him. But he knows, as he is a canny man, that there are one or two things that he should make adjustments to – not only to himself but also to his motor – before he pays a call on the nickery, it being a sensible sort of thing to do, under the circumstances.

So he asks the occupants of his motor to go to The Hundred House without him, which they do with much complaining.

Then Barney asks Willie the Pooh, another friend of mine, to slip him off to Littlers the Scrap to get some new boots for his motor off of one of the many wrecks lying thereabouts and Willie the Pooh, who keeps a pony and a trap, and who is also in The Buffalo just now, agrees to this.

So they goes back to his place and gets the pony, and fixes him to the trap, which is not easy, and they goes over the mountain, with some fermented damson juice, so as to quench their terrible thirst.

They arrive at Littlers.

And now, they go at it with plenty of spanners and tyre-getting-off kit, whatever, to get four new-old tyres for Barney's estate with the ladders on.

And then, being as time is running short, and the damson juice is moresome, with plenty of bite in it, Willie the Pooh sneaks off for a kip in a shed somewhere, and disappears, and so Barney, who does not know how to steer Willie's pony, or anything, has to ask Mr Littler to take him back to his car, in the village, and help him fix these new Brynners on, explaining all the while the nature of his problem and the business of the visit to the nickery, which problem Mr Littler sympathises with, and understands, and so does as Barney requests, very obliging.

Anyway up, come round about five-ish, Barney has new Brynners but no tax, which means a bit of a run-around, with MOT cistificates and whatnot, which takes time and is expensive, and as he is doing this he has to go and get his insurance from the insurance company, which is excessive in costs in every way and nearly causes Barney to have a very large cardiacal stoppage indeed.

But he pays.

Then he has to go to the motor tax office.

Again.

Once he has got his insurance papers after he has been home to find his Log Book, which is hidden somewhere very inconsiderate, and in which time he eats a great quantity of mints and drinks many cups of coffee and tea and pints of milk and everything else as looks as if it might do the trick to stop old

Silver Buttons sniffing all the medicaments he has been guzzling since dinner time, on him.

Anyway up, by six o'clock, Barney is stood beside his motor.

Now she has tax, and insurance, newish tyres, an MOT cistificate and everything else old Silver Buttons could possibly want, even a soberish kind of a driver – but all this has cost him too much corks in one dollop and is about to make his daily visits to The Buffalo come a very serious cash shortage affair.

So Barney, he nips in for a bit of a swill to get the muck off of him, and oil, and all the kind of small artefacts you become attached to from rootling about in scrap yards with Willie the Pooh of an afternoon.

Then he sticks on a cleanish shirt and some other strides and climbs in his motor and makes his way very careful to the nickery and he is very nervous about this visit on account of this and that, so he goes on chewing up these mints and toffees, and dried prunes, whatever.

He arrives in this Police Place at a dab past six.

Now he is very correct in everything he does.

He gets out the car and goes to this den of coppers.

He knocks on the door.

The door, it is locked.

Even though he knocks and he knocks no-one answers.

So Barney, he goes round the back, and there, playing football by hisself up against a brick wall, is a small kiddy. Barney now addresses this small kiddy like this: 'I say, small kiddy,' he says: 'is your dad, the Silver Buttons, in?'

And being as if he were took of a terrible fright this small kiddy makes for a big bunk to the kitchen of this house.

And Barney, being just a teeny bit still side-affected from the treatment he is receiving in The Buffalo and with Willie the Pooh – the squashed damson business, and whatnot – Barney, he has a good mind to clear off and come back some other when, just as his friends advised.

As he is debating with hisself as to what to do, presently, a very large Silver Buttons indeed comes out and he is carrying a spatula in one hand and has pink rubber gloves on and he is wearing a butcher's apron, and it seems to Barney, he is in fancy dress, or going to a party, or else is doing some kitchen chore, or other, and off-duty, and therefore likely not to be as fierce as if he was dressed up in his proper uniform, like a proper copper.

Anyway up, Barney he says: 'Good evening officer. It is a beautiful evening. I have come as you requested, direkkly.'

And he hands him at a very great arm's length, the piece of paper as was attached to his windscreen.

And he says, 'My motor, Constable, is a proper job. She is taxed. She is third party. She has these smart new tyres. You may, if it please you, inspect this vehicle as it is, I believe, probably the most taxed and insured van in the village. She is thoroughly legal in every respect, according to the law. I have changed the oil as well, on top, and have even given her a bit of a polish. She is one law-abiding vehicle, officer, sir, and very clean and not at all illegal.'

So now this Silver Buttons, he scratches his head and he looks at this note and he is, it seems, very mystified by the arrival of Barney in his place making these big-sorted claims about his motor, which Silver Buttons listens to very attentive, but cannot make out why he should be stating these things to him out of the bright of a summer's eve.

So then he looks at this note again and asks Barney when he finds it, and Barney is about to say 'at booting-out time down The Buffalo', but instead, very circumspect, he says he comes across it around about threeish.

So then Silver Buttons asks if he can see this motor, which Barney leads him to, parked as it is around the corner a small distance, and as soon as Silver Buttons sees it, he says: 'Ah yes: that car. Of course. I was thinking. I have a terrible big hole in the roof of my house. Which I am intending to repair. When I spies your motor in the village I puts the note on the windscreen as I wishes to know if you would be kind enough for to allow me to borrow your ladders for half an hour.'

So this story makes everyone in The Crown very happy and they are congratulating Barney on winning this round, somehow, as these go, you know, by and by. They all say as it is a brave and courageous thing to visit the nickery after you have been in The Buffalo or Hundred House or The Crown or The Three Tuns or somewhere, even if the Silver Buttons is dressed up in pink rubber gloves and an apron or something.

'Did you lend him your ladders?'

'Well,' says Barney, 'they ain't on the roof of my motor no more, that's for sure.'

So now they say that will give him points and if old Silver Buttons comes snaking up the valley one day and pulls him up for this and that he will be able to claim them and that will be good.

Well, that might be what they thinks but me, I don't think you win points like that with old Silver Buttons, not because he's mean but probably because he's got someone in the motor with him who he owes points and one way another it might go the wrong way.

The thing is, although they say these things, when it comes time for these people to go to their homes, they do not drive their cars. They rings up their missus or their girlfriends or mates or walks acrost the meadows back home; in fact, Barney's experience causes these people to think before they drink and drive their motors, anywhere. Even though, Barney, by chance, gets away with it, so to speak.

And so it is, that this night, when it is time for me to leave this establishment as my wallet is clemmed even though I went in with twenty pounds and comes out owing thirty, and also I am feeling upset on account of the ordeals my friend Barney has had this day to undergo. As I am leaving he says: 'Hey Burt, hang on, I'm coming with you.'

So out we steps into the darkness and since I have no motor of my own, I am forced to take the number 11 bus wherever I go, and Barney, he takes it with me.

'It is a beautiful night,' I says to Barney as we goes toeing it down the lane in the moonlight.

And he says to me: 'Burt, it is. And this day, I have had a lesson, in a round about way, even though I was not punished as I might have been, I have learned from it.'

So I says: 'Well, there we are then Barney, the mark of real stupidity is the inability to learn.'

So he says: 'How true you are. Barney, I think I was very lucky. I got away with it, though, didn't I?'

'Well,' says I to him, 'Barney: I think you were very lucky and it seems to me as you did get away with it, yes.'

As I am saying this we are passing this gateway and I says to him as I must stop there to shake a beetle out of my shoe when Barney says: 'Burt, is this not the place where you was earlier this evening this when I picks you up?'

So I says I do believe it was.

'What was it you was looking at then?' says Barney.

So I points to the sign as Old Ashe Able has painted and says to him: 'That,' I says.

And the sign reads:

Idle Deceiver, Thy Sins shall discover thee yet.

The Pearly Gates

A week ago last Monday, come round about mid-dayish, Ivor the Wellies, Knocker Morsel, Knukky Stubbs, Barbary and me are hanging on the straps in the bar of The Kangaroo. And this hanging on the straps, in The Kangaroo, is a custom in this place, as these straps, they are little leather handle dangler gadgets dangling from the rafters in the ceiling, and they are there to dangle yourself from, if you are in The Kangaroo of a Monday pitching down a quart or two.

And, but the thing is, as we are dangling from these dangler devices and formulating plans, and whatnot, it occurs as we are also in the state of enjoying a nice little game of Nine Men's Morris, being as this is, for us, a very commodious way to pass up a Monday when we should be out on the land, or somewhere, doing something.

Anyway up, but, the thing is, it being a Monday, we need – that is Knocker Morsel, and Ivor and Knukky, and Barbary and – I forgot to say also – Ray the Barbed, Duke Don the JCB, and George Gunter the F and Blast – what we need, all of us, what we require, is to take a further while so as to recover from the weekend a bit, which is most exploitative in every respect, being long, and dragging over three or four days in row.

That is, for some of us: that is, for those who began it of last Wednesday night.

Not Ray the Barbed, that is, who didn't start until Thursday.

But, George Gunter the F and Blast, he, in fact, begun his weekend on last Tuesday week's dinner time, and kept it playing along until we ganged up with him on this Monday I am on about, at a splinter past middayish, as I said, and he was a touch dilapidated when we encountered him, it has to be said.

Anyway up, however you look at it, it is a long old hooking and can leave a man fairly well conkered of a Monday. So he needs to have Monday off in time to recover for Tuesday, which is when he will feel more like doing something for himself or someone else, depending – unless of course it happens to be Tuesday's turn to be the start of the weekend again, especially for George Gunter the F and Blast.

And, but, so, in this game of Nine Men's Morris, Ivor the Wellies has got the upper stroke as he has a dab hand at this job. And Ivor, he is a mugger shot at angling the jack and hooking the swing spot-on so's it roisles very nearly all the skittles over every time, in one go. And although we each have put a pocketful of eeyore on this game, and are in some cases concerned about the cash shortage affair this might invoke, because this racket, it can cause you to be berefted of all your eeyore in one dollop, it is, as long as we plays it amongst ourselves, a sound bet as whosoever wins buys the next round and the next one and the next one so that, in the end, we are certain to come out pretty square, even if we went in The Kangaroo with twenty pounds and comes out owing thirty.

And but, being as it is a Monday, the Pendagon is quiet and peaceful and not full of the people that comes in of a Sunday, sitting on tables and eating dinners and drinking tea and coffee and carting their kiddies in and that, as is not really politic for an establishment like The Kangaroo, as the The Kangaroo, is, in fact, a pub, not a entertainment place for family outings, with their children running around, and wives, and girlfriends and that, wanting roast dinners, whatever, or tea or coffee and treacle tart and custard.

A pub is a pub: this is the venue where there's serious discussions to be done: by cow chasers and pony breakers, corn carters and potato scratters, who like to have debating sessions, about the European Union and slurry tanks, and whatnot, silage and Silver Buttons, the Tory party and cow cake, Cabinet Ministers and pig-swill, BSE and foot-and-mouth as well. And these cow chasers and pony chasers, they like to discuss, with language, about steroids and dewormers, about bull's equipment and sheeps' privates and the election of American Presidents and how is it they always seem to wind up with such ognels. These cow chasers and corn carters and that, they like to transact their business in confidential, over glasses of Bowel Vowel, or Liver Worm perhaps, or Dragon Milk or Noggin Splitter and such, without being interrupted by kiddies rummaging around playing hide and seek under the tables, or knocking their beverages over, or by wives stretching out for the salt and pepper or ketchup or mustard or something just while they was in full flood about politics or sheepdogs or the nuclear, or wind farms or lugging a dollop of pig muck up to London and pasting the House of Commons with a good blast of it, or something.

And but, the thing is, about these discussions, being as they are without doubt important and weighty – and however you hark at it, you will find as there is nothing at all on earth as these cow chaser and them don't yarp on about – even if there are kiddies in there running around and wives moithering about – there is one exception to their discussion as is to some of us most pertinent and noticeable. You will never hear them, ever, yarping on, never mind how hard you listen, you will never hear them yarping on about the window envelopes that drops through their letter boxes from the Subsidy Department in Brussels once every few months, no you won't: never.

Anyway up, never mind about that as that is nothing to do with this story.

This story is about another matter altogether.

It is about this: a week ago last Monday, come round about mid-dayish, Ivor the Wellies, Richard the Top, Knukky Stubbs, Barbary and me are hanging on the straps in the bar of the Kangaroo and we are playing Nine Men's Morris, with plenty of eeyore on this game when the door butts open and in scrawls Trouser Jabez.

So we give old Trouser a big 'how bist ee surree?' as you do, and but, Trouser, he's as a man stepped on a robin.

Trouser, he doesn't hardly take a scrat of notice of we at all.

Trouser, he sikes up to the bar as crowsty as a ground toad.

Trouser, he orders a half of mild.

Trouser, he sets hisself down in the corner and ganders at the floor. He is not cousins with hisself as is plain to see.

Trouser, he's got a rare old Charley on his back, whichever way you look at it.

Now, we, in The Kangaroo that is, are accustomed to people behaving in some kanky ways all the while but more oftener this occurs after they have been there for a long hooking.

I don't know why this is, but it is.

Sometimes, some people become so kanky as it is hard to stop them. Like George Gunter the F and Blast, for example. And old Heavy Behind. No sooner as they had about eight pints of the old viper venom down them than they begins to sling a few home truths about, without holding back a lot, so as you can get to follow pretty much what they are thinking. Which, it has to be said, is unusual in people, as usually you don't have a glimmer what they're thinking – but that's as, oftener as not, they don't either.

And, but, what is different about last Monday, and Trouser coming in as he come in, is that he come in as he come in.

Which is not to be anticipated.

The thing is, if someone you know is stepped into a place and is as chummy as a nest of hornets on a thundery evening, what we are not accustomed to, is people behaving like a nest of hornets before they have been having a long hooking. We understand it after, but not before.

Anyway up, as Trouser is sitting there looking as happy as a rat with the vermin stopper, and twiddling his fingers under the domino drawer, and got the knackerman stamp on him, Knukky Stubbs, he steps up to him and sets down beside him.

Knukky, he puts his arm round his shoulders.

Knukky he says to him like this: 'Old mucker,' he says, 'Our friend Trouser Jabez: gentleman of the valley. Do not worry about it if it is the crows is taken your taters. Do not alarm yourself in this style. We will sort out the old crows, later.'

But, old Trouser, he sniffs and he looks as if he is about to burst into tears and he says, very quiet: 'It isna the crows.'

So Knukky, he tries again: 'Old mucker,' he says, 'If someone is let the air out the tyres on your bike, well – that don't matter either.'

Trouser, he shakes his head and a tear rolls down his old hooter and dangles off the end of it and drops in his mild.

Knukky says: 'Well if someone is whipped the bucket off your rhubarb…'

Trouser shakes his head.

'Or nicked your pea boughs –'

'No.'

'Or loosed a bunch of heifers in your kale –'

'No.'

'Or filled in your thunder box –'

'No.'

'Well whatever it is then,' Knukky says with a big old sigh.

And, but, the things is, none of this is going to brighten Trouser no more as it is to keep Mr Renard smiling as long as the hunt's on the loose.

So Knukky, he tries again: 'Old mucker,' he says: 'Don't take on to your shoulders what you canna carry. If those ognels as dug up the road in The Castle got the traffic lights on too long, we will go to County Hall and have them impounded.'

But old Trouser, if anything he looks even glummer at this rabbiting on with Knukky, so Ivor the Wellies, he says to Knukky: 'Leave him be Knukky. It's a private matter as is gnawing away at our old mucker, Trouser. He don't need us to go moithering on at him about crows or taters or wind or traffic lights.'

This is in fact what Trouser wants and Ivor, he is right, so we goes back to handing all our eeyore over to Ivor the Wellies on this skittles lark as is, as a matter of fact, gone on a bit by now.

And but then, Trouser, he stands up and starts wringing his hands, and it seems to us as he is about to do an address, like a vicar in his pulpit, about Joel or Noah or someone, Moses, Isaac, Meshag, Toerag, Ragtag and Bobtail and them.

And so, we sets down in chairs about the bar, quietly, and waits for the sermon.

Presently, Trouser he clears his throat and he starts, and what he announces is this. Trouser announces: 'My friends,' he says, like that, like bitter news is about to be broadcast all over we.

So now we are all thinking that Trouser, he has been to see the old leech; and the leech has half scared him out of his wits and gone and told him summat dreadful, as no mortal man ought to hear, and his time is upon him. So Knukky says: 'Don't worry about it Trouser. That old leech in nothing but a skinflint and a yarb, and you don't want to take a scrap of notice of want he says: he is a old gargle head and a dootherer.' (Which in fact, is not true, as we knows old Doc White to be a rare old doc as never says bad things and never tells people stuff as makes them fretchit. He's an old gentleman and runs around in his old Riley car gadget of his, as is a fair a old motor as ever set wheels on tarmac).

But anyway up, Knuckky he says these things, to comfort Trouser.

Trouser, he replies: 'Oh no, old Doc White is a rare old doc as never says bad things and never tells people stuff as makes them fretchit. He's an old gentleman and runs around in this old Riley car gadget of his, as is a fair old motor as ever set wheels on tarmac.'

'Right we are then,' says Knukky.

'It is a different matter I am on about,' Trouser says.

And then, Dennis the Pigs, he ups and says: 'Never mind what it is,' but then Knukky jumps in and says: 'Dennis, let's hear what it is Trouser wants to say first as we do not know what it is as ails him. Go on, Trouser.'

So Trouser clears his throat again and he goes on: 'Last night, as I am getting into my stripes outfit, out of the edge of my eyes, I catch a glimpse of something rootling around outside my gaff. And as you know, my gaff is set up in the hills with the wind and the crows and no-one but me goes there, as no-one but me knows where it is. It is a awkward old place to discover unless you live there, as I do.'

And this is true, as Knukky Stubbs, Ivor the Wellies and George Gunter the F and Blast and me went to look for him one day and even after shouting and bawling and roaring and scratting up and down every brook and tummock and meadow and mountain from The Castle to the top and bottom of the Black Hill in Wales, we still couldn't find him.

'And so,' Trouser goes on: 'I looks out through the glass and what I sees makes me rub my eyes. What I sees is this. I sees this blue light squiggling and squirting about outside my gaff.'

'Oh,' says Knukky quick as a flash: 'That'll be old Silver Buttons from Ludlow apprehending criminals.'

'Well,' says Trouser, 'That is what I thinks for a minute until then, these blue lights, they go scorting up and down and round and round, all over the meadow and down the lane, then back, and over the hedge and then they stops by the spring.'

'Surely,' Knukky says, 'as that's old Silver Buttons out apprehending these yarbs as goes ripping around the mountains in the dark on these quad bike implements as they keep nicking.'

But Trouser, he says: 'No, it isna that. This blue light doesn't make a sound. And anyway up, then this blue gadget, whatever it is, goes haring up and down the banks, not on them, like a bike or a motor, but above them, flying, silent, then goes hurtling straight up into the sky, vertical, quicker as a lark, and goes into one big cuzum, then goes boof in a big flash and vanishes.'

The bar, thems as are in it, are silence.

No-one as we know has ever seen some blue arrangement go roaring round the country, then fly up in the sky into one big cuzum, go boof in a big flash and vanish.

No-one.

And, but, then, as no-one has any idea what this is, old Trouser he goes on: 'So, I dunna know what it is.'

So now, we as are in the bar, neither do we.

So Ivor says: 'You had a very long hooking then, yesterday, perhaps, in The Buffalo, or some other entertainment place, in the Valley, Trouser? Was it because you swapped from one to thother half way through?'

Trouser, he says no: as he was only in The Buffalo for four hours.

So George Gunter the F and Blast says: 'That's it then. If you had been there a while longer you wouldna seen this blue light gismo go cuzum and boof.'

But Trouser, he seems not to hear all this and he goes on and he says: 'I canna believe it is a thing I see, because there isn't nothing as can do that. There isn't anything as can scort about like that. So, as I am now in my third score year of this life, I am confirmed as I am addled in my head.'

'No, no!' says Knukky.

But Trouser goes on and he says: 'I believes as I am addled and lost my marbles. I believes as I are got this disease in the head lark as people get from drinking too much and that. It is called Delibrium Tremendous. And any minute now, they are going to come and cart me off in a sick man's transit, to the asylum, in Talgarth and throw away the key.'

And he sets down bang, heavy as a pile of tripe.

Now then: none of we know what to say.

We have never heard of this kind of thing, people making big claims about blue lights flying around in the sky over the Castle. Unless of course, they are stuck with delibrium tremendous.

And, but then, Trouser, he stands up again, as if he is going to make another speech, and what he says is this: 'And then, if that is not trouble enough for one man to have to wrangle, I repairs to my old scratcher, and canna sleep. On account of this blue light business. And even though I goes to the window a dozen times, I do not see it again. But then, presently, sometime in the night, I falls asleep.

'And then comes the worst bit: I has a dream, and in this dream I am died and, but, I don't see a coffin or anything, it's just me in this grey mist but I am not kitted out in white kit as I thought I would be. I am all togged up in a blue boiler suit with hobnail boots and black rubber gloves and a dairyman's hat. And then there's this ladder in front of me all of a sudden and so I gets on it, I ascends this ladder as goes on and on and on and eventually, it pops up through a hatch in the floor, and directly in front of this hatch is a pair of huge old steel gates, with heavy iron hinges and brassheaded studs in them, with a strip over and a sign saying: 'Pearly Gates', wrote out in copper plate. Only one of it hooks is broke so it's dangling off at a angle, flapping about and there's this bulb above it which keeps flashing off and on like its got a dodgy connection, or something. And there's a rare old wind howling as well, as ruddy near blows me clear over, as I creps out of this hole in the ground by these steel gates.

'Anyway up, I stare at this lot in this screaming gale and canna believe it as there isna a scrap of pearl to be seen anywhere.'

'In fact,' Trouser says, 'as these gates are well bolted up, and seem more like you'd have to defend a prison or for keeping people locked up in as you would expect to find for the entrance to Heaven. And, but, there's this little peephole you can peep through to thother side. And thother side, well, it's all in a fog.

'Anyway up, hanging beside these old gates, in amongst a ruck of ivy, all waving around in this gale, is this bell pull – I never knew till last night as they had a bell pull there, and a fair old donger it is too, not an electric job – and this sign as says: Pull. So I pulls and this old bell, he dongs out.

'And I seems to be waiting for hours, half froze to death in this perishing wind when finally, this scruffy looking angel floats up on thother side and he's kitted out in a dirty old vest, with the hairs on his chest all growed through, and these old long-johns as look as it's been a while since they seen the inside of a washing machine, and the hobnail boots and this scraggy grey hair, and his wings is not a bit like angel's wings as you see in church: no. his wings is like some sort of old hornet's buzzing away, with veins in and you can see through them.

107

And this dirty old angel – who could do with a good shave too – this dirty old angel, he stares at me with his bloodshot eyes though this peephole and he says to me: well, what do you want?

So I says, I am not sure, only I think as I am died and just come up this ladder as I thinks I was supposed to and, well, here I am.

So he looks at me up and down and says: Name?

So I tells him.

And he says something else. So I says: What did you say? I canna hear as this wind is screaming away and is blowing my eardrums out.

So he blarts out: What is your occupation? So I shouts back: Stone mason. Then he slams this book shut as he has been scribbling this down in and shouts at me: 'Well Trouser Jabez,' he shouts, 'why should we let you in here?'

'That's what he says. 'Why should we let you in here?'

So old Knukky, he says: 'Bloomin' 'eck!'

But Trouser, he goes on like he never heard and he says this: 'I couldna think of a single reason as they should let me in. Not one.'

So now the bar goes quiet as you can hear a spider piddle, and Trouser says: 'Then this angel says: 'Well, if you haven't any reason as you should come in here, then you better go to thother place.'

'And off he buzzes into this fog, like a big old horsefly.

'And then, I wakes up. And this image of this angel character is so strong in my head, and so real, as I have to ask myself well, Trouser Jabez, why should they loose you in there?

'And so I gets to looking back over my life and sees as there is nothing as I have done as been a sliver of good.

'All I have done is fineeging all the while. I have done nothing but been a old doonderer, poothering around with dominoes and Nine Men's Morris, and Shove Halfpenny, and darts and cribbage and quoits and spending all my eeyore in here or in The Buffalo, or The Lion, or The Hundred House, or The Crown, or The Kangaroo and my life, it is waste.

'I am ashamed.

'And now there is no time to make it right as I am too old and too beethy to mend it. And also I am gone warble-struck with seeing these blue lights scorting about in the meadows and in the sky and this angel has learned me too late as I am a failure and have to go to thother place, when it is my turn to go, and that makes me glum.'

As we all hear this – and Trouser, he says this very slow and heavy – it makes us all as miserable as maggots.

This is on account of, if Trouser is not allowed in, then for certain there's not one of we as is going to get close.

Not within a thousand yards of it. Especially if you have to climb this ladder gadget – I could never do it, I havena got a head for heights anyway.

So I shall definitely have to go below.

And, but so, this report of Trouser's, it dilemmas we.

Anyway up, as it happens, as Trouser is delivering these delivera-tions, who should slide into the bar as stealthy as a stalking mink, as Bill the Box. And Bill, he buys hisself a Liver Worm, and sets hisself down quietly, and harks at what Trouser is rattling on about.

Then, as when Trouser is said all he has to say and he sits down, Bill the Box, he says nothing. He keeps his counsel. But he asks Ivor, quietly to explain what is happened and what it is as Trouser is so bound up over. So when Ivor is finished telling him, Bill, he smiles as broad as baker pulled dough.

'Trouser,' he says: 'You're a lucky man!'

So now old Trouser, he ganders up and canna credit as Bill takes his predicament so light, and but, Bill says straight off: 'This blue light lark. Well, it is all over the Radio this morning. They been talking about it since breakfast, and even a bit before. This light you are on about, is seen all over Wales and up over The Long Mynd; they seen it on Beguildy Beacon and in the Valley and up on the tops, and loads of people seen it last night as they been ringing in the radio non-stop. They say it is a flying saucer gadget or else a UFO. Or maybe it is something as the Americans is experimentating out over Shropshire for trials before loosing off everywhere else. And the radio people, they are asking people what has seen it to step forward, and harking at the descriptions as you have given compared with what others have given, what you seen beats it all: you seen the best bit. You seen the real article right up close. And I tell you something Trouser as will make your day: they are offering for people to come forward to talk about what they seen and those as come up with the best description gets a hundred quid.'

Trouser says: 'You're having me on.'

Bill says: 'God's honest.'

And then, what happens next puts all of we in the finest temper as we have all ever been in, in all our naturals I shouldna doubt, as Bill is a clear-spoken man, and understands things better an most, and although he bungs people in the ground as a hobby, he is the best bloke around when things go wrong, and what he says is this, he says: 'And Trouser, my old mucker. This angel, when he asks you what you done, it is impossible for you to answer Trouser, as you are a modest man: you never call for credit nor take none neither.

'But I know things about you Trouser, as you canna see yourself. I know this: one winter's evening, a while ago, you are driving back to your gaff in the snow and what you seen in the lane, in the snow, is a new-born foal, laid wet and helpless and freezing. And that little foal is about to die. And I know this to be true as the yarb who seen it first drives direct past your place in his Landrover and says to me he seen a foal in the snow up on the tops. So I says to him, why didn't you pick it up? And he says to me, it's none of his business. So I gets in my Landrover and races up to where he says this foal is and when I gets there, it is gone. So that's when I knock on your door and find no-one is in. But then I peep through the window and sees a little foal cratched down in front of the fire in your sitting room.

'And then I looks around, and by now it is dark, and I sees this flashlight right up on the hill and hears you calling. So I know what you did Trouser Jabez: when you sees that foal, you stops your van immediate, and rushes out and picks it up and takes him straight back to your place and dries him off and puts him in front of the fire.

'And what you does then, not many would do: it is dark and the wind is howling and the snow is driving horizontal. But you goes out onto the beacon in that freezing wind and snow and you calls out until you finds the foal's mam. And you catches her and walks her home to your gaff. And you takes her into your front room, into the warm, where the foal is, and puts them together. And how do I know that? Because I goes looking for the mare as well, and about two hours later I is froze and goes back past your place and sees footprints leading to your door: and they are the footprints of a man and the footprints of a pony – that foal's mam.

'So I peeps in your window a second time and sees all three on you in there, with the foal suckling and the mare eating from a pail. And I know you keeps them there, in the warm until both of them is strong enough to go out into the shed and you feeds them both and looses them out onto the hill in spring and never tells a living soul.

'And that's not all: far from it: I know how you feeds the birds all winter, how when you goes home and first thing in the morning you puts food out for them. I know too how you look after all those old brocks as you finds hit in the lanes and you takes them home and patches them up and sends them off again when they're fit and

111

well – and you never said a word to no-one about it.

'And you say your life is wasted as you poothered around playing dominoes or darts or Nine Men's Morris and whatnot. Well, I'll tell you something else altogether, Trouser Jabez. Every time I have been in here all of my life and plenty of others besides, I have met in you a real gentleman: with good manners and with a way of saying things as few others have. You Trouser Jabez, have told us more stories as anyone else, and these have been the best stories we have ever heard, because they are so well said. And you have no clue as to how many people have gone away from here lit up with what you have said, and made to feel happy: blessed to have been in your company because you have said something as has changed their lives.

'So I can tell you this old mucker: when you go to them Pearly Gates, when it's your turn to go, you can tell that dirty old angel bloke to make way for better men, and loose on him exactly what I have just said.

'And you can tell him something else too: as if he asks you twice why you should be let in, you can say as Bill the Box, and George Gunter the F and Blast, and Ray the Barbed, and Knukky Stubbs and Dennis the Pigs and Ivor the Wellies and half the valley and more besides – all of we say so – and he better not tangle with we, because he will regret it. Yes suree, you can tell him that. And one thing I promise you, Trouser Jabez, as not only do you deserve to go to heaven when it's your turn, but when you goes you will get a front row seat.'

And that's when the next weekend begun on that Monday dinner time and that was the rarest thrashing we all took then, for certain, after that, on account of these blue light efforts of Trouser's and his dirty old angel.

The Terrorist

It is a week last Friday and I am sloping into The Crown to indulge in the alchemical art of exchanging one kind of liquid for another, when along the road comes this JCB driven by none other than my friend Duke Don the Digger. And Duke Don the Digger, as he draws up alongside in this machine, he cuts the motor and leans out and says: 'You are not thinking of stepping into that naughty place where they dispenses alcoholic beverages in order to indulge in the alchemical art of exchanging one kind of liquid into another, are you, Burt?'

Being as I am now a foot on the doormat and thother on the street, I say to him as, in fact, I'm not. It is just that I am testing doormat pressures in the neighbourhood, on account of doing a survey for the EU health and safety people in County Hall, Ludlow.

So Duke Don, he says: 'How many doormats have you done then, Burt, this morning?'

So I says to him, as this is in fact, the first one, being as I only just got the job, bang just now.

So Duke Don, he says as to hold on a minute while he parks his machine and will come along to give me a hand, or foot, to see if the doormat in The Crown is up to EU health and safety standards or not.

113

So I waits for Duke Don, testing the doormat the while, until, he comes round the corner.

So now Duke Don, he puts his foot on the doormat and gives it a bit of a prod and says like this: 'Burt,' he says, 'I think as the pressure of this doormat is not up to EU safety standards. Look,' he says, 'if you presses here, on this bit, it goes down more than if you presses here, on this bit. So my advice would be to go inside and interview the landlord and see what he has to say about it. Do you agree?'

So, in that I consider Duke Don to be a wiser and cleverer man than me in that not only does he own a JCB but also owns all the land over the hill and beyond and has heaps of houses and other tractors and forage harvesters and trailers and piles of cows and sheep and keeps a few horses just for throwing money away on, as well, whereas all I've got is my wellies and hat and jacket and pants. So I says: 'after you,' and traipses in behind him, as he also looks like a proper duke in that he is tall and slender and has swep back grey hair, and in fact, many people think he is a proper duke as well, until he gets cussing and then he sounds as ripe as the rest of we.

And who should we meet inside The Crown, quite by chance, as been doing some EU health and safety testing as we, and have also gone in to interview the landlord and his good lady Evie Floss, but Trouser Jabez, and Knukky Stubbs, George Gunter the F and Blast, Stan the Man, The Bishop, Kipper Northern, Typhoon Ted, Harold and Willie the Pooh.

'Well, F and Blast,' says George Gunter the F and Blast, 'I dunna suppose we are come in to see if everything is up to EU health and safety standard, are we?' says he.

'In fact,' says Duke Don, 'we are conducting a small test on behalf of the Commissioners of the European Union on thother side of the bar door,' says Duke Don quick as spark, 'known as Doormat Resistance and Counter-pressure Testing, as is vital to the health and safety of people entering and leaving Licensed

Premises, as per EU Directive Number 1357, 1999 Section (2) ibid.'

'Oh that does sound serious,' says George.

'And what we are discovered is of considerable concern to us, my friend George Gunter the F and Blast,' says Duke Don, 'and so we would like an explanation from the landlord as to why this is.'

'As a matter of a fact,' says George Gunter: 'I am also come in to test the hardness of the wood of the bar,' says he, 'for EU health and safety standards, and so far, I am unhappy to state as because it is a piece of King Henry's oak and has been here for about four hundred years and is hard as a mountain pony but, because it is not made of melamintic propyloptic EUrethane, has to be ripped out and a fresh one bunged in by next Wednesday or else the EU is going to have everyone as comes in here slammed up and the landlord hurled in pokey for the rest of his natural for violation of EU Directive 99786/95647 2003 Sec (i) ibid.'

'And me,' says Trouser, 'I am come in to test the heighth of this rail at your feet here, on the bottom of the bar, to ensure it is up to EU standards and is contrary to and in violation of EU Directive 4567/999768 1997 Sec (2) ibid. And,' he says with the knackerman stamp on him, 'I am sorry to report as it is in fact made of the wrong kind of brass and is also one and a quarter millimetre more higher than it should be and probably is responsible for the outbreak of verrucas as has been inflicting the sheep farmers as has been known to creep in here these past few years.'

'And does this have to be replaced too?' asks Don.

'Yes it does.'

'And that has to be made of polyclopyfooty EUrythane, as well,' says George, 'by Wednesday.'

'And me,' says Kipper, 'I am come in to try the quality of the beer, to ensure this is up to EU standards. Would you like to assist in this matter?'

So we helps with the beer testing and tapping the wood and

testing the heighth of the foot rest and agrees with George Gunter the F and Blast and Trouser Jabez about having to have this new proper EU approved kit by next Wednesday, and we helps Kipper test the quality of the beer and by the time a few hours is gone by and we are not satisfied with this, we gives it another blast, just to see.

It is then Harold, as has been sitting down quietly, not harking at anything as we has been debating, declares: 'It has to be as one of the peculiar things about our valley is why there is all we old bachelors living in there,' which in fact, is nothing to do with what we was on about. But, because we was fed up of the EU thing by now anyway, we stops and harks at Harold as he rabbits on: 'How it happens to be, I do not know,' says he: 'but it is. There is more old bachelors living in our valley as there are tups. Indeed, I am even one myself. Bachelor, that is. Although sometimes I wishes I wasn't. But, in fact I am glad I am. Since although I do not have a lie-by to crawl home to with a dinner cooking, I do not have to go back to a lot of moithering as well, which, if you were some of the old bachelors in this valley, you would be glad of, considering the state of some of we gets into the while, by and by.'

And as Duke Don is handing me a potful of the EU testing liquid and I am toasting the health and temper of King Offa and wishing him back instead of the EU people as there was probably not so much fuss in his day about doormats and rails and the hardness of bar wood, as I am gazing round considering what Harold has said. As I am looking about I notices that more or less everyone in there looks like they have been shaving with rotavators, with their faces all chopped up and ears full of bloody soap.

So I says that we are all getting on a bit these days and probably that is why we is all bachelors, because no woman in her right mind would want to wed a old wuzzuk as looks as if he is always chopping his face up with a rotavator every morning and filling his ears with bloody soap.

'F and Blast, you make we sound like a load of OAPs,' says George Gunter, 'Which we isna, not quite yet any rate. But,' he says, 'I can tell you something about OAPs as might surprise you, if you would like to know. As how, in fact, OAPs is nothing but terrorists and rage artists and is causing grief in the town and is nothing to do with the EU safety standards, but ought to be, if you ask me.'

So now we are all listening to this, as George, it seems, has made some sort of a discovery and it is always good to find out what these discoveries might be. So we all goes quiet and waits and then George Gunter he ups and spouts: 'All these OAPs from off as comes to Ludlow to die, and don't, are commencing to clog up the streets of a Saturday morning chatting about their diseases. Have you noticed?'

'How true you are,' says Trouser Jabez, 'only I was thinking the same thing myself, last Saturday, when I peels off into Ludlow to see Ivor the Wellies in The Feathers. I arrives in Ludlow, sticks my motor somewhere handy, gets outs and the first thing I overhears is this old wuzzuk stating: "I have had three new hips now and two new knees, or my arthritis in my hands is got so bad I have had to have two new ones. And my back is so crocked as I has to have this new motorised zimmer perambulator gadget, isn't it a rare tool?"'

'See what I mean?' says George Gunter: 'this is exactly my point. You gets all these old wuzzuks all admiring one another's diseases and crocked backs and new knees but most of all they stands about admiring one another's new motorised zimmer perambulator gadgets, like it's some sort of pavement rally. Then all of a sudden there's about twenty of these things like a heap of old snails, creeping up the pavement in a swarm with these old wuzzuks clutching on the handlebars – and they're half-blind and deaf as you dunna need a test for one of these gadgets, no you dunna, surree.'

'In fact,' says George, 'the more worse you are in every

respect, being blind and deaf and with diseases and crocked back and new knees and hips and stuff, the more likely you are to get one of these motorised zimmer permabulator gadgets, and these things goes inching along at about a quarter of a hour making this big whining noise and taking up more room than a bunch of Alice Chalmers on a seed bed.'

'How true you are,' says Trouser: 'and they gets everywhere. In the bank, in Woollies, in the bun shop, in the bookshop and the supermarkets like a go-cart-having-a-very-slow-stroke race in there, of a Saturday morning. It takes me three-quarters of a hour queuing behind a pile of these things trying to get into The Feathers last Saturday. And in there was all these old wuzzuks in white linen jackets sipping shandies through straws, and being handed pre-chewed bacon sandwiches before going out and terrorising the pavements again. Me, I think something should be done about this.'

'I agree,' says The Bishop. 'I think some of these old wuzzuks in Ludlow and Clun and The Castle and Church Stretton are nothing but terrorists as they are periculous and dangerous to the health of ordinary citizens under sixty years of age as they gets pavement rage if you don't jump out of their way immediate they commence lambasting you with their sticks.'

'And there is one in particular,' says George Gunter, 'as I knows of as has a bright yellow motorised perambulator gadget as is a powerful piece of kit, I don't mind saying, being bigger and wider than most. And the old wuzzuk as tools along on this thing, well he must be a hundred and five years old, if he's a day. And he comes to Ludlow to die fifteen years ago and is still terrorising the place and getting worser by the week. And he is blind, and deaf, and got three new knees and four new hips and arthritis in the nose and ears and hair and is as savage as a Limousin bull with a fly in his groin. And he goes scorting off round Ludlow on Saturday mornings and then creeps off to Church Stretton on the train in the afternoon to do a bit of grief there. And the thing is, what he does this old gaffer, is to collect a load of OAPs with motorised perambulator gadgets to go along with him, like some sort of OAPs' Hell's Angels outfit and they cause some havoc, you hark my words. Why, only last week I seen them lambasting this young kiddy with their sticks and bawling at everyone to get out their way as they comes crawling down the street. I tells you, they have got that much pavement rage they are too violent to deal with and old Silver Buttons won't touch them as if he does he will be done by the Political Correct people, straight, and lose his job immediate and get photographed all over the papers and be bunged on the telly for being brutal to old codgers. But these old wuzzuks, they are the real terrorists and trouble-making-octaganerian-trikers and something should be done about them.'

And as we are discussing this business, I notice as Duke Don notices as the Landlord, Spud, does not seem to be taking part in this conversation very much and is thinking, probably, as perhaps his wife Evie Floss's dad is one of these old wuzzuks as does people grief in his yellow perambulator, or something, as is not very proud of this and wishes to keep it a secret. So Duke Don, in that he knows as Spud's dad is died when he is very young states: 'What ails you, Spud, my old friend? Is your wife's dad one of these ninety-year-old Hell's Angel types as goes about doing grief on a 3 mph Ludlow trike?'

And Spud, he shakes his head and says it is not this, even though his wife, Evie Floss's dad is, in fact, an old wuzzuk but has not got all the usual diseases is not bad enough to get a free motorised permabulator gadget to go out Hell's Angeling on but has to hobble about on his sticks, instead. Even though he lives up with all the wind and the crows on the mountain on his own, down a five mile track and can't drive a motor and there's no buses and if he wants something from the town he has to creep there on his sticks to get it.

'You only get given a motorised permabulator gadget if you have over a million pounds,' says Spud, 'and live in a town with buses and a phone and your Mrs and family and maids and home-help and private nurses and have all the diseases,' says Spud, 'so my Mrs' old man does not count as he lives ten miles from the town and is as poor as a grating spider and is not yet got enough diseases and lives on his own on top of the mountain where there is no buses or phone nor ever will be.'

'Oh dear,' says the Duke, 'I am sorry to hear about Evie Floss's dad on the mountain. But if it is not this as makes you sad, what is it, Spud my old friend? Perhaps you are sad on account of the new EU regulations forcing you to make you higher your doors to 198 centimetres as none of we know how big this is?'

'No, although I do not know how big 198 centimetres is, if it is very high or very low either,' says Spud, 'on account as I cannot do the sums to make this into proper English, as I do not speak European. But you are right they have asked me to do this but why I do not know as no-one has ever brained themselves while coming in or going out yet – not on account of the heighth of the doors anyway.'

'These EU Regulations are mischievous and evil things, I do credit you,' says Duke Don.

'And they have also told me to deepen the cellar by 134 centimetres, however deep that is, but why I do not know as these cellars was built by King Offa and has been good since then, so what the problem is I canna understand, only the people as dishes out these rules is so officious and niggly as I think they have got a dose of the evil maggots in their livers, to make them so cruel.'

'How true you are,' says Trouser: 'only yesterday as I was setting up my ladder against this wall to do some masonry and this officious official slithers along in his officious motor, leans out the window and declares as he can see as the rungs on my ladder are not metrified and are illegal and that it has to be throwed out and I have to get a new EU metrified ladder to do EU standard steps up on, or else I am breaking the law and will have to pay a big, heavy fine. And the thing is, I canna afford one of these so now I canna work and am unemployed and destitute as a result.'

'I knows how you feel,' says Spud, 'and all these things is true, but it is not this as is making me sad, today, although from now on I have to wear rubber gloves to serve the beer in white plastic overalls and white plastic hat and face mask and goggles and anyone that comes in to drink it has to come dressed in polycloth super-jammer zipper suit with rubber gloves and face masks and goggles and has to speak through tubes and telephones to each other and put on these white boots. But still, it is not this as is making me sad, today.'

'What is it as is making you sad today, then, Spud?' the Duke asks him again.

And old Spud, you can see as it is hard for him to say, of a sudden he blarts out with tears in his eyes: 'in the midst of the night last night I creeps in here with my Purdey and blasts away with both barrels at all my whiskies and gins and vodkas and rums and bottles of beer and everything and now they are all gone and broken and busted and blown to pieces and this has cost me a fortune, on top of everything else.'

This now causes we some mighty interest on account of why Spud should blast away all his whiskies and gins and rums and vodkas and beers in the midst of the night, with both barrels of his Purdey.

'What makes you do such a thing?' asks Duke Don, as he is wondering, as we all, if Spud is gone a bit rattled in the bonce just now, or else has had a bit of a fisticuffs with his Mrs and perhaps she is all blasted away as well.

'It is on account as I have had no kip for nights and nights and am apt to do strange things just now.'

'Is your Mrs all blasted away as well?' asks Trouser Jabez, weaselly careful.

121

'No,' says Spud, 'she is cooking my dinner for me right now.'

'Oh that's good, then,' says Trouser and has another swig of beer.

'This blasting away all your whiskies and gins and vodkas and rums and stuff – does this help you solve the problem with your not having any kip, then?' asks Don.

'No,' says Spud: 'it is not that I am come in here in the midst of the night just to blast my pub to bits on account of it making me kip better, it is another thing.'

'Ah!' says Duke Don, 'And what is this other thing?'

'It is this terrorist as has come to abide in the village,' says Spud, 'I was after him with my Purdey.'

'Hellfire!' says Don. 'An intruder! But, the thing is Spud, you have to watch out for that kind of thing these days as if you does that you will wind up in pokey fairly smartish, even if they shoots you first. But tell us, was it that old wuzzuk in one of these yellow motorised permabulator gadgets as has bought up the manor and is now skimming about the place on this thing lambasting people with his stick? He is a terrorist for sure. And probably an intruder too. You needs to keep an eye on these old wuzzuks, you know, as comes to live in the country from the town with their yellow permabulator gadgets.'

'No,' says Spud, 'in fact, it is not this, although you are right in saying as this fierce old wuzzuk has come here, to live in the manor, with his yellow permabulator gadget and million pounds and home help and private nurse and telephone and bus. I seen him creeping past here yesterday, peeping in the windows, with his big white eyebrows, wrinkly old eyes and spotty-brown hands, and he is acting very suspicious like he is plotting something, as he has this great big net with a big long handle, like one of them huge great things they uses for snatching butterflies and landing salmons or sharks or something.'

And now it is clear to see as Spud is near enough about to breaking as everything seems to have got on top of him just now and we feel very sorry for him and think as perhaps he is beginning to imagine things as is making his brains addle and cause him grief and sorrow in his heart as normally, he is a great, big, jolly fellow, full of fun and mirth.

'Tell us what it is as ails you, Spud? Who is this terrorist in the village that we might go and get him and dangle him from the withy stump?'

'I am afraid,' he says, very slow, doodling his finger in a puddle of beer: 'I am afraid, it is something to do with you, Duke Don,' he says, very sad, just like that. 'It is something that you did as is causing me such grief and agony that I have not slept now for six whole nights and my brains is addled and I have got sacks under my eyes black as silage bags and am worn-out and weary and exhausted in every respect and shoots my pub apart as a result.'

And now of course, this fretchits the Duke complete as he is not the sort of man to go about dishing out injustice for the fun of it and he is total shook-up as something that he did is causing Spud, the landlord, so much vexation.

'What is it that I have done?' he asks, very worried-like.

'It is to do with a certain commodity you know by the name of Lance.'

'Oh no!' says Duke, 'not Lance! That Lance is a mogger and mischiefer and is fit only for the narrow eye but how is it that he is troubling you?'

'This Lance, as you brings to the village for my chum, the Detector, to keep his chickens happy, is a savage beast and noisesome and troublesome in every respect. Ever since he arrives in this village from your place up on the mountain he has caused more harm and havoc than if Napoleon and all his horses and cannons comes up the valley from Clun and starts loosing them all off every morning at two o'clock every day, non-stop.'

'But Lance, he is a fine bird,' says Don, 'Lance Cockerel is Champion Cock of the Clun Valley, as is why The Detector wants him, for his hens, so that they can have babies to scort about the place.'

'And make as much racket as Lance Cockerel, no doubt. But the thing is,' says Spud, 'as when you brings this Lance Cockerel down for The Detector to borrow, not only does this bird escape, but he goes strutting about the village all day and all night blarting this cock-a-doodle-dooing at the top of his voice, only this bird, he does not have a small voice. He has a very big voice. Did you know,' says Spud, turning to Trouser, 'that this bird stands nearly three foot six in heighth?'

'Well,' says Trouser, 'I never knew that. But I knows about Lance Cockerel as Champion Cock of The Clun Valley. But, the thing is, his heighth must be against EU regulations straight, as if he is not the proper heighth in centimetres he will have to be shot at dawn for sure.'

'And did you know,' says Spud, 'as this bird, when he cock-a-doodle-doos, does not cock-a-doodle-doo like a normal cock-a-doodle-doo, but sounds like one of them black spiritual singer blokes, his voice is that deep and big and brassy. And this bird, he struts up and down this road outside my window, just as I am grabbing some kip at two o'clock in the morning having just tossed the last customer out of my pub and then he commences this racket and prevents me from kipping, at all. And, but, the thing is,' says Spud, 'last night I leans out the window to give this bird a good blast of lead with my Purdey, just as he's strutting down the road blarting his silly head off, and then, as I gets the bead on him, who should come purring round the corner but old Silver Buttons, in his Raspberry Ripple, from Ludlow. I can hardly loose off a couple of barrels of Ely straight out into the night, can I, and not be accused of being a random assassin, like them nutters in petrol stations in America, can I? So what do I do? What do I do? I let this bird go by, blarting his beak off, cock-a-doodle dooing away with old Silver Buttons, like some sort of Al Capone protectionist society, cruising along behind him.

'Then when old Silver Buttons finally streaks off, I nip out into the night to do for this bird, once and for all, and although I stalks the village with my Purdey as now it is three o'clock in the morning, in my pyjamas, and I have had no sleep for five nights, and am apt to do something very dangerous – for this bird, although I look for him everywhere, he is gone.

'So then I scrawls back to the pub and hands-and-knees up the stairs. I crawls into my scratcher, keeping my Purdey beside me. My wife Evie Floss is also tossing and turning on account of this bird as well and she is near to breaking as a kindling stick. She snaps at me as though it is my fault. But we are so exhausted we tries to grab some kip. But then I hears this scratting. And then this scratting gets louder and louder. Suddenly I knows what this scratting is: it is the sound of a very big chicken scratting. So I ups and grabs my Purdey, thumps down the stairs and who should be in the bar, standing slap bang right on it, and is about to give us one big blast of his cock-a-doodle doing but Lance Cockerel.

So now I gives him both barrels.

Boom! goes this gun.

How I miss him, I do not know.

But I do not miss all the whiskies and gins and rums and vodkas and bottled beers as is all blown to bits behind the bar as is why this place is full of holes, this morning.

And this is enough to make me weep all alone.

'And this bird, he disappears and although I look for him all day long, I canna find him. But I know he is still about, in hiding, somewhere, like a terrorist, waiting to make his next break.

'I tell you, I am exhausted, as this Lance Cockerel is causing me financial and moral loss in every respect and I demand now, Duke Don, that you assists me to trap and capture him so you can take the wretched thing back home with you, for ever, and promise never to bring him to the village again. Please.'

And so it is as Duke Don sets out to capture this Lance Cockerel bird of his. He makes this plan.

He says the best time to catch cockerels, especially this one, is near enough at dusk, when he goes off for his kip.

'If this bird gets any kip,' shouts Spud, 'before me, or ever again, and keeps the rest of we awake all night after, I shall wring the blighter's neck in person when you catches him and hang and draw and quarter him, so help me God I am that fed up with him and his cock-a-doodle-dooing as there is no punishment as I can think of as if fit for him except the torments of hellfire and destruction.'

So, now, the thing is, we all is beginning to realise Spud is a little gone over the top with this one, specially since he blasts his pub to bits in the midst of the night with his Purdey and it is perhaps wise not to come to this pub in the hours of darkness as maybe, he is apt to do it again, only with we in it.

So, what we arranges is, to go to The White Horse instead, and let the Duke and the Detector sort out this chicken, without us, lest we are all likely to wind up the same way as Spud's whiskies and gins and rums and vodkas and bottled beers and all.

A week goes by and we are in The White Horse dinner time next Monday when we hears this JCB come rattling up the street and park somewhere handy outside and in should come none other than Duke Don.

He 'how be surree's?' we and we 'how be surree's?' he, and then gets to asking him how it is he is still alive and has not been shot by Spud with his Purdey.

So he tells us this: he says as the day we all ran away to hide in The White Horse and left him alone with a very tired Spud, who by now had got hold of his Purdey again and was moithering on about lying in the dark in the bar, waiting for the first sign of movement before blasting off both barrels. Don says as he himself, thought it more safer to go and look for Lance Cockerel outside and leave Spud lying in the bar with his Purdey on his own.

By now, he says, dusk is fallen and he is creeping about the bushes here and there and in barns and through hedges and stuff, trying to find this chicken. But, he says, he canna find him. Spud, he says, at the time, is still lying on the floor in the tap room with his Purdey aimed at the door. But Don, he says he does not like to think about what is about to happen to the first person as wanders in for whatever it is he wanders in for.

And, but, as he is thinking these things, he harks at this strange whirring sound as comes as starts and stops, and then starts and stops, and then he hears this whooshing sound and a clump and this old wuzzuk shouting: 'Got you, you beggar!'

Then there's all this squawking and screeching and flapping and then silence.

So now Don runs out and what he finds is this old wuzzuk in his yellow perambulator zimmer gadget, with Lance Cockerel in this very big net, all trussed up tight as a broiler and this old wuzzuk lambasting him with his stick.

Only this old wuzzuk his face is all lit up and he is bawling 'Aha! You can't get away from me, you know! Joss Horrocks of the Himalayas! Master Trapper and Mercenary, Terrorist and Jungle Warfare expert! No-one escapes me! Aha! Aha!' and he continues with his lambasting, blarting these things at the top of his croaky old voice.

Anyway up, Don goes up to him, eventual, and says as he has done a rare job in trapping this bird as he has been causing the landlord of the pub not a few nights' problems, of late. So this old wuzzuk he says: 'I knew it! When I went past his pub in my yellow permabulator I fancied I saw this bird creep in but then my eyes aren't what they were, you know, in my youth. I knew the only way to catch him though was with my snake net, see? I've been tracking him for days, you know.'

So anyway, Don then says as how Spud will be very delighted to know this and will give him a reward, probably, as he will be that happy to hear this bird is caught, only to watch out before going in as he is presently lying on the floor of the tap room with a well-loaded Purdey.

So this old wuzzuk goes down the pub in his permabulator and this very duffed-up cockerel and does a lot of shouting outside first so that Spud gets up from the floor and looses him in.

So now he and Spud have a long old chat about this bird and very shortly they are getting on like pigs at the swill, as Spud thinks this old boy is a grand old fellow and full of stories and experiences and used to be a mercenary and in this war and that war and has that many medals if he put them all on he'd fall over.

'It is a very good outcome to this story,' says Don. 'I am happy about it. Also since the old duffer gives me back Lance Cockerel even though he is a bit duffed-up, he is now back at home, terrorising the buzzards but no-one minds on account no-one lives up there except me and I dunna notice him anyway.'

So we are all very happy about this, and say that was a good job then, and we can go back to The Crown without being shot, then.

Duke Don says yes, more than likely, unless of course Spud goes mad again.

Anyway up, a month or two tips by and we all goes back now we are not likely to get shot no more and find this old wuzzuk in there, on his yellow permabulator gadget, snorting away at this pink-gin kit as he whacks back by the bucket, whirring from the bar to the gents to here and there in this perambulator.

And we gets on with him fine, even though he is a fierce old devil and dunna mind what he says to no-one, and is, in fact, when it comes to plain-speaking even worser than George Gunter the F and Blast.

Anyway up, all the while he is scorting about on his permabulator gadget, George Gunter the F and Blast is taking a big interest in this thing and very soon it is very clear to we as he takes a bit of a shine to this contraption and says to this old wuzzuk can he have a go in it? So George has a go in this thing and creeps about a bit and asks about a licence and this old wuzzuk says as there is no need and says to George, if he likes he can have his spare one as he has got back at the manor.

No sooner is he said this as George is up the manor and gets hold of this thing and the last we sees of these two is them trundling from pub to pub all the way down the valley and getting into any kind of mischief and Trouser says when he peels into Ludlow last Saturday, he sees these two, in The Feathers, on their yellow motorised permambulator gadgets, knocking back a yard or two and then creeping out into the sunshine and lambasting at thothers in the street with their non-EU regulation length sticks.

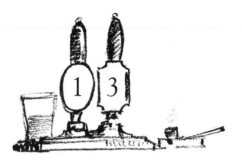

Third Party

Will Perverse is in the back of his van in The Castle Vaults car park one night, having plenty of rumty-tumty with Mrs Moonstrike Morgan, a few weeks ago, while Moonstrike is in The Castle thinning the wedge in his wallet.

Any rate, Will Perverse forgets it is about fullmoon time which is not a good time to be on the wrong side of Moonstrike, so keeps on peeling away at Mrs Moonstrike, which is not easy because Mrs Moonstrike is a fairly well-wintered sort of lady and jams herself into her kecks tight as a roll of spring swath in a sack of hot silage.

Anyway up, these two, being preoccupied by what they are doing, and enjoying themselves much to the exclusion of the rest of the world outside, omit to ear-hole Moonstrike come thumping out the bar at whenever it is, and, but Moonstrike, on surmising that all this left-a-bit and right-a-bit, and ho-ha-hum is emitting from Will's steamed-up van, reckons he'll have a bit of sport on Will whom, he reasons, has got some sort of a local lie-by warming up his motor, but which bit of local lie-by Moonstrike does not twig is his missus.

So he creeps up very weasel on this van and just as it is sounding as if the occupants are nearing some sort of crisis, he slams his fist on the roof and hollers:

'Oi! What do you think you're doing, then?' at the top of his voice – and very like a Silver Buttons – which causes the occupants within to suddenly desist in their activities.

With a big bellow Moonstrike then hurls the back door open and what should he find himself gazing into but a flowery sort of a parachute of a frock affair, and suspenders, and a pair of hefty D-cups, and lacy this and frilly that, which is the sort of clobber he remembers his Missus having.

Anyway up, he sticks Will one.

He sticks him in his breakfast-box with his foot-rot knife.

And this sticking causes a lot of grief: suddenly all the Silver Buttonses from Ludlow and everywhere are swarming all over the place, and half a fleet of sick man's transits pitch up, and here is Mrs Moonshine swanning round the car park bawling her eyes out, and Will all bent up like a knackerman's offal sack, and Moonshine doing the third degree in a puddle with a six blokes standing on him, and goodness knows what.

So, they bracelet Moonshine and slip him off to Ludlow nickery, and toss Will in a sick man's transit, and blue-light him off to the local patch-up, but no-one seems to give much hoot about Mrs Moonstrike who is left standing in a puddle with her hanky in her face bawling about having no home to go to.

Anyway up, later that night a bunch of blokes in green outfits pump the beer out of Will, stitch him here and there then turf him out the hospital come tea-time next Thursday.

Two weeks after, the whole thing is blowed over and Will and Moonshine are wading into the brain shriveller in The Vaults again like nothing has occurred, and Moonstrike buys Will one for the dyke, or maybe two, for old time's sake, then they get booted out at booting-out time and Will crawls into his van and goes thumping in and out of the ditch on his way home when Silver Buttons nails him and causes him to stop.

Then as Silver Buttons opens Will's door and is about to say, 'Breathe into this,' Will says: 'It's me, Buttons: Will Perverse. I can't do heavy breathing. I'm the bloke what's in the papers. The one what gets stabbed,' and as he pulls up his shirt so Buttons can shine his torch onto his stitches, Buttons says, 'Strewth, Will:are you fully recovered?'

And Will says: 'Oh ay, 'course: third party, fire and theft.'

Phantom's Revenge

If you live in a town, these days, or even in some village in the country, nights are no longer nights on account of there being lights on all the while as ruins a good sleep for those of we who don't mind a bit of dark.

And, but, the thing is, these lights, at night, do harm to some small creatures, bats and owls and stuff as needs the dark to get by.

And, but, the other thing is, these lights at night, they don't stop them others from breaking in if they has a mind to because half of them break in in the day anyway, and if the night is all lit up like day, then you can say as the other half break in the day as well, even though it's night.

And the other thing is, these lights, they have done for the ghosts.

There usened to be more ghosts than there are these days but I think it is these lights as have done it and they have died out from sadness not being able to lep out on people no more, and give them the cardiacal stoppages, like they usened to.

But, there's still some old places as still have ghosts, like Ludlow for instance.

And Ludlow, Ludlow is heaving with them.

Trouser reckons as there's more ghosts packed into Ludlow

than the whole of the rest of England put together. Ludlow ghosts, they aren't afraid of light at night not one bit and they are as alive there as when there weren't any lights, or so Trouser reckons anyway.

There's more ghosts in Ludlow per square yard, Trouser says, as there is cockroaches.

Trouser, he says as if you went to Ludlow to count them, you'd run out of numbers.

And although they are died out in the rest of England, because they've driven them off with street lamps and car lights and pop music, because there's no street lights or pop music in the lanes down our way, you find them. Any amount of them, especially in old gaffs like Bentpenny Castle, Catchmace Court and The Pendragon.

And, but, the thing is, I don't know what it is about young people these days as they don't seem keen to talk about ghosts, which is different from we, as we used to rattle on about them all the while and spy them regular, in barns and old houses, in villages, in the boneyard and in the lanes – in daylight even. I spied one once outside Steve the Coat's place. A young fellow with a bill-hook, in leather leggings, a weskit and collarless, standing slap bang in the middle of the lane. I thought he was a lad doing a bit of pleaching. Then I had to ask myself how is it that a lad is pleaching at this time of year, as it is the middle of July? And what kind of outfit is he wearing? When I looks back he's gone.

Next time I see old Steve the Coat and tells him he says: oh ay, he knows about him as it would have been his great uncle as I seen, as was a lad when he was killed there with a runaway hay cart behind a pair of shires in July 1922. Nobody seems to know why he has a bill-hook, though.

Anyway up, even though the young ones aren't keen, there's some of us of an age round here are interested by these things and about mysteries and phantoms and that, and weird wolves and ghouls and things as go creeping about in the moonlight. We want to know what these apparitions are, what they want, what they are supposed to be all about, and one night, it is the eve of the First of May, in fact – as is the night witches are abroad as they call it Val Purges Night, as is the worst night in the year for havoc with ghosts, as it is the night when old crones gets their crystal balls and books of spells out and starts chanting magic on people as done them grief in the village or something, for not paying their milk bill, or something – on this night, Val Purges Night, we are in The Pendragon, debating this subject.

And, but, the thing is that's in fact a bad old night to go waffling on about this kind of stuff, as you need to be extra cagey lest you invite the whole caboodle in on you and give yourself a clammy fright and fetches up with creepy things flitting about you all the way home and whispering round your scratcher for the rest of the night. And it's alright for them as drives home, but I has to take the Number 11 bus, and that lane's as black as, well – a witch's hat – at night, and there's been moments walking back up that track when my skin is turned to putty – and that's been on an ordinary night, never mind Val Purges, and that's got nothing to do with the beer neither.

And, but I don't know who this Val Purges is, or what sort of an article she was. But the thing is, she must have been a evil old buzzard as to get a whole night called after her, for her mischief.

Anyway up, so for me and for Knocker Morsel this is not a good plan as Knocker, he has to creep off up the beacon, dead smack past the boneyard – and there's no light where he's going either – so it's a bit of a clencher to talk along these lines, deep into midnight, and then scrawl back home, on your own, in the dark.

And worst, in The Pendragon: strangers who have been in there drinking and nipped outside of a night instead of using the proper facilities and have come scorting back in twice as quick, white as a goose and very quiet for the rest of the session.

No locals round here do that. Never. They knows better.

The Pendragon is very particular like that.

As is why it is in fact, not the best venue to have discussions like this, about ghosts, even if it is with Trouser Jabez, George Gunter the F and Blast, The Padre, Knukky Stubbs, Spud the Landlord, Stan the Man from down the valley and Knocker Morsel from up the tops.

Anyway up, we are, and as the night goes on, we gets swapping tales about this ghost and that ghost, where the toff from up the tops hid a dose of gold in the garden and went back to dig it up only to find it gone and then got axed to bits, and about the coach and eight as plunged off the corner on The Anchor tops road one winter's night and killed all the horses and all the passengers and the driver and the man with the blunderbuss – all of them. And they say as you see it by and by, of a dark night, this coach and eight, go rattling along.

Then, just as we are discussing this point, in very low voices, and the air is thick with smoke, and you can feel the nerves, and all of us are leaning forward, heads together, eyes straining, harking at Trouser saying about this coach and eight, as how his dad seen it one June night, spanking along, eight black horses, two dim lamps and the horse's eyes flashing in the moonlight, the crack of the whip, the coachman calling out – then as he says this, there's a soft jingle from outside, like chains, and all our skin freezes over.

The clock, it strikes midnight, bang on the moment.

Then this little jingle, it comes again.

'Hark!' Trouser hushes.

Our eyes all swing to the door.

The door knob, it turns, slowly.

The door, it creaks open.

A hand slides round.

135

No-one breathes.

A face in the darkness, out of the glow of the light of the bar, in the half light: 'Is this a private party?' it asks.

Well: the air as gets let out in one puff blasts all the smoke out.

'Come on in,' says Spud, the Landlord.

And in strides this kiddy as about fortyish something, who is an incomer round here, as we have seen about in his Jap job, his brown Subaru station wagon.

His name's Hugh Janus.

And this Hugh Janus, he's got some scrat as that, is true, as he has bought Catchmace, out along the tops, a place as catches all the winds as God invented of the winter. But of the summer: well, there's a view from there to thother side of the world. And, but, Catchmace is a biggish old gaff and goes up for auction eight months previous and we all knows what it fetches and it isn't local money as wants to pay that kind of eeyore for a wind-ridden barrack with no land round here, no it isn't.

And so this Hugh Janus incomer geeser, it seems, has got plenty of corks.

And, but, the thing is we knows this Hugh Janus gets in the hostalries around and about very late at night for some reasons, we don't why it is: he never comes down at six or seven or nine or in the day: he creeps in at midnight and then stops until three or four and goes crawling back up Catchmace along the tops on the Anchor road, which is all upsy downsy road to drive along, at three or four o'clock in the morning.

'How bist 'ee suree,' says Trouser to him very cordial, and he says very cordial back as it nice to be in there in the warm, in such nice, polite company and such a splendid old pub – and this is how to make friends and influence people, so it is.

And so we gets on prattling along all amicable and presently he says as when he came he heard as we was talking about ghosts and so we say, yes, that's right what does he think of that?

So he doesn't say much, because he's never seen one and then he says as he overhears Trouser saying something about a coach and eight, so what's all this about, then? So Trouser tells him. And Trouser tells him as he tells us: eight black horses thundering through the darkness; eyes glittering in the moonlight; sweat-steam pouring off of the horses; the wind whipping across; tails and manes flying; the coach rolling from side to side, the spokes of wheels flickering round, the coachman calling out; the man with the blunderbuss sat beside him and the two little outrigger coach lamps burning dim.

So this Hugh Janus, he sits and harks at this in silence puffing away at his cigarettes. Then he ups and says as: 'There is always a logical explanation for these things. It is not possible', this Hugh Janus says, 'for ghosts to exist. This coach and eight is part of the local psyche: it has become legend so people imagine it very clearly with their mind's eye. So when they are in the place where this accident took place, the truly creative mind will see it: just as it imagined it happening – as real as a dream seems to be, when you are dreaming. Yet,' he says, 'in fact, it does not and cannot possibly exist. There is no such thing', he says, 'as ghosts. Ghosts', he says, 'are not paranormal things: they are a phenomenon, yes, but of the mind. They can be directly related to incidences in that person's life without him even knowing it: in short, they are figment of the imagination: a very frightening one at times, yes, but nevertheless, unreal.'

Knocker Morsel and me, as we are harking at this, we are thinking of something else, I know, as we don't like to taunt Lady Providence in this way as we are the only two in here who has to leg it up the hill in the dark, after, on Val Purges' own particular night.

We don't want to hear him banging on and on about no ghosts as there is probably swarms covening up in the trees and bushes and the hedges and brooks right now just itching to pounce out on we as we goes groping about in the darkness trying to find where on earth we are, especially when they harks at this Hugh Janus shooting his mouth off about them not being real.

So we keeps on clearing our throats and staring up at the ceiling and knocking the Nine Men's Morris skittles over and trying not to listen, but he goes on: 'No,' says he, 'they are figment of the imagination. There is not one shred of scientific evidence that finds proof of their existence. Ghosts, spirits, coaches and eight rattling along high roads in the middle of the night are pure mental images: deluded pictures on the screen of the imagination, projected out into the darkness. They are, phantoms – but not external: they are phantoms of the mind.'

Well, to be honest, I'm not that bothered if they're phantoms of the external or phantoms of the internal, whatever they are they scare the goosegogs out of me, and so I says: 'Well what about the lad I sees in the lane then, above Steve the Coat's place? And him being his great uncle and that?'

'Well,' he replies: 'perfectly logical: you had heard about this, perhaps as a child, and all your mind has done is to deceive you: first of all by apparently forgetting it, erasing it entirely from your memory banks and then, secondly by deceiving you into believing it by reproducing it at the precise moment when you were in the circumstances that provoked that hidden memory, suddenly to divulge its contents and relate the story, in visible form. An optical trick: the eye working in conjunction with the brain: the exact moment arrives and hey presto: the spook appears. The genie is out of the bottle of the mind, so to speak.'

'Well I don't know about that,' I says, 'and I suppose it is true as I could have heard it, only I never did. I saw this lad, plain as day.' But then this Hugh Janus bloke goes on and proves me wrong.

And then he goes on: 'There are no mysteries in life,' says he. 'All life is totally explainable: it is run upon logical lines. What appears as a mystery is just that: appearance. The truth lies in scientific explanation, in logic, however bizarre it might seem.'

'The best way to prove yourself against ghosts,' he says, 'is like the story of the monk and the wolves. How they haunted him and came closer and closer and closer, until he was so terrified, he knew the next night they would kill him. A tiny voice inside his head – his patron saint – said: go out into the darkness and put your hand into the hand of God: confront them: tell them you do not believe them: tell them they do not exist. Do this and they will shrivel into nothing and disappear and you will never be bothered by them again.'

Then he stops.

A minute goes by.

'Well?' we says: 'what happened?'

'Well he told them of course,' he says 'and they disappeared: poof, just like that.'

'Well, F and Blast,' George Gunter the F and Blast says: 'I dunna credit that!'

So this Hugh Janus says: 'It's true: try it. If you see something you don't understand, don't run away from it: face it. Confront it – and the problem will be halved, the fear will vanish.'

Well, we'd tried that kind of tactic with old Silver Buttons from Ludlow, hiding in the car park, or in the lanes and that – but if he's going to get you he's going to get you and that's that, so we don't think this kind of talk is much good.

But there was no telling this Hugh Janus that.

Then this Hugh Janus, he gets up, swills his beer, wishes us good night and he's out.

After a minute, Trouser says: 'Well, I don't know about him but my life's a big mystery to me,' says Trouser Jabez, 'maybe he's got it all sorted but I don't know what's going to happen next and whatever does, I canna explain it.'

'That bloke lives a dry old way to me,' Knukky says: and we all agrees with this. 'Me, I see wonder in everything,' says Knukky, 'even the little minnows in the brook is a marvel and a mystery to me. And why's there so many different kinds of birds?

So what's that if that's not a mystery? And how is it the wild flowers are all so different, so many colours and shapes and sizes? They could look like lumps of stone, if they wanted to, couldn't they? And smell just as dull; and the insects be terrible things, and bees make poison honey – but instead, we have butterflies and grasshoppers and little black and yellow beetles and bees as make sweet honey. What's that if it isn't a mystery and a marvel?'

And then old Knocker Morsel he says: 'And grass; it is wonderful stuff. It stays quiet all the winter, all couched down, then bursts out in spring and feeds the stock. And then you can cut it and keep it to feed them all next winter too. It is a marvel.'

'F and Blast,' says George: 'and I dunna hold with him and his sykees and all that twaddle about the mind. When I see a ghost, the thing is as real as you stood there, and I ent about to go marching up to tell him he dunna exist or for sure he'll frit me to death and that'll be the end of the job. And I'll tell you something about that Hugh Janus: if he sees the coach and eight coming straight at him, he'll be the last one to go up to it and say: I say, go away, we don't think you're real. No, he'll be the first to run, you hark my words.'

And that's pretty much as we all thinks and then Spud the Landlord says: 'Well gents, it's three o'clock and if you haven't got homes to go to, you can kip in the car park if you like, but me, I am off to my scratcher as tonight is Val Purges night and what we have been going on about will draw these ghosts to we, as pigs' snouts to acorns. Good night!'

And, although we all turn to go and say ta-ta and goodnight, this is the moment as Knocker and me have been hoping would not come.

And, but, so we all clears out the bar and stands about yakking in the car park for half an hour, then they all jumps in their motors and clears off.

Spud, he turns all The Pendragon's lights out.

Knocker Morsel and me – we are left standing alone in the

carpark, in the dark.

And by God, it is dark.

Then old Knocker, wherever he is because I can't see him, he says: 'Hey, Burt, are you still there?'

So I says, yes, as far as I know, I'm still here.

Then Knocker he says: 'By God, it is dark.'

So I say: 'By God Knocker, you're right it is. I canna see a single thing – it is as if I am struck blind.'

Knocker, he says 'It is as if I am struck blind too.'

Well then, says Knocker, as he is going to walk up the hill to his place now.

So I say as I am going to walk across the meadows and up the hill to my place. Then Knocker says as he has to creep past the boneyard only he's thinking of running.

And me, I say as I have a obstacle as is a periculous old job too, only I canna think how to tackle it just now. So we says goodnight to each other and turns and goes our ways.

Only, the thing is, on the way to my gaff is this little bridge effort over the river. It is only a small wood footbridge, but it is where the river is deep and quick and it is not altogether easy to find, especially in the dark. But the other thing about it is, that the Council footpath outfit is doing work on this bridge just now and have taken down both handrails so the only way to cross it after you have been in The Pendragon, especially in the pitch black, is to get on your hands and knees and crawl – if you can find it, that is. So when I says to Knocker as I am going to walk across the meadows and up the hill to my place, I remember about this bridge and this no handrails lark, and do not say about crawling. I'm thinking about Knocker running past the boneyard – maybe he will decide to crawl past it as well.

Well, but, the thing is, I won't keep this story running on too long: only to say it takes me till the sun rises to get home this Val Purges night and what I went crawling out on on my hands and knees across the river to this day I shall never know. But whatever it was it put me in mind of those men in the olden days as used to drove their beasts along those tracks in the pelting rain and snow and must have half froze to death because by God that water was bitter.

Anyway up, after all this caper, the summer is going along and we forget all about this Val Purges night malarkey and think more about the Festival as comes every year in the village. And this is a fair old to-do, with everyone turning out in some sort of arrangement: they are King Henrys perhaps, with these turny-up toes on their green boots and yellow leggings on and green jackets and crowns, or the girls are kitted out pretty as pictures in tight bodices and buxom as serving wenches, they make an old man's heart thump. Then there's Ivor the Wellies and he comes along with his bride and his Suffolks drawing his big yellow haywain and that takes up half the street and it's a good job he keeps on nipping off with these horses carting kiddies about for rides otherwise he'd cloff the whole place up.

So the old sun is blazing away and this is as fair a day as ever, full of smiles and sizzling sausages as Frank the Plank is frazzling up on a griddle, outside The Buffalo. And Knuckky Stubbs has got his tub cart there with his old cob Domino, shining like the squire's Bentley, and here's someone dressed as Jack Mytton the Highwayman on his horse, with his big cuffs and tricorn hat – he doesn't look a bit out of place here, as though time itself stood still for him and what is out of place there, if anything, is the cars.

This Festival of ours is a rare do, and it brings all the valley together and has everyone trading all kinds of stuff as they've got jammed away in their attics for the past forty years or more.

But the really big show of the day is when Richard the Horse comes. When Richard the Horse comes, this is a sight to behold.

You can hear him smacking down the road, even above all the rattle in the fair: you hear all these hooves thundering along the tarmac as it sounds like a whole army is wenting along. Then comes the sound of big metal wheels grinding along the road and then above that Dave Lerman the Music, as carries the blunder-buss for the day, he blows the coaching horn so as everyone knows to keep clear as these horses swing in pulling the coach.

And when Richard the Horse comes, and the horses come clattering over the little bridge, and up the hill and turn left into the square, everyone gives them plenty of room because they needs loads of it to turn.

And they comes in all snorting and eyes glaring behind their blinkers and the leather is all shone up to a sparkle and the horses, they got a good sweat on and their manes and tails is flying, the spokes of the wheels flickering round, the coach rolls as they thunders in and Richard is up there with handsful of reins and Dave is giving the coaching horn a rare tooting – and if ever there is a sight as whips the breath from your body, this is it.

Then Richard pulls the horses up bang in the midst of the square and by the time the horses have stopped, and the air is full of dust and the smell of horse sweat and leather, and you look at the length of this thing and it seems to take up the whole square as eight horses in harness is a lot of horseflesh, so it is. Specially Richard's horses, as they are all black and sixteen hands a-piece.

So we 'How bist' ee surree!' to Richard and he hollers back.

So he rests the horses for a short while then he calls down to we, and Trouser, and George Gunter the F and Blast and me climb up onto the coach with a ruck of kiddies and a bunch of bulling wenches with dimple smiles and pert arses – they make an old man very happy – or very sad – and Richard hoy-ups the horses.

Then we smacks forward: the horses stern in their breast plates, muscles straining, thirty two hooves plugged into the dirt, heads bowed, necks bulging, haunches rippling, that is power as no motor whatever can come within a thousand mile of.

The speed we takes off at tosses you back in your seat and we go hammering down the main road half a mile or so, then

Richard flips the rein and turns us off the main road onto the Castle lane and that is the fairest way to clip through the scenery and no mistake, better than anything else on earth.

It makes you feel like a king.

But as we are going along, Richard says a strange thing happens to him on his way to the fair today, something he canna explain.

Richard he lives out along the tops, right along the upsy downsy road, well past the Anchor. He says he sets out from home at three thirty in the morning, in the dark with the coach so as to be with Reuben at Crackspur at seven thirtyish to give the horses a bite and a rest the horses before coming to the fair.

He says, Richard, that as he's coming along the tops with the horses going up and down these hollows and dips in the road, he sees this car streaking along, with its headlights streaming direct at him, which he thinks is very early for someone to be about, or very late for somebody else. So what Richard does then is to stand up from his seat, wave his arms about and start shouting at this nutter roaring towards them, but then, as this car comes along, suddenly it jams to a halt, stops, reverses, stops, then rushes forwards, squeals to a stop again, then goes screaming backwards again, brakes hard, then comes rushing forward and suddenly takes a plunge off to the right, goes crashing through a five bar gate and hurtles off down the hill across the meadows and through a hedge to Stan the Man's place, deep in the valley below.

Richard pulls the horses up and gazes down into the valley and wonders what on earth all this is about? Then Stan's lights go on in the house. So he thinks to hisself, should he go down there and see what's what, as this is a very strange way for someone to behave. Richard, he thinks it be someone stole this motor, or a nutter maybe. And should he go down and help Stan to sort this bloke out? But the thing is, here's him and Dave half froze up on this coach with eight steaming horses in the dark and he can't leave the horses and the only lights he's got are two dim coach lamps burning on either side of the coach, so what does he do? He hoy-ups the horses on to Crackspur.

So now of course, we are all very interested in this story as we can sort of guess as what this is and so we canna wait to get back to the Festival to see if we can rootle out old Stan the Man from somewhere.

It is in The Sun we finds him, standing at the bar like Sir Oliver Lawrence, the big actor, enjoying telling this story, putting plenty of part into it. He has told everyone in there five times before we arrives. So we ask him to tell it again. And he does, as he likes to do this. What he says is this: he says Catchmace across the tops is on the market from today and why? Why? Because this incomer bloke as lives there, is going to sell it quick as he has had a nasty fright this last night. He seen a ghost. He seen the ghost.

Well, says Stan, putting a bit of time into this – this Hugh Janus bloke comes piling into his yard about three thirty this morning with a very bent motor. Only this bloke, Stan says, doesn't come down the drive like normal customers: he comes howling down the bank from right up the top, screeching across the meadows, smashing up two gates and a hedge on his way down then wrecks his car on a stone wall in his yard.

So, when he harks at this rattle going on outside, Stan smacks the lights on, grabs his Barbour, duffs it on top of his dozing livery, and nips out into the yard with his Purdey to see what all this commorando is about.

And there he finds this Hugh Janus bloke, sobbing in his twasted up motor, all covered in blood and jibbering on and on and on about the phantom coach and eight on the tops. He sees it, real as real can be, eight black horses thundering through the darkness; eyes glittering in the car moonlight; sweat-steam pouring off of the horses; the wind whipping across; tails and manes flying; the coach rolling from side to side, the spokes of wheels flickering round, the coachman calling out; the man with the blunderbuss beside him and the two little outrigger coach lamps burning dim.

Lying Doggo

Hoofface-Henry got a smack in the snozzle by a Section C Cob when he used to be a stallion-man and he's called Hoofface-Henry because of the impression this made on him, at the time.

So Hoofface jacks in this stallion-man caper and skims about in a beat-up old Bedford TK horsebox now, ferrying ponies from here to there, by way of making a bit of scratch for himself. Anyway up, Hoofface has a filthy old mutt called Arsenic, and Arsenic is some sort of a diesel-hound cum-collie or other, and rattles around with Hoofface in his waggon, and the other day Willie the Pooh creeps off with Hoofface and Arsenic to collect a pony from down country Cirencester way, which is a fair old pull from the borders, where Hoofface lives.

And, but, the thing is, Willie doesn't much like Arsenic, but he knows that actually, Arsenic only ever bites Silver Button merchants which is why Hoofface never bothers much to tax his waggon. So down they all buzz to Ciren' when Willie says to Hoofface that actually his waggon is a pretty ropey old affair and really shouldn't be allowed on the road but Hoofface says that if Willie wants to go and get his new pony in a Rolls-Royce then he should have said so and he could have fixed it, only he might have hit him for a bit more bleat from his bank, in that case.

So this shuts Willie up. Then, a while later, they pitch into this horse-coper place or other, and argy-bargy the price of this pony, with a bit of luck money here, and a bit there, which takes most of the afternoon, and gets people worked upsome, narked even, and eventually the horse-coper is so keen to get rid of Hooface Henry and Willie he lets the pony go for what Willie has got in his top pocket.

So they lug the pony in the waggon and come rolling back to Knighton at midnightish when the local Silver Buttons pops out the hedge in his Raspberry, sticks his Stop Lights on, and pulls them up.

Silver Buttons ambles very slow over to the waggon.

He taps on Hooface's window for him to unwind it so he can say whatever he wants to say. So now Arsenic looses off with a string of barking fit enough to wake the boneyard skellingtons. And Hoofface doesn't open his window in case Arsenic goes piling out which Hoofface isn't keen to happen because he could be in bad enough bother as it is.

So they shout at one another through the window while Arsenic goes rabies in the cab with Willie trying to smother him under his Barbour.

So Silver Buttons hollers: 'Where's your tax disc then, eh, Hoofface?'

Hoofface shouts back: 'Dog ate it.'

Then Silver Buttons goes inspecting round his waggon looking at this and tapping that, which seems to take a long time, and when he comes back to Hooface's window, he gets out his booking pad and bawls: 'I should get rid of that dog if I was you, Hoofface: he's ate all the tread off your tyres as well.'

By Example

These little village schools nowadays, like ours, in the village, they are very small, with maybe twenty kiddies in; less even: fifteen; perhaps fourteen, I don't know, somewhere thereaboutish. Being as these schools are out away from towns, and remote, with an average kiddy age-ish round about six or seven years, these government toffs, they want to shut them.

And, but, our school, it is a very fine little school, being sited hard by the river, in amongst a heap of trees, and this little school, it is run by Annie Rook what is a lady of all of a keen way with her, and strict with discipline, yet she is also very fair, and bunged full of understanding of schoolish things, about books and whatnot: the sort that kiddies like, with pictures of chuffa-trains and postmen; doggies; pussy-cats and ponies, whatever, in.

Anyway up, Annie, who runs this school is, one day, passing by The Arms come dinner time of a Friday, as The Arms is but a short stepping distance from the school, and, Annie, who should she meet on his way in for some barstool therapy but Trouser Jabez.

And Trouser, being as he is a polite man, he 'how be you be's?' Annie Rook, enquiring after her health and temper, and she says like this: she says that she is total confounded as to what these people in County Hall want to shut down her school for.

So Trouser, he asks: 'What will happen to all the kiddies if they shuts down your school?' And she says, they will have to go to town.

So Trouser says, this is a long way to expect a kiddy to go, all on its own, ten miles there, and ten back, and is periculous of a winter's night, in the dark, on the roads, with nutters abroad.

And, Trouser says, there are already too many kiddies in the town school anyway. So he tells her not to take a gnat's worth of notice of what these County Hall vermin say and just carry on, as before. But Annie Rook, she says as this is probably not as simple as all that, as nothing connected with County Hall ever is, and, but, she says her school is, in actual fact, better than the town school on account there are less kiddies in it, so she can attend to each one, individual-like, and sort of encourage them-like, to learn whatever, and have manners.

And Trouser, he says she can give the little blighters a good clopping as well, if she likes, and sort out straight who be's boss round here. Which is right, says Trouser, and in fact, he says, he remembers when he is a kiddy, his dad used to give him a good clopping every day, whether he'd done wrong or not, just in case he was about to. And he says to Annie, she should do the same.

But she says, you cannot do this these days on account of if you do, you will definitely wind up in the local nickery and get wrote about all in the newspapers, as well, on top.

So then Trouser, he says he can see no way out then because if you cannot give a kiddy a good clopping when it needs one, how are you to get it to do right?

But Annie, she says you do it by example: you act right, and they will copy, and have good manners, and sound sense, and so Trouser says, she is right, and this is why she is boss of this little school, and not him.

Then as he is saying a good afternoon to her she asks him if maybe he would like to come to the Carol Concert in the little school in a week's time, which is a nativity job, on account of it being near Christmas, and a very important occasion because the chief school inspector gaffer from County Hall is supposed to be tipping up and she is hoping as to knock him flat with this play, so as he might decide not to pull the rug out from under her.

Also, she says, if plenty from the village come along, this would be handy.

So Trouser, he says he will be there; she can bet the vicar's guzunder on it.

It is a week passes and it is the evening of this play and Trouser, he is in The Arms again, getting a swift one down before the performance, when into the bar swings this foreigner, and Trouser can tell at once that this bloke is from off, from County Hall probably, on account of the way he is decked out, with a suit and tie and stuff, and not wellies and duffed-up Barbours like everyone else.

So, as he is ordering his beer, Trouser, he sidles up to him and he says like this, he says: 'Good evening, Mister County Hall. If you are come to shut this school down you had better think twice on account of me what was at this school and everyone else here as well, and we is very proud of this little school, even though it is little, because we was heducated gooder as anybody else in this 'ere Monarch's realm and don't you mistake it, no surree. And, what's more, as well, Mister County Hall, is that this night you will see the finest performance of this carol service play job effort as what you have ever seen before.'

And then Trouser, he nods to agree with himself, and this bloke he just wanders off to sit down in a corner on his own and opens up the evening rag.

So now Trouser, he thinks he is iggorant this man, and none too friendly, and is the sort of fellow as would merit from a good kick in the jodhpurs by a pig-swill lady in size 10 Dunlops.

So Trouser, he does not bother to let on what he thinks of the school, to him, personal. Instead, he blarts it right out loud to everyone what comes in, until everyone knows the little school in Big Duley is gooder as any other in the whole world and ought not to be shut down by people from County Hall, with no manners.

Anyway up, this bloke gets up and clears off, in a huff, slamming the door behind him, when suddenly, outside, scorting round the corner on her way to school, comes this little kiddy.

And she wallops into Mr County Hall.

They both go flying.

But, quick as a flash, this little kiddy gets up and goes scorting off, as she is in a blinding rush, and, but, Mr County Hall, he looses off after her with a string of common blasphemy as is fit enough to fell a herd of Hereford cows, never mind a small kiddy from school.

Now Trouser, in The Arms, he harks at this language, through the window, and though he is terrible shocked, he says nothing: he just scratches his chin and slips another couple of pints down, and sort of ums and ars, then nips across to the school hall for this play.

Anyway up, he arrives.

He sits at the back.

He looks about.

And this is what he sees: he sees this little theatre, been done up special, with a big old red curtain across, and these seats for the kiddies' parents and everyone, sat in them. And over near the front, Trouser, he spies the head teacher Annie and she is with this bloke from County Hall, who is a very serious looking commodity altogether, being as he is in actual fact, very dour, with the knackerman stamp on him, and he seems pretty fed-up with all this, already.

Anyway up, after everyone is settled, and the lights goes dim, as people gets their coughs out the way, and blows their noses, and wriggles, it all goes mum and the curtain, it edges back.

And there, lit up on the stage, are these little kiddies.

They are all kitted up in their Bible clobber, whatever, with long stripey coats, and sandals, and funny hats, with tassles, and they are a very pretty little lot, with grease-painted beards and all; and here are the three kings lugging big parcels with murphys and gold and frankersense in, and here is this little kiddy with big paper wings, who is supposed to be some sort of a angel, perhaps, all done up in white with a wire halo strapped to his bonce, and there's even old Tom Bevan's donkey in there with them, and a few bantams; and rabbits; a hamster; a few kittens; a puppy; and really, this is all a very fine picture, indeed.

Anyway up, these kiddies, they get to do with this story a bit, and presently, this little tiny little child of someone's daughter affair, she is in the front with this little dolly in her lap, and she is rocking this dolly back and forth, and, she: she is supposed to be the Virgin Mary.

Then, one of the other kiddies, a little boy, from the back, strolls across to her, bringing Tom Bevan's donkey with him, and this little boy, he is Joseph.

He stands beside Mary.

Then this other kiddy, a white angel gets yanked up in the air above everyone's heads on some sort of a pulley gismo and he lands in a bit of a heap near enough right on top of this little Mary, and, but, he steadies hisself and he says to her like this, he says: 'What child is this as is laid to rest on Mary's lap is sleeping?'

This little Mary, she says nothing.

She is silence.

So this angel, he gives her a good prod with his magic wand, and tries again: 'What child is this as is laid to rest on Mary's lap sleeping?'

But this little Mary, she isn't speaking.

So this angel gives her another go, and this time lets her have a real hard prod in the ribs with his magic wand: 'What child is this as is laid to rest in Mary's lap sleeping, eh?'

So this little Mary, she looks down on this little babby, and she strokes his little face and she says: 'Colin.'

So this angel, he gawps at this Mary.

'No', he hisses.

'Yes', she whispers.

'No', he hisses, again, even louder.

'Yes', she whispers.

'No', he says, again, 'you're not supposed to call him that, you silly nit.'

'Yes,' she says: 'Colin. I'm going to call him Colin.'

So now this causes people to snort somewhat, and snigger, and look across to the head teacher who is up-sitting in her chair and leaning very much forward and is wearing this expression of surprise: disbelief even; and this school inspector, he is holding one hand over his nose and what he is thinking is sneered all over his face. And these others, they look around for the vicar as is perched on the edge of his chair with his mouth open. And one or two of these people is nudging one another and winking, as though to be saying: well, maybe it isn't such a bad idea as they are going to close this school down after all, considering.

And, but, then, this little Virgin Mary, she takes not a tad of notice of any of this, and she bangs on about this Colin being the King of Kings and Saviour of this and Redeemer of that, then winds up with all the others singing Away in a Manger, and even then she gets to the little Lord Colin asleep in the hay.

So by now most of these other kiddies, they are not a little out of hand and are falling about, and very shortly everyone has lost the storyline here and this little play, it ends abruptly and the curtain falls.

But, the thing is, these people in this audience, in that this is their little school, they clap and shout and whistle like this is the last performance of Vera Lynn and this new Colin King of Kings character is just the job for this play and their village and that'll be that, then. They get these kiddies to do about twenty curtain calls.

Then the whole caboodle is over, and everyone is in this Common Room swigging cups of coffee, and in come all these kiddies from the play with all their make-up on, and they are very lit up, and, but, Annie, the head teacher, she cannot believe quite what has happened here, so she collars this little Virgin Mary, because Annie, she knows that in fact this little Virgin Mary is bright little spark, even though she muffs her words at the wrong moment and gets to calling the chief villain of the plot by a duff name.

So then, now Trouser, being a kindly fellow, he picks this little Mary up, and as Annie Rook is about to give her a bit of the old right-now-you-little-perisher-may-the-Lord-make-you-truly-thankful-for-what-you-are-about-to-receive – up pops this inspector bloke, smug as a cock on a midden, and he says to her, he says, 'I see you don't seem to know the name of our Saviour, the Son of God? Do they not teach you this in this school?'

This little Mary, she says nothing.

So he smugs it again: 'Eh? Do you not know his name?' in a very big-sorted way.

Then Trouser, he says to her, 'You tell him, my little shusty,' being as Trouser twigs as to how this little kiddy thinks.

So this little Mary, she looks this school inspector gaffer deadsmack in the beezer, and this little Mary, she's got very clear eyes, and she says to him, she says: 'as you come out the pub tonight, you sent me flying, and frightened me, shouting like you did, so as I thought as you seem to s'pose His name was only for swearing, I used another in our play, so's as you didn't think as I doos swearing too.'

Love's Harvest

Ivor the Wellies lives over the hill from our valley, closer to The Castle, you might say – perhaps six miles or so – which is why he has friends over that way as well as friends over this way, which is why if you go over that way, you will catch him in The Three Tuns, or The Six Bells or The Bull or The Castle Vaults or somewhere, of a market day.

Barney Dawes, Trouser, George Gunter the F and Blast and me are thinking to pay him a call last Wednesday, in The Three Tuns, as we haven't seen him for a while and are thinking as maybe he could do with an outing, to steady his nerves.

So we piles in Barney Dawes' motor, as he's got a bit of a knack on this skimming about the place job, and we tips up over there bang on High Noon.

Anyway – this last Wednesday I am on about is the most beautifullest day, being more like spring, even though it is in fact, winter, official, being February.

And, but, if you drive over to The Castle when the weather is like this, as you come over the tops, The Castle lies in a mist, like houses in a lake, while you up on the tops is in the sunlight and this makes for a very pretty picture indeed, which is when George Gunter the F and Blast says as he wishes he has a camera.

155

As to why he wants a camera no-one knows as who is going to look at the photo, ever, even him, is the question.

Anyway, so, when we gets to The Castle, as Barney Dawes is finding somewhere handy to jam his motor, George Gunter the F and Blast and Trouser and me, we jumps into The Three Tuns.

And no sooner as we are in as the landlord, who is the person as we are familiar with, says as Peter Gurney is died last week and today is his funereal.

This is, for us, a very sad moment, because although we don't know who this Peter Gurney is, or why he is died, it is very sad as he was probably someone's mucker, somewhere, and they shall miss him, whatever it was he did. And no doubt, there will be a church service job, with hymns and the vicar going on and someone doing a bit of a speech and those things.

All this is very miserable making so we are decided then to stay in The Three Tuns, even though Peter Gurney is died, because The Three Tuns is as good a place to be miserable in as the Six Bells, if you think about it.

Anyway up, Barney Dawes, he harks at this news when he comes in.

So then we buys some of The Three Tuns beer as is very pale beer in colour and palms one of these acrost to Barney to give him a moment to ponder on this Peter Gurney business, whoever he is, and him dropping dead just like that, and this funereal job of his.

So Barney, he does this, quietly, and scrats his arms a bit and says: 'mmm...' then he screws up his eyes and gawps up into the rafters and says: 'mm....well, well, well: poor old devil.'

Then he snuffles about a bit and stares down in the flags and says: 'Poor old boy.' Then he runs his hands through his hair, and scrats his hairy old chest and has a good rootle about in his belly button and wipes his hands on his trousers and has a few draws on his beer, then wipes the froth off his mouth and then says: 'Well I never.'

'You knew him, then?' says the landlord.

'No,' Barn says: 'Never heard of him.'

So the landlord just looks at him and dunna say nothing.

'Well, there we goes then,' says Barn. Then he says: 'Fancy a game of pool?'

So we do this.

Then he says 'What about darts?'

So we do that.

Then he says: 'Shove halfpenny's a good crack, let's give that a whirl.'

Then we does Nine Men's Morris and quoits and by the time we've lost all our wallet grease to him, Ivor the Wellies scrawls in.

And although we 'how bist 'ee surree's?' he, he dunna reply. In fact, Ivor the Wellies is as miserable as maggots.

He thumps hisself down on a stool.

He joggles with his hat.

He looks along the lines of bottles.

He wipes the beer off of the bar with his sleeve.

He puts one foot up on the stool foot rest and then thother and then he puts them on the floor and stands up. Then he sets down and then gets up and then sets down again and Barney says: 'For heaven's sake Ivor, you'm jumping up and down like a tom-tit on a pump handle, you got a bee in your drawers?'

'No,' says Ivor, 'I just been to the boneyarding of a consider-able friend of mine,' says Ivor, 'by the name of Robin Oates, and this Robin...'

'Wait a minute,' says Barney, 'who?'

'Robin Oates,' says Ivor.

'Not Peter Gurney?'

'No,' says Ivor, 'who's Peter Gurney?'

'I don't know who Peter Gurney is,' says Barn: 'Trouser tells me when I comes in as this Peter Gurney is died and then Mart – the landlord – asks me if I know him, and now you, and you say you've just been boneyarding this Robin someone, and I still don't know who Peter Gurney is.'

'Mart told me and Burt here about this Peter Gurney as soon as we come in,' says Trouser, 'but we don't know him neither.'

So then Barn says to Mart: 'Do you know who this Peter Gurney is then, Mart?'

'No,' says Mart, 'I don't know him. I thought you might though.'

'Well how come you got to hear about it then?'

'In the paper shop this morning.'

'Well they must have known who he was, then,' says Barn.

'No they didna,' says Mart, 'as I asked them who he was and they said they didn't know only that he was died and his funereal is today, in the church.'

'So who's this Robin fellow then?' asks Barn.

'Robin Oates is a considerable friend of mine and we have just been boneyarding him in the church as well.'

'As well as Peter Gurney?'

Says Ivor: 'I never heard no-one say nothing about no Peter Gurney.'

So now this is getting in a bit of a mess all of sudden and so we decides either to stop talking about this Peter Gurney bloke, or to go and find out who he is, but then Barn says as there's not a lot of point in doing that because he's dead now and it's too late.

So, instead, Barn asks Ivor about his friend Robin whatever it was. And Ivor says this: 'This Robin Oates as I am on about, is fifty-three when he dies – too soon for a man of his quality and standing. This Robin Oates, you never know a better man for leaving his dinner aside not to spoil his appetite for draught bitter. And this Robin Oates, he gets these Capstans down him something chronic and can fug up a room quicker than the Flying Dutchman. And this Robin Oates, he is a maker of breeching for horses when he is alive, and it is this I shall miss him for, as there has never been a man so skilled at fitting breeching for big horses as was bore from the time of King David and his harlots to this day.'

Although this is a big-sorted claim to be making about this Robin Oates character and his thimbles and this breeching job effort, it is plain to see as Ivor is took it bad that he is departed to thother side.

And so, although none of we know who this Robin Oates is – never mind this Peter Gurney – George Gunter the F and Blast says: 'F and Blast,' he says, 'He's in a finer place now I doubt, and quaffing some fairer kit too, I doubt, as the stuff they brews on thother side is a sight better than this mallard water they pokes across the bar at you here – and free too. So you don't want to worry about him Ivor, old mucker, he'll be better off where he be than where we be, and I'll have another pint of that duck slosh, please,' and he hands him his empty glass, 'while you're about it.'

So old Ivor gets them in and now, because of what George Gunter has said is right, it lifts Ivor to a higher spirit as he was before and so we drinks a toast to his old mucker Robin Oates and this Peter Gurney, whoever he was, and imagines as they are now probably sat in heaven knocking it back by the yard.

Then Ivor says: 'You know, I can glean it as I have been to that many funereals in this valley this year, maybe ten, as I am thinking that the population of the place is descending faster as it is rising, and the reason I am sure it is true, is that I am asked to that many funereals in my lifetime, maybe a hundred, but I have never once been asked to a birth.'

It has to be said, as we are in agreement with this. No-one as we knows is ever asked us to a birth.

Never.

But everyone asks us all the while to go to this funereal and that funereal, the ones in Big Duley, and in our valley and in Ivor's valley and over Llanbister valley and Trouser's valley and this is not to say as we do not wish to go. We care to make our respects to the deceased, yes we do.

But it does take up more time than you would credit.

And, but, set against this is that whenever there is a

boneyarding in the locality, usually, they slap on a fair old sending off spread for whoever it is as is hoyed over, as is right and polite. And it also has to be said as there's not many as comes away from there as knows their home, straight off, either.

There have been occasions when one boneyarding is followed direct with another on account of the boneyarding they just been to, and the spread after and the amount of whisky as gets rivered about, as they crunches one another up on their way out, and runs over them with a Fergi or something, or scraggles them up under a Landrover, whatever. Like they done to Troy the RSJ, down the village and ranned him over with a Volvo as he was guiding them from there. Only they only broke all his arms and legs, that's all. He was alright again in the twelvemonth.

So, even though what Ivor says is not a lie, Barney says to him: 'Ah but the thing is Ivor, people don't ask people to deaths either. They asks them to the funereal.'

'Well,' says Ivor, 'that's obvious because nobody knows when they're going to pitch over so it'd be hard to arrange a party for them when they was about to kick the bucket just in case they don't.'

'That's the thing,' says Barney, 'they don't know when they're going to get born either, so that's why they asked to go to the Christening instead, as you can more or less fix up some sort of date for that.'

'Well, that's what it must be,' says Ivor and he says as Barney is right.

'But,' says Ivor, 'I still get asked to more funereals as I do Christenings as there's still more people dying as there is being born. And I doubt as I will ever be asked to a birth and none of you will neither, you hark my words.'

None of us makes a reply to this.

The thing is, you must never taunt Lady Providence.

We knows this.

From little 'uns we are taught as we must never taunt Lady Providence.

If you are going to make some sort of a claim, you have to whisper it under the rose – if it please Lady Providence – or else she will sour you a harsh lesson for trying it out on her.

And if you make some big-sorted sort of claim, such as you have found something cheaper than you have or that you have something that you haven't, as duck eggs is blue, Lady Providence will make you cough up the bitter-regrets for that when you get it, if you get it, and it will fall to bits and not work and conk out and royzle it about as if it's got Lucifer hisself in it and you will be much worser off by a mile than if you'd kept your trap shut and not said a dickie on it and just gone about quietly, without it.

And the thing is, this is true as I tell you, as Ivor is to find out, as Lady Providence has an uncommon addiction to springing the trap on you for trying her out, so she does, and what Ivor says this day, one way and another, he gets to recall.

Ivor the Wellies is a mid-high man, being always turned out in cleanish trousers and a collar and tie, and this old jacket job, and flat hat and – even though he looks as though he shaves with a rotavator and has ears and nostrils plugged with shaving cream – is clean shaven, and is in most respects a nice-looking old ruffian even if he is a touch over half way, if that's what fifty-five is.

He's got a rare thatch of hair, long and white as a barn oolert, eyes as dark as a pool in a spinney, snowy sideburns and these wellies as I thinks he's glued to. Even if it is a scorching summer's day and everyone is burned to a cindered pig, with their shirts off, Ivor is in his wellies.

Anyway up, he's got a bit of a place over Mardy somewhere, all painted white and cratched up with stone, with a big old inglenook in it and a settle and telly and chair.

And, but it's a fine place, being of vintage and made by people as made things beautiful because they took time.

People in those days, they loved to see fine things, even if it was a bit of a cottage, with only two rooms upstairs and two down. They made it so that it would be a pleasure to live in, minding they didn't have half a rind of flitch to live off hardly, and some spuds perhaps and kale maybe and an apple or two growing in the patch out the back.

When they made these places, they took care how to site them: off the wind and facing the sun, so as to make the best of good weather and least of the worst of it. Because they made their own places, their work was riven with care, and attention, and most of all, respect, as is why these old gaffs are sought out these days as what went into them in the first place canna be took out as they still anchor that power, unlike the ones they slings up today, just for money, without a glimmer for how they look, where they're sited or who shall live in them, as is why people keep having divorces and committing felonies and that, in them.

Anyway up, Ivor the Wellies farms just under a score of acres and has done all his natural as his dad and grandad before him.

In fact, they say of his dad as they remember him going about the place in a stove-pipe hat, dressed in black and driving a big old tub cart drawn by a pair of Suffolk Punches, as is how, I suppose, Ivor comes by his taste for this breed, as he keeps a pair of these heavy horses, in his place.

And these two horses he has, they are huge.

They are the biggest Suffolk Punches you ever seen.

They are that big that the place they live in, their stalls, has to be biggered to fit them in, they're that size.

And Ivor, he loves them.

He loves them that much, that if you are with him in The Buffalo say, or The Hundred House, or The Three Tuns or Six Bells or The Crown, The Sun or The Pendragon, when it comes to three o'clock, no matter what he's doing, even if he is winning at Nine Men's Morris, or at spoof, or cribbage, or dominoes, he ups and outs and goes skimming back to those two horses, just to be with them.

He's that smitten with them.

And it's not as if he was smitten with them for being new: he's had them for twenty-five years, these two, and they are a pair of old scallywags, there is no doubt.

Before these, he had another pair as his father left him, in his will, and when they died, they lived to over forty years old apiece, and that's a fair vintage for a Suffolk Punch, indeed it is.

And he moithers about these horses and spends half a day sweeping them and unclogging the mud from them, and picking out their feet and untanglifying their manes and tails and getting their buzzies swep that clean as the Queen herself could eat her dinner from there.

And these horses gets the best they can have, flake barley and peas, steamed maize and wort from the brewery. And he bangs them full of linseed with barley mashes and he looses them to scrut about on the land as he keeps as clean as a cat's jacket.

His farm, the land, this nineteen acre, he looses these horses on along with half a dozen Welsh Blacks, as he keeps as well.

And in the summer, when all this lot is gannetting their heads off, Ivor, he sets a patch of land by for winter fodder, there being no extra for him and what with needing 500 bales for winter, he makes best use of any grass he can find and he's the only man left alive as I know of as grazes the long acre.

So if you go round the lanes by Mardy in June or July or August, you might find these lanes all cloffed up with beasts and two heavy horses, who dunna care a twaddle about motors and tourists and that.

And these horses, what they do when a motor creeps up is to go running direct at it, which is alarming for townspeople, not expecting two monsters to come piling at them when they are out and about on their holidays, doondering about the countryside, with their kiddies, from Birmingham.

And these horses, like I say, are collossal, very, very big and make the ground thunder as they booms along and then these horses, they jams their heads in the windows either side of these motors and do snapping with their lips, and lays their ears flat and glares their eyes, until they get lumps of sugar or sweets or sandwiches or oranges or apples or anything, which people give them, on account of being frit to death because if they do not give them something, these horses duff the panels of their motors in, as they are a canny pair of old yarbs as you might ever meet in a lane, of a summer's afternoon, in your motor. You won't find Ivor to complain to neither, as he'll be coutched down, in the feg, on the adland on thother side of the hedge.

Anyway up, as it is, these horses graft about the place for Ivor, as he has no tractor nor nothing to do the farm work, only these horses. They do the harrowing, rolling, fingerbar mowing, hay bobbing and cart the grub cart for the cows. The baling Ivor gets the Bishop to do, with his baler gadget.

And the thing about working with these horses is that they go along without you, more or less, unlike a tractor, which you have to be jumping on and off all the while as it is a senseless implement and can't think for itself. But big horses, two of them, think plenty for theirselves and when Ivor is mowing or tedding or lugging bales, these two horses they lends their weight as though they know it is for them anyway, and I swear to God as they put their hearts and minds into it.

Anyway up, this last July past, last year it is, of a Thursday evening, when Ivor is at the rumps of this pair of sweating giants, sitting on the spring seat of his fingerbar mower, casting his eyes across the swathes they just cut on his top meadow, satisfied it is done proper, he flicks the rein and hoy-ups the horses back home.

When they pulls into the courtyard, Ivor hasn't to touch the reins at all.

Those horses know how to back the fingerbar straight into the shed, then wait for him to unshackle them and drop their breeching off.

Then they stands over him waiting for their dinner.

Ivor, he is very studious about this, and never gives them too much nor too little. When they dust this lot off, he opens the five bar gate for them and out they thunders and plunges about like a pair of colts and as soon as he sees them settled, he goes in the house, has a swill and a dose of pickled eggs, changes his pants and hat and by eight o'clock he's down The White Horse playing Nine Men's Morris with the rest of we.

This particular time, we has a long weekend of it.

Ivor buys all the beer.

None of us puts our hands in our pockets.

Come Monday, Ivor, he breeches his horses again, this time to the acrobat and works that crop all day.

By next Thursday midday, The Bishop has baled it all up and Ivor is out in the meadow with his horses and four-wheeler waiting to pick them up.

And up in that top meadow, is George Gunter the F and Blast, Trouser Jabez, Barney Dawes and me – as now we have to earn all the beer Ivor bought the weekend before.

Any rate, this particular day – it is July 29th I do recall – as we are pikling the bales up to Ivor, who is stacking on the trailer, with the horses going along nice and steady, drawing the flat-bed, so as we keep pace nice and even – when a sight appears on the meadow as to make a man's chest hair fall out.

This day, it is a scorcher, and we all has got our shirts off as sweat is running off us like Niagara Falls, Africa.

To keep cool, we have got tucked away on the flat-bed, in the bales, a brace of cases of contagious flagons. And these flagons is full to the brim with some sort of jungle spirit as Ivor has devised, from the ellern flower, and this kit has got plenty of spike in it, is cool and quenches your thirst, only it makes you crave more and more, as is why, we have got on the flat-bed, twenty-four bottles, which amounts to forty eight pints, in English.

Now the thing is as we are pikling this hay up to Ivor on the flatbed, the thing as makes us stop dead is this: striding across the meadow toward we, appears this apparition.

It is plain to see as this apparition is headed deadsmack for we, by the way it is bearing down hard.

As it gets closer, it is plain to see, as this is some sort of woman, and, but, what it is we can see as she draws near, is that she is definitely not the sort of woman as takes her corned beef straight from the tin.

This woman, she has jet black hair, to the shoulder, and you can see as she is very nicely made, being big where she ought to be big and little where she ought to be little, and here's us lot, with our shirts off, sweating away like a load of old boars on a dung-grub rootle, snouting about in a meadow on a beautiful summer's day.

And, but, then, this woman she comes direct up to we as now we have all stopped and are gaping at her like she is a apparition from outer Mars or somewhere, as we do not know who she is or what she wants, striding so purposeful to we.

And now she's near enough right close beside us and she says: 'Good day, gentlemen.' Like a lady.

Course, this is the correct thing for her to say, as it is a good day, a beautiful day, and here is she, spectacle enough to make a tree curtsey.

'I was wondering if you needed a hand,' says she, 'there seem to be lots and lots of bales here and since I wasn't doing anything, I thought, perhaps, another pair of hands might be a help.'

Well.

That's the first time anybody's volunteered anything in this valley since God decreed it should have a dent in it.

And, but, the thing is, Ivor, he is froze like a statue, with his white hair blowing about his face and his sunburned skin and white sideburns and white hair on his chest and belly, and he's fit enough, Ivor, for an old one, and well-muscled, and here he is gawping down on this woman like she's the first woman on earth, Eve, or someone, or that one as belonged to King Solomon: Delilah.

Ivor, he is speechless.

Then this lady, she strides over to the horses, who have also noticed as she has come by and have stopped. She goes over to them and smoothes their noses, which is a brave thing to do as these two horses have eaten people for less, and she says: 'Aren't they beautiful! What a sight! Do they have names?'

So Ivor, he comes to, all of a dither, drops down off the flatbed, rubs the sweat off his face with his shirt and goes up to her with his white hair all sticking out on his chest and he looks like one of them rag-rugs you drops in front of the fire where some old long-dog has been kipping on for a decade only nobody bothered to shake off the sheddings.

'This 'orse,' says Ivor, and Ivor's very strong Shropshire: 'This 'orse, he's a touch older than thother and his name is Melilot, and his friend here, we calls him Nonsuch, although his name is Medick, as is the same as a little wild plant as grows hereabouts, in the grass.'

'Those are beautiful names,' this young lady says: 'and so nice Nonsuch has two names.'

'F and Blast,' George Gunter gets in quick: 'and Melilot has other names too, you hark my words!'

'We was just about to have a bit of bait,' says Ivor. 'You can join us if you likes, Madam, and then perhaps, if you likes, after, you can jump up on the flatbed and help with the stacking.'

Ivor takes the bits out of the horse's mouths and slips them under their chins and lets them rousle about for whatever horses rousles about for in a bit of cut while we sets down beside the wagon out the power of the sun with these flagons and pops a few corks.

Now this girl, she sets down with us, straight, and she's smiling and very polite, and got lovely little white teeth and these deep brown eyes and this olive skin and when we offers her a swig of ellern, she's game enough and takes it and says: 'This is delicious!'

'And it's got a pair of boots on, so mind out!' says George, cracking the stopper on another.

'Haven't you got any sandwiches or anything?' she asks.

'No need,' says Trouser, 'this kit has plenty of power: that's enough for we just now,' and hands her the bottle for another draw.

She's called Karen, this young lady, we learn, and she's in her mid-thirties, and she is no hobbledehoy or mollekin, and she is definitely not the sort of girl as stirs her beer with a five-inch nail.

In fact, she's a librarian.

And what a librarian is doing sat down with a bunch of smelly old hay carters, I do not know, but there she is, large as life and twice as pretty. She is renting The Coffee Pot for three weeks, as is a tiny little cottage in the hills that stands on its own and you can just see it from the meadow we are in. Which is how she comes to spot us. She's here for three weeks for her summer holidays as she does not want to go to Spain and these places and not knowing much about our part of the country, thought she'd come by and see for herself.

And we find out she has come alone.

After about a ten minute, we get back to the bale lugging nice and steady and she gets up on the flat-bed and helps Ivor to stack. Although it's grand to have her help, she stops we chatting, as we do not know what to say when there is a lady abroad, it happens to we so rare.

After we've got about seventy bales on we all climbs on the flat-bed and the horses turn for home.

And that's when Ivor gets this Karen to sit down beside him, and hands her the reins and as long as Englishmen been eating mustard I know that is the first time anyone in the world except Ivor has ever held a rein on those horses.

Down we go to his place as is called Foss-y-Carreg, and this Karen, she canna believe what she's seeing.

Something about this place knocks her dead flat, we don't know what it is.

The old horses pull up by the barn and now she has to go into the shed to stack the bales as they comes off the trailer and that's heavy work.

By and by Ivor cottons her fingers is getting raw from the strings and her wrists is getting scratted from the rough of the hay, as this is good, hard horse hay with plenty of ryegrass in it, as well as bents, and timothy, crested dogtail and meadow foxtail and a dose of medick. So he gets her some gloves as are a pair of the rattiest old mittens as ever man handed a lady, they looks like they was the ones them Vikings used for waging war on Julius Caesar. Karen doesn't mind though, even though they keeps falling off and as the work goes on she keeps having to stop and stretch her back as the weight of the bales is getting to her.

We stops for a bite in Ivor's house after the next load and Ivor brings the horses in out of the sun, waters and nosebags them and we nips in the house and this Karen, it is like she is seeing something for the first time, ever.

It is nice and cool in the house and Ivor hooks out a jar of pickled duck eggs and a flitch of fat bacon, a raw onion and a handful of radishes, then opens another couple of flagons and I'd say although she ate and drank along with we, it probably near killed her. The ducks eggs were grey in colour and tasted well of pond. The onions was Trouser's specialities: the-rip-the-top-of-your-head-off variety. The radishes was George's: the instant mouth-incineration species. You needed the ellern to put the fire out and that, and wadges of smoked, fat bacon are not, I don't suppose, what young ladies eats much. But if the top of her head

169

was about to explode, she never said so, although I did notice it made her eyes water.

Anyway up, she stays with we for the rest of the day and then by tea time we've nearly shifted three hundred and seventy bales and leave the rest for the morning.

And this Karen, it is plain to see, is boiling hot, like we, with sweat across her forehead and down her back, but she looks the prettiest thing I ever saw and that goes for George Gunter the F and Blast and Trouser and Barney and Ivor as well.

Then she says she must go home now but will be back to help tomorrow if we like, and though we say no, no, no: no need, you'll do yourself a mischief, these is heavy old bits of kit these bales, she says she'll come, and although Ivor says he'll drive her back to The Coffee Pot, she says no: it's only a short walk.

We says our thanks to her and off she departs.

And if I tell you not a word of a lie that she takes all our hearts with her, I would not be making too much of it. But, if there was one heart as you could almost see wrench itself out of his chest, bound to the door and go galloping across the meadow after her, it was Ivor the Wellies'.

She's there next day, good as gold, and helps with the bales and brings sandwiches as is the tastiest I ever had and a welcome change from the flitch and exploding vegetables we normally pigs out on.

In the late afternoon she goes back to her cottage.

And although Ivor offered to pay for her help, she said certainly not: it has been a joy for her.

If that was a hundredth of a joy it had been for we, she'd have been proud to know it. But you dunna say, do you? You dunna say.

Anyway up, summer tips by, we lugs more hay, wraps more silage, greases more tractors, maggots sheep and I don't know what.

By and by we gets back in The Crown and The Buffalo and

The White Horse and The Sun and the Hundred House and July comes and goes and August comes and goes and then September, and all this while we haven't heard a whiff off Ivor, nor seen him once.

It is Saturday dinner time and we are in The Pendragon, of the fifth of September, as is a nice soft day, playing quoits: that is Willie the Pooh, Oonty Tump Tom, Vernon the Vermin, George Gunter the F and Blast, Trouser Jabez, Barney Dawes, Knukky Stubbs, The Bishop and me when we hears this. We hears this great rattle larrapping down the road like the legions of the Roman army is roaring by, with their chariots, horses neighing and harness jingling and when we looks out, smacking down the road with their manes and tails flying, their ears up and shouting their heads off, high stepping and making the ground boom and thunder come these two monsters drawing a big yellow, iron-rimmed haywain, and sat up there driving this lot is Karen, grinning like a Amazon Queen, with Ivor at her elbow, white headed, grinning, stern and grand, like the King.

She runs the wain up into the car park and wings the horses round so they are pointing home, drops off the wagon, takes the bits out the horses' mouths and slips them under their chins, like Ivor. All the while he is watching, admiring.

She hooks the nosebags on and shouts: 'Hello boys! How about a drink?'

Into The Pendragon she and Ivor jumps and we how bist 'ee's they, as you do, as it's such a rare sight to see them.

So we have plenty of viper venom and swaps a few tales and this and that and then after we get the little talk out the way, Ivor, he turns to Trouser, and he says to him: 'Trouser, my friend, I have a request for you, if I may.'

Gentleman of the valley that he is, Trouser replies: 'You may.'

Ivor the Wellies says: 'I wonder if you would be so kind,

Trouser Jabez, my old butty, as to do me the honour of being my Best Man?'

I canna remember what happened to the rest of the day after that but the wedding was set for a month later, in our little church, up on the tops, as is the prettiest place for a wedding to be.

So we all togs up for this malarkey, and Trouser, he gets in a twirl because he has to make a speech and the only things he can think of about Ivor he canna say in public.

When Ivor says that we shall be going back to his place for the wedding breakfast after this job, we says to him, you leave that to us, which is what he does.

When he asks where it is going to be, we say he will find out.

When he says how will people know where to go? we says: they'll find out as well.

So along comes the wedding and this is not a big to-do, as these things are better for being smaller, but what we done in the church was this.

Being as we are only a bunch of old blokes and not one of us with a wife, we don't know much about bought flowers and such, from shops, so what we done is to go and collect as many different feg grasses as we can find in the hedge at that time of year – it's when they're all feathered and gone to seed, but the stems are good and long and there's loads of them and they are fine and pretty to look on: fescues and bents, oat grasses, quaking grass and tall couch even. We garners heaps and heaps of them up and as many wild flowers as we can keep fresh. And the aisle of this church we plaits with these grasses so that when Ivor and Karen come in it is like walking on a meadow, with the smell of grasses with it.

Round the walls of this little church we strings all the flowers of late summer, harebells – blue and white – and mulleins and hawksbeard, scabious, hardheads, knapweeds, meadow cleary and meadow sweet, ragged robin and bell flower and even a few foxgloves as is still with us and dozens of others beside.

Come midday of the Big Day, Ivor rattles up to the church with Melilot and Nonsuch, splendid as Drum Horses with flagged manes and polished hooves, glossy as sideboards and decked in glittering harness and drawing the big yellow haywain, all sparkling like new.

He pulls up outside the church a touch before twelve o'clock, and goes straight in with Trouser Jabez, both as smart as each other, I never would have recognised them. And that's the first time I seen Ivor without his wellies, too.

I am left holding the horses outside.

Then Karen comes about ten minutes after and Knukky brings her in his trap, drawn by his Welsh Cob, Domino. And they come spanking up the lane with the wheels flickering round and the sun smarting off it brilliant as a river, and old Domino in his patent leather harness, as fine a Welsh Cob as set hoof to hard ground.

They pulls up outside the church, the smartest rig as cut ridges in the grass of that little church since Queen Boadicea raced across here with her chariots chasing out the Romans in the old days.

It is Knukky Stubbs as is to give away the bride, as her dad is died and she says as there is no-one she'd rather do the honours, than Knukky.

And she is kitted out in some sort of apparel, I canna think how she got in it. But there's enough material there to sail a fourmaster across the Pacific Ocean to Spain.

The service is a quick kind of affair, without no-one making speeches inside as Ivor says he dunna want to give the vicar a chance to get going or they should be there till Boxing Day.

The service being over Ivor says: 'Where are we going to creep off to for the wedding breakfast, then?'

This is our little surprise, although we had prayed to God

and every elf and sprite and spirit as lurks in the place, as the weather would hold.

Trouser takes the reins off of Ivor as he and Karen gets in the back of the haywain, which we'd decked out in straw with a bed of mallow, and he drives them up the hill past The Tack, then cuts down into the old oak wood as stands half way between the hill and the manor.

In that wood we'd set the wedding breakfast.

From the trees we'd hung this bunting, and little flags, and put bales about to sit on.

The thing is, the Mote Wood, it doesn't need anything for decoration.

The Mote Wood is the most beautifullest wood you can imagine.

It is as if fauns lives in there, and protects it as it is so quiet, with moss and this little brook running through and these smooth old rocks and the grass is short there ever, and dark green, and there is broome round the edges as keeps the wind off. In amongst this we'd set the tables, with white cloths and I reckon God hisself had fixed that day as it was the most gorgeous end of a summer's day as I ever recall.

We'd asked everyone as comes to bring some grub with them and whatever they wanted to drink, and people, they bring plates and plates and plates and firkins of ciders and beers and Jock the Toff, he carts in cases of wine for them as like to swill it. Half the valley turns up with more of this and more of that and with presents of all kinds: here are the Barrant boys and Keith and his missus and Tom Vaisey and Mark White Dog and Nick the Utensil and his lot and Barbary and his gang and Trev and his Anne, and The Bishop and his boys and missus and Spud and Evie and everyone from everywhere.

For music, we has the birds.

And, but, Willie the Pooh sings Suzannah's a Funniful Sow, and George Gunter the F and Blast sings a song as gets ruder and ruder and someone has to shut him up, then The Bishop gives us a dose of some wild song no-one has ever heard of, then Dave and Jen sings summat about roses and winter and I dunno what. Then Mark White Dog gets his Salopian Tube as he calls it, as is in reality a four-foot length of hosepipe, which you blows down like a trumpet and he gives us a version of If You Go Down to the Woods Today, You're in for a Big Surprise, before going the colour of a damson and toppling off his bale. That tube of his makes the weirdest noise and even shuts up the birds.

Then when night falls, Ivor, he takes his bride off in the moonlight with Nonsuch and Melilot stepping out into the dark as proud a pair of horses as pulls the stars across the sky.

That party goes on in the wood for the rest of that night, and I don't mind admitting as I falls asleep in a pile of leaves somewhere not very handy and when I wakes, dawn is cracking across in the east and Trouser Jabez and George Gunter the F and Blast are singing Rudolf the Red-Nose Reindeer.

So what's all this about?

Well, it's autumn, then it's winter and spring and soon enough hay harvest again next year. A lot of us are in The Buffalo one dinner time when the phone rings and it's Ivor the Wellies: 'Come quick,' says he: 'Urgent. Hurry.'

His voice sounds shook up.

So we piles in Barney Dawes' old motor, George Gunter, Trouser and me and goes roaring over to Ivor's place and as soon as we pitches up, the first thing we sees is old Doc White's black and white Riley outside the house and we're thinking oh no: catastrophe.

We runs in the house and Ivor he is white as a barn oolert.

Karen, she is not there.

Ivor points upstairs.

Then we takes another look outside to check as it is the Doc's Riley, and sure enough, it is.

Ivor, he looks as fit as a footrot tup.
We set down, quietly.
And so we are thinking the worst.
Ivor, he won't speak.
Then we hears it.
A slap, and a sound, not hardly bigger than a kitten squeak.
So there, see.
Now we all been invited to a birth.

Oonty Tump Tom

Round about family-falling-out time, three days before Christmas, a small section of society hereabouts are helping to polish the brass rail in The Buffalo, in Clun, at midday, one o'clockish, this being the custom. And while this small section is aiding with the shine on the brass lion's heads as grips the rail in their teeth, George Gunter the F and Blast, says this: he says: 'It is a crying shame that some of us do not all have the kind of noddle as Oonty Tump Tom,' he says, just like that.

Looking around to see if anyone is going to make some sort of a contest out of this, he continues: 'Old Oonty Tump Tom, in as much as many people think he's just an old scratter, sniving about, here and there, in his van, up to mischief, is, in fact a good friend of mine, as it happens.'

So then, there's a bit of a pause, as there always is with George Gunter the F and Blast. 'And old Oonty Tump Tom,' he carries on after a short while, 'makes his home in a pile of tin sheds and a old barn and bit of a cottage three or four valleys across from here – more even if you go by pony – into Wales, up by the rocks, top of Llandegly – a place not many from round here has call to go.'

'Oh,' says Trouser butting in, 'that Oonty Tump: I was mixing him for a moment with Vernon Vermin, the rat stopper –

177

but it's not him, it's this other one you are on about, I think he is a cousin to him, if I am not mistaken – go on.'

'Right:' says George Gunter the F and Blast: 'this old Oonty Tump is a crafty old wuzzuk it has to be said, as he has total cornered the market for oonts in these parts. In fact, he is an oont millionaire.'

This comes as a big sort of surprise to most of us, as we didn't suppose as people went about the place collecting oonts, or indeed that there was a market for them, so now we do not know what George is on about.

'This is most mysterious to me,' says Knocker Morsel, 'as I do not credit as anyone creeps about picking up oonts and then passing them on, in trade.'

'Aha,' says George Gunter the F and Blast, 'and this is why I am telling you as it is a pity as none of we seem to have catched hold of the same kind of business noddle as Oonty Tump Tom.'

So now just as we are very keen to know what his special business trick is, just in case we can copy it and make a few shilling ourselves, as is always a bit of a leg-up if you spend more than five hours a day in one of these sort of places, like The White Horse or The Crown or The Radnor or The Anchor or The Wharf or somewhere. So then George Gunter the F and Blast says: 'I think it is time to pay our respects on Oonty Tump Tom and allow him to convey his own tale as it is a miracle and mystery that a cracked-apart old duffer like him, who can hardly read or write or tie up his boot laces should these days be scorting about in a brand new Landrover.'

And, but, the thing is, some of we are not keen now to go lugging all the way to Llandegly, in the cold, just to go and see this old Oonty Tump Tom, even if he is a oont millionaire. So we grumbles and complains about having to climb into the back of cold Landrovers and whatnot when there is a good fire in The Buffalo, which we are now basting nicely in front of. But George Gunter the F and Blast, does not give up so easy and then shoots us another bit of a surprise when he says like this, he says: 'It will not be of a great inconvenience for we to go and hark at Oonty Tump Tom directly.'

So, though nobody says much, we think as George must have been in The Hundred House all night or something if he thinks as going to Llandegly from The Buffalo is an easy manoeuvre, three days before Christmas, for a heap of blokes as is happy where they are.

'The reason for this being,' George Gunter the F and Blast rambles on, 'is, sitting outside The White Horse, opposite, is a brand new Landrover. And, it happens that when I am passing this brand new Landrover just now, not knowing whose it is, I catch sight of something in the back of this vehicle as is familiar to me but for a moment I do not know what it is and have been thinking about this gadget ever since I come in here.'

So then he stops and has a pull on his ale and just stands there, and doesn't add anything, standing stone still, staring away.

'George!' Trouser says: 'Are you died or something? What are you on about now? Where is all this going?'

'Well,' says George, coming back to we from wherever he's just been: 'This gadget as I am on about I shall describe to you to see if you can make out what it is. But before I begin, I shall state that this thing is one of the craftiest money making gadgets I have ever heard of, even though it is, in fact, a ordinary kind of thing as most of we have chucked away by the score.'

So now we are all impatient for this explanation, as we could be set to make a fortune on this one, which would be a bit of a change since most of George Gunter the F and Blast's tales do not lead to ways of earning your keep, never mind becoming a millionaire, even if it is in oonts, so we're pretty keen to know what the outcome of this one is going to be.

After he's recharged his glass, he says: 'This gadget is, in fact, nothing but a big old enamel basin, such as your granny usened to have about the place, and, such as we have all flung out on account of we prefer the new. But, what makes this enamel basin different is that attached to it is a kind of cover, just hanging about three inches above the surface, more or less like some sort of an umbrella spread over it. There, that's what it looks like. What do you suppose it is?'

We all get along guessing about this thing and has to give up as no-one knows what on earth an enamel basin with a little umbrella on it can be and how it is as such a gadget ever made anyone a penny, never mind a million.

'It is when I remembered what this thing was, as I recalled it belonging to Oonty Tump Tom himself.' George says: 'No-one else as I ever recall ever has owned one of these things. That's because no-one else knows what it is – excepting, of course, for old Oonty Tump and me. After I remembered.'

'Well then,' says Ivor the Wellies, 'that's marvellous, but are we going to find out what it is?'

So George Gunter the F and Blast, he says: 'On remembering what this device is, and on recalling as Oonty Tump Tom is to be seen these days driving round in a brand new Landrover, and on surmising as he is not in here, then I would ascertain it more likely as he is in there, in The White Horse, opposite. So I was thinking as we could all go and see, and he can tell us himself what this gadget is, and we can learn how it is as he has got a lot of noddle more than most.'

Charged up now to find out what this thing is, and whether we can make something like it ourselves and get hold of some of the money this thing seems to be able to magic up, as is always handy, especially before Christmas, whether you go in for family-falling-out or not, we pitch back the stuff in our glasses, which is a smarter job for some than for thothers, and out troops George Gunter the F and Blast and Barney Dawes, Knocker Morsel, Knukky Stubbs, Trouser Jabez, Ivor the Wellies, Willie the Pooh and Kipper Northern.

And into The White Horse steps George Gunter the F and

Blast and Barney Dawes, Knocker Morsel, Knukky Stubbs, Trouser Jabez, Ivor the Wellies, Willie the Pooh and Kipper Northern and, I forgot to say, me.

And who should we find sitting on a stool, sleek as a old oont himself, but Oonty Tump Tom.

And, but, the thing is, as we are not so common as to go barging in demanding as to what this gadget in the back of his brand new Landrover is, we says our 'how bist 'ee surree' to him, as you should, as is polite and proper and says what a rare job it is to catch sight of him round these parts and get chatting and by and by it swings round to him and how it is he's come our way – trying not to talk about the gadget in the back of this brand new Landrover even though we're itching to find out.

And but, also, Old Oonty Tump is not so daft as to throw away all his state secrets to any section of society, as just creeps in The White Horse three days before Christmas, just like that. He's a canny man, and even though Knukky Stubbs is a canny man too, he's not as canny as Oonty Tump Tom. So it takes a fair old while to drag this story out of him and on the way, it is becoming expensive into the bargain and then finally, on account as it is Christmas and he is come to Clun to celebrate his retirement, on account as he is giving up the oont commodity traffic altogether, he tells us all about it.

And what he says is this: he says as when he was fifty years old, and has been grafting all his life about the place, on farms, for people, and has been having a thin old time of it trying to get any money to stick. One day, he is passing by a farm and he sees a man wandering about dropping worms down oonty tumps. So he goes over to this man and says, why is it you are feeding the oonts? And this man, he says no, he is not feeding oonts, he is killing them as these worms is bunged solid with poison and as soon as an old oont gobbles one of these he'll drop dead straight and there will be no more oonty tumps and that'll be that.

Well, Tom thinks: that's a bit of a rum old do. Poor old

181

oonts. There's got to be a better way.

'Oonts,' says Tom, 'they are a marvel and a mystery. How they have invented themselves to go tunnelling about the way they do is a miraculous sort of a job,' says Old Tom. 'They aerates the soil and makes little drainage channels, they eats up the leatherjackets along with the worms and land with oonts is good land. It's a sign of it. But land without oonts is a sad old place and to me, to see this man getting rid of them like this was never right. 'Anyway,' he says, 'it's bad business, isn't it? Getting rid of the thing that keeps you going. No, no: you don't want to kill them,' says Tom, 'you want to breed them.'

And he winks and grins and you see his old eyes twinkling away and his old skin all wrinkled up and here's a wise old adder, and no mistake.

'Any road,' Old Oonty Tump Tom goes on: 'I go back to my place and forget about this man and his oont malarkey for a while as I am busy with other things. It happens then, by and by, as I am laying down a piece of garden to lawn at my place and instead of buying turf as they do nowadays, I seed it. This grass comes up very slow as in fact, this piece of lawn is laid beneath an old walnut tree and these old walnuts, they can be moggers to get things to grow under. But, soon enough the dog's mercury is up in the woods, and jack-by-the-hedge is coming up, and Queen Anne's lace and so is my grass. One morning I go out to inspect my hard work, and who should be in there throwing up the biggest oonty tumps all over it but Mr Oont hisself. On and on he goes, flinging up tumps here and hummocks there, burrowing there and here am I wishing he'd go and ruin someone else's lawn, not mine what I have just laid. Then I think to myself: small wonder it is as people get in a froth about these creatures: this little blighter has just gone and cost me all my winter's work.'

'So I set out to get rid of him.'

'And then I think, well how? I thinks about this man and his poisons and how easy he does it. But I don't want poison on my place: it's bad old stuff: the dog'll pick it up, or the cat, or old Mr Broc or Mr Renard or Mr Buzzard – and we don't want that, do we? So then I am thinking well how do you catch an oont?'

'Off I goes to the farmer's shop to see what kind of oont catching equipment they've got and do you know what? There's nothing. There's only these poor old traps as you bung in the ground as snaps shut and breaks a oont's back and I thinks the same about traps as I do about poison.'

'Then this gaffer tells me to bury upright empty bottles in the run as'll frit any oont away. 'How is that, then?' I asks. 'When the wind cuts across the tops,' he says: 'they make this ghost sound, so the oont thinks as his tunnels is filled with oont spooks, away he runs, skidaddling off somewhere else, straight.'

'And though I bury these bottles all over my lawn – anyone would wonder what kind of a wino lives there – it does not work. Mr Oont, it seems, is not a scrap frit by oont ghosts and carries right on making as big a muddle of my bit of lawn as he can.'

'To trim this story back, one night, I don't know why I do this but I do, I bury an old enamel basin in my new lawn. In it shoved a few grubs and big old lobb worms and a little sliver of bacon. I bury it up to its rim as I am thinking well, if Mr Oont pops out of his burrow and comes along here to sniff this lot out, he'll drop in but he won't be able to scramble out.'

'I nip down to The Lion later for a refresher of this and that and a chat with Edward Dog Days and when I come home I hear this weird noise: a kind of squeaking and squealing and complaining and shrieking. So I whip out my lamping lamp and sneak out to see what all this commotion is. At first I think it must be a weasel jammed in somewhere, or a rabbit trapped by a foxcub. Shining around here and there, I find nothing. Then when I creep over to my enamel bowl – from where I realise all this rattle is coming – I shine the torch in and what do I find? Not one but eight oonts in there, all yelling their heads off.'

'This is a big surprise to me and I am amazed. There they all are, scorting about, squeaking and complaining and bumping into one another and I feel sorry for them, then. I think what lovely little things they are. How can anybody want to kill these? With their little pink flipper feet and shiny coats and their funny little snouts, working away. So now what? I thought I only had one in my garden not a fleet of them. First I think, I'd ought to do them in for the havoc they have just caused me – but then I don't want to do that: blind little things all struggling around in this bowl. So I think: well, I know what I'll do: I'll leave them there and see what happens: old Mr Oolert will take them probably, for dinner for his wife and children.'

'I go to bed.'

'In my bed, I cannot sleep. And I can hear them still, all squealing away. And I think it is a merciless thing to do to leave little oonts all alone in a bowl on the lawn for the savage old oolert to pick off as he please.'

'So I get up, go out to my lawn, count them again and finding there's still eight in there, pick the lot up in the bowl and take them all into the kitchen, cover them in a sack and leave them with a dollop of bacon and small bucket of worms as I happened to have.'

'In the morning this problem of what to do with them is not gone away. How do you get rid of oonts?'

'Poison them. That's how. Or drown them?'

'But I think well, not so fast. So I sit down with a cup of tea and think about them as everything has a commercial advantage one way or another if you have the kind of mind to spot it. That day, I go off to the library and learn all about them, and reading is tricky old job, but I get the gist of it quick enough: what they eat, what they do, where they live – all that, and pretty surprising it is too.'

'As I drive home, slowly, I get a bit of an idea.'

'I keep these oonts, tease a bit of soil on them, more bacon, more worms and by now they're quiet. I go off in my old van. I go round these farms, looking to see oonty tumps and by and by notice that some farms have plenty and some don't. All the while, I am keeping my little brood at home fat and happy and pretty soon, these little furry monsters have bred and there's not eight oonts in there, there's about forty and I have to expand their quarters to accommodate them, and believe me, that is another story altogether.'

'Anyway up, I keep going round these farms where there aren't any oonty tumps and knocking on their doors. I tell them that I am a oont catcher and they say they don't have any oonts on their land. I say, well, you never know, here is my business card anyway, which by now has got on it: Tom Silverthread: Master Moler, with my address and telephone number. As I hand them these cards I am thinking – you might not have any oonts just now: but you very soon will.'

'Well – I expect you can imagine how my business grows.'

'Soon enough my telephone is red hot with these farmers all ringing and always saying the same thing: it's a funny co-incidence, they say, but just after you come here we got a oont invasion, bang, just like that.'

'And I'd say, right-you-are, I shall be round just now. And round I'd go, in the night with my enamel bowl as now had a bit of a refinement on it, which is a lid, of a sort, to keep the rain and oolerts off my precious little herd. And back they'd come, shrieking and yelling, then drop in the bowl and in the morning they'd all be gone and a couple of days later I'd go back for my earnings, which, when you've about fifty enamel bowls on the go can add up to a fair old bit.'

'Well, that little bunch is the best travelled oonts in Britain, I'd say. They've dug up land from Brecon to Builth by way of Bishop's Castle. Why, I have had some of them so long now they've gone white. And they've earned me a rare old packet over the years. I am truly grateful to them. They are my friends.'

Well: some of we are thinking that this is a bit immoral, what with cheating people like that. But old Tom he says: no, he sees it that his little oonts does as much good for their land as any mole plough ever did in aerating the soil. They never did anyone any harm, in fact, all he as doing was renting them out to perform a good service for a few days, reducing the pests in the soil and bring good heart to the earth. And for his part he kept his pact with the oonts, to see they came to no harm neither. So they repaid him, in the way all things, in the great mills of life, do, one way or another.

And as old Oonty Tump Tom bids us a goodbye, old George Gunter the F and Blast he says to we: 'Now there's a fellow who knows to work with God, man and beast – or the devil or someone. Only one thing I was thinking – didn't old Harold get Vernon Vermin the rat stopper in the other day, down the grain store?'

'By heaven, so he did,' says Trouser.

'And didn't you say as Vernon the Vermin is a cousin to Oonty Tump Tom?'

'I did too.'

'Are you thinking what I'm thinking?'

186

Pit for Pat

Queenie, who runs The Pendragon, is really not a very large lady at all. In fact, she is quite small. And Queenie, she keeps this little tiny withery husband bloke called Nat, and Nat, she parks on his fianola on an old windsor, round the back of The Pendragon somewhere, tight up against an old range, because Nat, this little old fellow, he is always coughing his guts up.

And he is always coughing guts up not on account of having any problems all of his own, or anything, but on account of Queenie's Capstans which she is always puffing away at, non-stop, from the pip of the peewit til the oolerts' blart, and most the dark as well.

And Queenie, she keeps this Nat jammed tight up against the range because she thinks he has, all his life, an evil dose of the TB, which is about to clop him one, so she will not let him loose, never, not out of the building, not even in the woodshed, nowhere, except bang tight up against this old range, because she thinks he will get worser, if she does.

And nor will she allow him any of the Black Cat she hauls out the pump in the bar, or anything; and she keeps shovelling this stew down him, and this stew it has been is burbling away on the range since back from before she and Nat first got spliced, when Queenie got left The Pendragon by her granny, old Mol Swodgey.

And, but, the thing is, old Mol Swodgey, she abided in these parts til Jim the Post handed her a bill from the Monarchy saying as she had lived five score years and that, and old Mol Swodgey kept this stew burbling all her life, as well, and then she upped and pegged it, like all of us has to, one day, somehow or other.

Anyway up, Queenie, this stew of hers, she keeps topped up level with the lid all the while with a lump of chicken here, a bunny carcass there, a carrot, maybe, or a swede, or an armful of sprouts or half a sack of turnips, or something; a few pounds of onions, or a chunk of fat bacon, whatever, and this stew, in that it has burbled out the top of the pot over the years, has got sort of welded to this range somehow, and Queenie, because she loves this old Nat of hers, she keeps lugging this stew down him, which she thinks is good for him, and wrapping him up in eiderdowns and blankets and stuff, even on a boiling summer's day, because he will not stop coughing his guts up.

So, as time goes along, this old Nat, he gets to becoming extra crowsty looking, what with his rowzeling about in these blankets all these summers, and with all this gwathelly stew, and stuff, and, but, if you ever see Nat, it is very hard to imagine he was once a young Nat with plenty of fire in him and a lot of zip, and it is even impossibler to imagine Queenie is a young maid once and that these two were singing out the same book together, or something, and doing plenty of staring up at the sky from the fescues in the meadows round The Pendragon, or somewhere; but they must have, sometime, because one day, Queenie ups and puggs out round as a Gloucester Old Spot and farrows down to a little pink boy, she calls Spud.

Anyway up, Queenie, she is very proud of this little boy, Spud, even if she does blow Capstan smoke all over him, and, as this boy grows up, Queenie, she gets plenty of this stew down him, just like Nat, and, so he grows and grows and grows. But, she notices Spud is, in his upcoming, more or a less a day behind, pouring milk in the teapot, and such, and shoving salt in the sugar bowl, or sticking ice in the oven, or peeled potatoes in the fridge and such, and sometimes, Queenie gets to thinking the Lord has not finished him, properly.

Yet he is clever in other ways, and though he is cakey-handed, he is good with his head, even if he does lock the hens out, and chucks sawdust in the bread-bin and throws breadcrumbs on the floor.

And, but, the thing is, he grows into a huge great bloke, over six feet tall, even more, maybe six foot six, and he has brown hazely eyes and he has a big belly and a big laugh and he is full of fun and plenty of Capstans and Black Cat by the time he is seventeen.

But he is not a bit like Queenie, nor Nat, nor anyone else anyone else can think of, not at all, and if it wasn't for the fact that Queenie whelped him herself, in the bedroom upstairs, and never took her eyes off of him for ten years straight, she might have doubted he was hers, at all.

Anyway up, this boy, Spud, he grows up very popular in The Pendragon, even if he is a touch keffel, and everyone likes him because he is kindly natured and curious as a kitten about everything, especially small engines, and even more especially with a little steam job old Nat gives him one day, which is of a sort you whack a load of meths in, then fire up with a dose of strikes and set her rattling across the floorboards in a big puff of steam and sparks and plenty of leaky valves.

So Spud, he gets to playing with this gadget while he is a kiddy, all the time, and Queenie, after about fifteen years of this, is about had it with the stink of meths all over the pub, and puddles of water, and oil marks everywhere, and Spud, he is keen as mustard with this thing still, and over the years has made one or two improvements to it, so now it is some pretty high-pressure article, and travels at a rare speed, and whereas he has made it to take more pressure, he has not made it any stronger, and so, in fact, this is kind of like a kind of a bomb, and is bound, one day, to go bang.

Now then, there is also another problem with all this in that Spud, being as he is an enormous kind of a bloke, he takes up most of the pub just by being there, and is never quick enough to keep out of his own way, because The Pendragon is not a huge place: in fact, it is fairly small, and low in the beam, and narrow by the door, and after he is seventeen, Queenie, who is getting more crowsty as she gets on, finds, one day, Spud is just too big for The Pendragon in every respect.

She begins to get fretchit with him, not only because of his size and his steam engine, but also because he is took up with much attention by a certain young lady, with the name of Evie Floss, what creeps in The Pendragon, with her dad, of a Friday night.

And Spud, Queenie can see, is thinking, probably, to do some exploring as to what Evie keeps inside this spotty frock of hers, and this Evie, Queenie can see, will let him, even if he can't see this himself.

Queenie can see as that these two are set to make plenty of trouble, whatever, for everyone, and Queenie, she does not like this, no she doesn't.

So one Friday night, Queenie, when Evie Floss comes in, she tells her straight to clear off and leave her Spud alone: she is nothing but a mischievous hobble-de-hoy, and a hussie, and not worthy to be Spud's girl, and a dirty little mollekin in every way – even though this girl is only fifteen, and very pretty and a sweeter little dark-eyed rosy you would not ever meet, certainly not in The Pendragon of a Friday night, even if she is the sort of girl who stirs her beer with a five-inch nail.

Anyway up, this little girl, she bursts into tears, and runs out, and Spud, he is stricken with shock, and filled with bitterness and does not get to see this girl in The Pendragon of a Friday night again.

So he plans plenty of revenge on Queenie, even though she threatens to give him both barrels of her Purdey if he dares take one step out the door in pursuit of this maid.

A couple of months tip by, and Spud, he now is become a total mogger.

He moons about this pub smashing his fist into the plaster and whacking back plenty of puss-cat, so's he's always squirted up to his eyeballs, and will not speak to Queenie, and takes money from the till, and leaves the puss-cat taps open at night, and, instead of being in the bar helping, and making jokes, as he is before, he is upstairs in his room, tinkering with this engine of his, and drinking, and smoking these Capstans, and smashing things up, and all this goes on while old Nat is busy croaking it in the kitchen, by the range.

So what with Queenie being kanky and the boy being kanky, and people in the bar wanting puss-cat, no-one much pays much attention to old Nat, who is pegging out, quietly, on his jack.

Anyway up, it is at the deepest part of a night, somewhen, when Queenie is in her bed, and Nat is sweating his heart out in front of this range all wrapped up in his eiderdowns, that Queenie, she hears this chuff-chuff-chuff coming along the corridor to her bedroom, along the floorboards, sort of bouncing along the walls, clattering about here and there and this sound wakens her up.

She turns on her light.

She goes out into the corridor.

In the corridor she sees this: she sees, coming toward her, this big pot of stew, on wheels. And being as she is part asleep, she cannot make this thing out.

But on it comes, with blue smoke and steam, and it goes chugging past her and into her bathroom, which is straight down the corridor and when it hits the wall, by the bath, it explodes.

So now there is stew dripping down the bathroom walls, and

all over the ceiling, and plenty of pieces of clattering metal, and it is oozing all down the thunderbox, and over the sink and on the ceiling, and Queenie, she is taken of a very big fright, and thinks then, this Spud of hers, he has got to go.

And, she thinks, all this exploding stew business is on account of that hussie, Evie Floss.

So then she marches off down the corridor, with her Purdey, to Spud's bedroom to give him one piece of her mind, and maybe a little lead, as well.

But, on going in, she finds he is not there.

The window is open.

The curtains is blown.

Spud is gone.

Only he leaves a note which is pinned to the pillow which says: 'I am run away forever, Spud.'

So now Queenie, she sits down on his bed and she weeps long and loud as she is in deep anguish.

Then she pulls herself together.

She straightens her hair.

She wipes the tears from off of her face.

She pulls her dressing gown tidy and she sets herself against Spud.

She decides she never wishes to see him again.

Nor let him set foot in The Pendragon, never, not as long as he has this Evie Floss person hanging round him.

Especially after he makes a bomb from her stew, with his steam contraption, which Nat gives him.

So she has a mind to hate Nat as well, and next morning when she goes down to tell him, she finds he is croaked, dead, and so she blames Spud for this croaking as well, which makes her lungeous at him even more.

And so now, Queenie, she hates her Spud with some power, and she cannot abide to hear anyone merit his name.

She thinks now he is devilled, and out of his wits, and made for her and Nat, life in The Pendragon, very intolerable indeed, while he is there, what with his sticking the wrong things in the wrong box all the time, and bunging the wrong lids on the wrong jars, and whatnot.

After twenty years is passed, and Queenie is clocking on a touch, and crowsty as a ground toad, she has decided that if she ever sees this Spud again, by chance, she will get him somehow, for what he has done running off with this mollekin, and making Nat to die, and everything else.

Then one day, while Queenie is in The Pendragon all by herself, and this is a hot summer's day, a car pulls up in the car park come back on oneish, and out gets this great big bloke with a bushy beard and big belly and big laugh, and he has got with him this darkish sort of a womanish person, with black hair and brown eyes, and, but, these two, they saunter into this pub smoking a lot of cigarettes and this and that, and it is easy to tell, somehow, that this bloke is very familiar with the surroundings of this Pendragon pub by the way he looks at it, as if he is recalling something, from a long time ago.

Anyway up, they steps into the bar.

And, but, the thing is, by now, this big bloke, he is seeming to be not a little anxious about something and casts his eyes quickly along to the place where Queenie used to keep her Purdey, and seeing that Queenie does not make a dash for this place, cools down somewhat and goes to the bar and orders a couple of pints of Black Cat.

So now, old Queenie, she looks at this big bloke very steady for a minute, and screws up her eyes and all the time she smokes her Capstan and she keeps looking at this big bloke and this dark-haired woman, and then she goes over to the place where the Purdey is which is when this big bloke thinks it is time to leave, suddenly, but instead of pulling out the Purdey, Queenie fetches out a pair of pince-nezes and sticks these on her beak and says like this:

'Your are familiar to me. I knows you. You are that miserable son of mine what runs off twenty summers past in the middle of the night with that Evie Floss. And you makes a bomb from my stew which is over one hundred years old.'

And this big fellow, being as he is touched by Queenie's recollection of happier days, his eyes turn water, and he says: 'Yes, Queenie, my mother, I am returned. And I am brought back for you to see my wife Evie what, twenty years ago, I become wed to in the registry.'

Queenie, she chews this one over.

Spud, he does not know what she is thinking, excepting that, in the next few minutes he is likely to be a shot man.

He says more: he says: 'We have come back on account of this and that, and whatnot.'

Queenie, she says nothing.

Spud, he does not know if this is good or bad.

Then Queenie turns about and draws two pints of Black Puss Cat, and sets these on the bar in front of these two, and when Spud offers to pay, she says no need and shuffles off out somewhere, then she comes back and she says, 'If you wish, you and this Evie can stay for the night.' Just like that.

So now Spud, he is very delighted and makes a big noise about this and he smiles and whacks back the puss-cat and says this is the finest scrump in all the land and he becomes very convivial, and sets himself down spread all over the place, like he owns it, and is very familiar with everything, and Queenie, she gives him a long long look, and she smiles, but the smile she smiles is not for him: it is for her.

By and by, the day goes on, and Spud is wandering around and getting in the way, and saying as how not much is changed in twenty years, and here he is pouring milk in the tea pot, and buttering his bread with sugar and sticking jam in his tea, and all this kind of stuff.

Then, come the right side of six, when Queenie opens the

doors of The Pendragon, customers, like Knocker Morsel, and Trouser Jabez, and Willie the Pooh, Bill the Box and Knukky Stubbs and all, they come in, and as Spud is now standing behind the bar, they recognise him at once, and Evie, and they buy them many pints of puss-cat, and remember the old times, when Spud was a nipper and had his steam engine, and how when he and Evie done the bunk, and everything.

And even old Queenie, she seems to be enjoying this, and smiles, and she even cracks a joke or two, and Knukky Stubbs says he hasn't seen her so light since Nat was braising, out the back, by the range, on his windsor.

So this party bashes on and plenty of black puss slips down and then, come the morning star, Queenie boots this lot out and sets Spud down by the bar quietly, and fills him up with a load of gin, so's by the time he hits his paliasser he is as clipped as a shorn cob.

Next morning, Spud, he is not feeling so good, when he gets up.

This is not only on account of the gin and the puss-cat and the Capstans, whatever, but also on account of being squashed up in bed with Evie, what is a single scratcher, what was his when he was a nipper, which he sees, when he wakes in the morning, to be covered in a good layer of dust, as if it has not been cleaned, for maybe twenty years.

Anyway up, he chucks off the bedclothes, and on making his way to the bathroom, passing Queenie's bedroom door, he knocks and says: 'Good morning, mother, I hope you are slept good. Me and Evie, we are slept like sawed timbers in my comfortable old bed. It is lovely. I am now going to the bathroom to brush my pegs and wash my chops.'

Spud, he waits for an answer.

But Queenie, she just says back: 'There is a tin of Liver Salts in the cupboard above the sink.' And though this seems to Spud a strange reply to his good morning, he thinks no more of it. He stumbles into the bathroom in his snoring overalls.

He stands in front of the mirror.

It is here he notices he has noises in his head like a smithy's anvil.

He thinks he needs curing.

He opens the cupboard.

He reaches inside.

Inside, he finds this big tin of Liver Salts, just as Queenie says.

He opens this tin.

He reaches for a glass.

From this tin he puts two heaps of these liver salts stuff in this glass and places it down on the back of the sink.

He holds the tin under the tap, fills it up, bangs the lid on, and puts it back in the cupboard. All of this he does while looking in the mirror. Then he takes the glass and pours these liver salts into his mouth.

Now he seems to have a swarm of bees in his mouth, which is when he looks into the empty glass, which is when the cupboard explodes and the door flies off, and this tin of Andrews Liver Salts goes flashing past him in one big froth, and he staggers back and falls in the bath and brains himself on the taps and the room is full of hissing sounds, and above this, is the sound of Queenie in her bedroom, cackling.

An Opportune Moment

One fine day, yesterday in fact, I am gazing up into a bright blue August sky with my friend Ivor the Wellies. And as we are gazing up into the sky, looking at all these swallows and little martins that are sniving about, twittering, Ivor says like this: 'It is amazing when you comes to think about it how these little birds ever manages to get along the way they do.'

So I says, how true he is in saying this.

Then he says this, he says: 'Burt, you see all them little swallow gadgets larking about up there in the blue, we dunna hardly know a thing about a single one of them, although they have been around now all the while, ever since we took the first cut of hay this year and even a bit before that.'

So I say, how true he is: we none of us knows hardly a thing about any one of them.

'You know, Burt,' he says: 'these little tiny birds as is no bigger than my little finger hardly, they will shortly be getting together, in a bit of a swarm, even the ones as was born here this summer, and they will set off without telling no-one and fly all the way to Africa non-stop, bang, just like that and go and have another heap of babies out there. Isn't that amazing?'

'It is amazing and astonishing,' I says to Ivor, 'and the marvel is how they knows how to get to Africa because even if I had wings and a bit of a map to be getting along with, I doubt I'd be able to find my way there, hardly.'

'Me, I think they are able to do it on account it is their purpose in life.'

'Their purpose?' says I, 'how do you mean?'

'Everything has – or should have – a purpose in life,' says Ivor. 'If you dunna have a purpose in life,' Ivor says: 'then you won't be able to find yourself nowhere. Not even if you haven't got a map.'

So I thinks about this for a minute and wonders what Ivor is on about, as I am not able to follow him, altogether, properly.

'That is one of God's great gifts to they,' says Ivor, 'in that they have a purpose: to go there, to Africa in the summer and then to come back here, for our summer. Just to keep alive, to keep their numbers, to keep on with the very important business of being nothing other than a swallow or martin. 'Course, they got homing instincts as makes them able to find their way, like pigeons and buzzards and bad luck.'

'How do you mean, then, Ivor?' says I.

And Ivor says, 'Well, there's some on this earth, like these little swallows, who seem to go about courting bad luck as if it was a special gift, or something. They seems to goes off and deliberately arrange to collect bad luck, no matter if the sun is out and everything is going their way and trying to push them onto the path of good fortune and prosperity, all the while.'

'How can this be, then?' says I: 'What do you mean?'

So then, Ivor he goes on to say as how some people, even when things is going their way, arrange for themselves to be total benighted, and turn the whole caboodle inside out so that it works against them. 'You take old Heavy-Behind, for instance,' says he, 'old Heavy-Behind is not a stupid man by any means. In fact, he is a very clever man. But, the thing is, whatever he does, it runs out bad for him.'

'Yes,' says I, 'I have observed this.' And now Ivor and I are stopped peering up into the sky as our necks is near enough broke, and we are sauntering along, instead, to The Castle Vaults, to make up the shortage we have just been suffering from staring up into the sky.

'What I have observed about old Heavy-Behind is, that he is apt to spend more than five hours a day in The Pendragon or The Radnorshire Arms, or The Crown or The Hundred House or The White Horse or The Buffalo or some such other place.' says I.

Ivor says: 'This is true. But,' he says, 'so do a number of others as I know and if you looks at them, some of them does well, while thothers dunna. How is that, then?'

So I says as I suppose it is down to luck. Good or bad.

Then Ivor he says, 'It inna.'

Ivor he says this: 'You hark my words Burt, what makes people have good luck is not chance so much as the choices they make, how they turns opportunity to them and not turn it away: how they does things as makes money stick and not tossed away. You know the expression "Save a match and buy a farm"? Well, that's true too. And these people who do this are no more clever than no-one else, it is just that they have got the knack of using opportunity when it comes their way and make the most of it, and they're not wasteful. And, but, the thing is if bad luck comes their way, they have a way of making the least of it and not wallow around in it, as so many people seems to do. Most of these farmers around here are very canny in this respect.'

'This is true,' says I, 'as you do not meet many poor farmers.'

Says Ivor: 'These people bends to circumstances. Yes, they might bitch about hard times, who wouldna? But they're quick to turn the corner and take another road. It's them as tries to hang onto the old road when her's all wore out, is the ones as lands the trouble. Making the right choices, is what it's all about – choices. It's nothing to do with how many books they reads or how much news they listens to on the telly. Any silly clot can do that.'

By now, we are in fact arrived at The Castle Vaults and it being a very close day, we nips in, just for a minute, and who should be in there, by chance, but Trouser Jabez, and Knuckky Stubbs, Kipper Northern, George Gunter the F and Blast, Typhoon Ted and my friend The Bishop. So, by way of getting this conversation going with these gentlemen this morning, I tells them as what Ivor has been saying, as he is off gathering the beer mugs together and recharging them with the stuff they doles out behind the bar, from these long-handle pump efforts. So Trouser Jabez, he says: 'What Ivor says is true. Good fortune comes by because of correct choices not because you can read a book, or have got a degree or summat. You take Knukky Stubbs here, for example: Knukky is in fact a wealthy man, even though he spends more than five hours a day in one of these places, and why is that? It is because when Knukky goes out from home in the morning he sets up the day so as to make it work out alright. Is this not right, Knukky?'

So Knukky says as this is more or less right although sometimes things doesn't work out quite like he expects and that can be a bit of a nuisance. But what he says is that he gets money to work for him rather than him having to work for money. It's easier that way, he says.

The thing is, this all sounds very easy but some of we haven't got any money to begin and so the chances of getting it to work for we, don't really come about, says I.

Knukky says, this is true, but also, there is a kind of a knack in being able to see things and then have a go at them, just like that.

So I says, well, this knack thing, I dunna seem to have got it.

Knukky, he says: 'Well, it's a bit like some people have got a sort of a turbo-charger in them.'

So I says, 'Well, how is it that I don't seem to?'

Knukky, he says, 'Well, people are mostly born with this turbo-charger gadget in them and they can turn this thing on and off, if they wants. But other people, it seems, haven't got one, or even if they have, they dunna know how to turn it on.'

So, I says, 'Do you mean to say as you are either born with it, or without it?'

Knukky he says: 'Well, yes.'

So I says, 'This is handy then, isn't it?'

Knukky he says, 'Well, yes.'

So now this is a bit of bitter news for me to get hold of this morning, when the swallows are all up in the sky and I am sat in here with this lot and thinking there they all are, with their farms and Landrovers and sheep and horses and cows and houses; and me, all I got is my wellies and jacket and pants and hat and this mug of beer.

But then I gets to thinking as maybe Trouser is a bit like me – neither of us has much of anything but then Trouser is a very contented man, it seems to me, and happy to live up with all the wind and the crows, on his own, in the boondooks.

And I has to ask myself if I am a contented man and when I thinks about it, I am forced to admit I am not. So I says this.

So Ivor he says, 'Well Burt, course some people was born with opportunities spread out already for them and all they has to do is keep on working with them and they'll be alright. Mind, there's plenty as has been gived opportunities,' says Ivor swigging his beer, 'and throws them away, and that's a big problem for them as they feels like half-wits then and that'll not help them think well of theirselves, which kind of doubles the burden. But then,' he says, 'there's them as has arrived in the world with no opportunities, but they is like the martins and swallows. They gets the purpose of their lives and sets out to fight for it. They don't let nothing get in the way of that, and if you do that, then you make the right decisions because every choice you make is made to point you toward that goal. So no matter what comes along, if you sticks to that purpose, you will get there. That's how it's done. That's the turbo-charger Knukky is on about. Purpose.

If you haven't got one you won't go nowhere. And the thing you dunna want to do is keep chopping and changing, because that won't help you, and it'll keep putting you back. If you sticks to your plan, your hopes, then opportunities will come along as will assist you as you would never have dreamed of. And then you will be able to forge ahead. It dunna mean to say it'll be a doddle. Things will get in your way. But be determined and it'll pay off. Then if bad luck comes by, you deal with it, straight, but don't change your plan because if you give bad luck a room to live in, you've got it for a long while.'

'I knows all about that one,' says George Gunter the F and Blast, 'I let bad luck into my life once and by havoc, he took some fetching out from there.'

'That's right,' says Knukky Stubbs, 'it'll try to get in, but you got to be strong enough to stick it then stop it. You gets up and goes on on your road and sweeps it aside – like The Bishop here – you ask him about not letting awkward things get you down.'

'That's right enough,' says The Bishop.

'Let me tell you a little story,' says Ivor, 'about how people is clever with opportunities and very canny and perhaps you will gather something from it as will help you to see how to make the right choices for yourself.'

Then, as Ivor is stating these things, into the bar comes none other than this big-sorted tourist creature, of about forty-five years of age, with grey hair and dark blue knee-length shorts, and red laces in his boots and big woolly socks rolled down and with a huge great ruck-sack, as is the size of a two-hundredweight bag of King Edwards. And this tourist, he has a big, puce face from the effort and sweat, it is pouring off of him like a Margam furnace stoker.

And this bloke, he dumps all this lot on the floor with an enormous crump, with these tin mugs and saucepans and all rattling about, and he says like this:

'These farmers is the dirtiest devils I ever known,' says he. 'Why, here am I, taking this long hike through England and Wales and what do I find? What do I find? In all the way I been, I have not yet found one farmer who polishes his tractors or trailers or muck carts or anything. And they leave them all scattered about their yards, parked up here there and everywhere, and jammed in the hedge and all over the fields and waggons all stuffed everywhere and all full of rubbish. And even though some of these tractors is brand new, not one farmer in the whole of Britain ever polishes or even tries to clean one of them. It is a disgrace.'

Well: what this makes everyone in there do, is to shock we into silence for a minute as this bloke is probably best left un-encouraged, or else he'll go on and on and on, whereas what everyone in there wants him to do right now, is to go off, and keep going off until he's about fifty mile away.

Then he says: 'And this place,' he says: 'outside there are about ten of the filthiest Landrovers I have ever seen, which is another thing: why do farmers never polish their Landrovers, what is the matter with them?'

And so now, Ivor the Wellies, he says: 'Well,' he says, 'I don't know about that, I never seen any farmer polish his Landrover, but some of we as is farming don't have tractors nor Landrovers, as a matter of a fact, so has no need to polish them.'

So this bloke says: 'What is it you use then?'

'Horses,' says Ivor.

'Horses?' this bloke says. 'Horses? I seen that many filthy horses and cows on my journey as I canna hardly credit it. And as for the sheep round here, they are the filthiest. There's not one clean one to be seen anywhere. Sheep should be shampooed every day before being let out so they looks nice and clean and tidy and as for the cows, well they should be shampooed every day and the horses as well. I mean, what do you think these foreign tourists are going to think coming here and seeing all these filthy animals and filthy tractors all scattered all over the place, and filthy landrovers all over the roads and everywhere you look a muddle? What does that tell you about a place?'

So now this is a bit of a thing really as we were not expecting this, and do not quite know what to say to this man.

And so Knukky, as is a steady sort of a bloke says: 'As a matter of a fact we do shampoo our sheep by and by only we calls it dipping, in these parts.'

'Well,' this bloke says: 'that's a silly name if ever I heard one, either you shampoos them or you don't. In Germany they shampoos their sheep every day and their pigs and cows and horses and if you go there, you will find all their tractors lined up in rows in their yards and all polished and shiny, like they should be. It is a disgrace it is to be in the Welsh countryside with all these filthy animals and filthy tractors, never mind the filthy farmers, as well, in their filthy yards.'

So now Ivor he says to this man as he better have a beer and calm down or else he will give hisself a large cardiacal stoppage and come and join we.

So this bloke does this and it is not long before we gets to find out as this bloke works for the Welsh Assembly, which is handy as he comes from Doncaster, and is something to do with their agricultural department, which is also handy since he's got a degree in Marine Biology, (whatever that is), canna speak Welsh, has never been to Wales, hates the countryside and farmers and is set out to try to get rid of farmers, and turn the countryside into town.

Other than that, he's not a bad fellow, in fact he is a bit of fun to have about, especially as he goes on and on and on about how filthy farmers is and says so: most particularly to Ivor the Wellies, as is sat there, steaming away, humming well, in The Castle Vaults, along with the rest of we.

Presently, Ivor says to me: 'See this bloke here? Well, he is the future.'

'Oh', I says, 'God forbid'.

Ivor he says: 'No, no,' he says, 'probably, most people will agree with what he is saying, these days.' And then he says to me: 'You know what Burt?' he says, 'if you make friends with this bloke as works in this Welsh Assembly, and goes about with him a bit, it is almost certain as within a short while you will find yourself with a Sheep Shampooing company set up and funded by the EU.

'You will also find yourself set up with a Tractor Polishing Company and Yard Tidying Company and also with a Filthy Farmer Counselling Company funded by the Welsh Assembly, as that is how things are these days. What people like these days, he says, is not real jobs. They like service jobs as has no real point. And if you are canny, this is what you should do. That's the future.'

So I gets to thinking about what Ivor says and thinks as maybe he is right. But, the thing is, I don't want to do this.

So then Ivor says, then I shall have to be content with what I've got.

But when I thinks about what I've got, which is my wellies and hat and jacket and pants, I has to think as maybe Ivor is right.

Anyway up, what happens next is that this tourist bloke, he is getting partly ratted up by now and he says as what needs to happen in Wales and here on the Borders is that money from outside needs to come in so as to make people proud of the place and tidy it up.

So Ivor says, how does he mean? So this blokes says business needs to come here, show these people how to make real money.

Ivor goes quiet for a minute, his face darkens a touch, he slants a look at this bloke and says this: 'Listen suree,' says he, 'dunna imagine as because the man you are sitting next to isna dressed up in posh clothes as he is poor, or silly, or canna handle money, no surree, dunna make that mistake.'

So this bloke says as if anyone has any money, they'd be living in a big house and skimming about in a Jag with a blonde in the seat beside him.

George Gunter the F and Blast now says: 'You are making a big mistake, my friend,' says he, 'as in fact, most of these farmers round here although they goes about looking like tramps is very, very far from it. And if you think as because they looks at you gormless as they haven't got you weighed up straight, you better think twice, mister and that's a fact, you hark my words.'

'And as for big business coming in here and upsetting the apple cart, bringing in their clocking-on and clocking-off and statutory day's work and minimum this and maximum that, things happen in a different and better way round here. Them's as is round here,' says Ivor, 'looks after the place and each other pretty well, I should say,' says Ivor, 'in fact, when someone wants a hand on their land or whatever it is, their neighbours or friends or whatever it is, goes along and, instead of working for them for money like you do, just for money, they goes along and gives them a hand and in this way they helps each other out, for a bit of help here and there, and that swings all ways. And that, mucker, is the difference between here and what you're on about. And let me tell you about real money, too. I was just saying to my friend Burt here,' says Ivor, pointing to me, 'about canniness, how it's in the blood, here's a little story about this big American outfit as comes here one day, to make this big film.

So now Ivor has a new pint of beer and has a big swig and he goes on: 'This is about big money, this one. It's about this big American outfit, from Hollywood, they comes gawping about here a year or so back saying as this countryside is the most beautifullest they seen in Britain. There's plenty of oaks here and hedges, and rocks and rivers, and fern and gorse and heather and hill and old farmhouses and cruck barns as has been here since Moses was dishing out his Proverbs.

'And these Americans, they skims about in this Cadillac,

whatever, looking for somewhere to make their film.

'Presently they see this real old farm shoved away in a bit of a dingle down the valley somewhere. So they turns down the drive and runs up to the house. They gets out the car and knocks on this huge old studded door as has been hanging there for six hundred years, probably. Above this old door is a huge great carved lintel, with a sword embossed on it, entwined with a dragon, and these Americans, they canna believe their luck.

'They looks about at the buildings in the yard and what they sees takes their breath away. There's these old stone sheds there as is the most ancient old buildings as you can imagine, with huge boulders holding them up and great big oak doors with yards long wrought iron hinges. And out in the meadows is these long-horn cattle as is a very ancient breed, indeed.

'So now no-one answers the door, except out the barn shuffles this real old specimen. And this old specimen, he's about four foot ten in heighth, all his teeth is black, he's got this filthy old mack on tied up with baler twine. He's got odd wellies on – one green, thother black, and both is more patches than they are wellies. He's got this flat hat on as is solid with age and he says hello to these people, can he help?

'So they take a look at him down their noses and says they would like to speak to the owner of this place.

'Well, he says, he'll see if he can find him. What was it they wants?

'So they say: well – and at this moment these Americans shoot looks at one another and then around at this yard and at this ancient, rambling old barrack, and what they are thinking is to lift this old place out of the hands of whoever owns it, for nothing more than a song, which they should be able to do, since it is all fell apart. What they could do is throw out whoever lives there – who could obviously do with some money – toss them out into some pokey little bungalow somewhere, with a load of empty promises to help them on their way. So they say: they are interested in discussing terms with the owner about this property.

'So now this old boy, as is called Tom Owens, says he doesn't understand what they mean.

'So these Americans, they say they want to speak to the owner directly and talk to him about it.

'So now Tom Owens tells them to come in the house. So they goes in the house and as he's making a cup of tea for them, they takes a look around. Inside it's all oak panelling and flag stone floors, and the sink is a huge great old stone trough and all the furniture is threadbare and the carpets are wore out and but, the thing is, this place reeks of age and has never had a lick of paint across it. It is an untouched, border fortified manor. So now these people wants to buy it even more.

'Tom Owens, he puts the tea on the table and sets down and they says, well where is the owner? And he says: he is.

'This throws them a touch as they canna understand why he did not say this in the first place but then they goes on and eventually says how much they'd like to buy this house and what kind of money would he reckon that this place is worth?

'So Tom Owens says as he's never thought about that.

'So they ask about the land and he says as he's got four hundred acres.

'They ask what land is fetching these days and he says, well, maybe land like this, here, is worth about £2,500–£3,000 an acre.

'So they do their sums and think things over for a minute and then ask if he lives alone.

'He says, maybe.

'They say, it must be tough.

'He says he's used to it, by now.

'They say, maybe he would like to retire.

'He says he retired twenty years ago.

'They say, he looks to them, as if he's been working.

'Well, he says, what else is he supposed to do with his time?

'So now they say as he could go and live in the Bahamas or

somewhere, and have whatever he wants, with the kind of money they could give him on this place.

'What kind of money are they talking about? he asks.

'They say maybe two, three million.

'He says, what kind of house would that buy in the Bahamas?

'They say a beach property, with fishing and tennis court and pool.

'He says he dunna care for the sea, dunna like the sun, got plenty of fish in the river here and canna play tennis.

'They say, he could have parties all the time, people to stay, barbecues.'

'He says he dunna want anyone to stay, dunna care for parties and canna think of anyone he wants to stay. And he dunna like meat all frazzled up outside.'

'Then he says he doubts any house in the Bahamas was a patch on this place, anyway.

'So he's got them and at least they got the sense to know this, that this awkward old duffer isn't going to part with this place for this kind of money – so they up the offer. Then Tom says as he owns another two farms over the hill so it would be a bit awkward selling this place because those two is tenanted out so he'd have to buy another house and what would be the point of that as he's already got this one?

'These Americans are now getting to feel a bit out-manoeuvered here but they still need to make this film and think that maybe he'll agree to that at least, and maybe they can tackle him again. So they ask him and he says yes.

'This surprises them that he agrees to making this film here so quick, but they're not going to lose this opportunity so they argy bargy about prices and before long they've got down to a bit of a figure. Tom Owens has told them that he can let them have the grass keep for £75 an acre, but it should have been a £100 only they come a good bit after Lady Day so they can have a bit off.

'So now these people are thinking that they have got one heck of a deal here as they are used to paying thousands and thousands for making films on land and here's this genuine ancient place offering them facilities over 400 acres, with period animals already on it, for £30,000 for the year.

'Tom Owens points out that grass keep money usually comes up front so soon he has a cheque for £30,000 and within the fortnight these Americans starts to ship in the film equipment.

'The film they are making has got a lot of horses in it as it is a film about knights in armour and stuff and so not only do they bring a lot of horses along but also 150 mobile stables. When Tom Owens sees this lot arriving he asks if they need any hay, which they do and a bit of hard feed, which they do, and so he sells them hay at £4 a bale – which he'd normally sell locally for £2, if he was lucky – and a dose of rolled barley at £300 a ton. Then the thing is, as there's not quite enough horses, these Americans ask him if he knows anyone with any horses and soon enough he gets hold of about thirty or forty boys from the valley with horses and charges the film company £350 a day each for these and pay the lads £200 each, which suits them fine.

'So now the filming starts and they begin in this old courtyard and this means that the Dutch barn as Tom bunged up in the 1950s has to come down because it's in the way. So these American agree to taking this down as long as they put up another in its place after. So they do this. They also need to film inside the house and because the house is a tip, it need to be sorted and painted and Tom only agrees to this if they leave all the new film furniture there after they have finished. So they agree to this.

'So after a week or so they are filming out on the land and as they are doing some extra difficult bit, this little MF 135 creeps along straight into camera shot and who should be driving it but Tom Owens. So they shouts at him as he is in shot and that he has mucked things up.

'But he says, there's a hitch.

'So they ask what this hitch is.

'He says that grass keep means grass keep. It does not mean eight-wheel waggons scorting about cutting it up, and it does not mean sticking up 150 portable stables.

'So they say, what did he want?

'Tom, he says £1,000 would fix it.

'So they give him a £1,000 in cash and off he goes on his tractor.

'Next day, they are filming again when along comes this tractor, again, straight into shot at more or less the same time.

'Now what is it?' they say. 'Well,' he says, 'they're doing it again.'

'Doing what again?' they ask. 'Driving around the field with eight-wheel waggons and these portable stables are still there.'

'We gave you a thousand pounds yesterday!' they screams. 'Ah yes,' says Tom, 'but that was yesterday.'

'So now they have to sit down with him to do a new contract and this contract is very, very weighty. So they have to think this one out and what they realise is this: that they are so far into filming now and are so committed to this landscape that they can't quit. To go somewhere else would be even more expensive. So they are forced to agree to Tom's terms and Tom's terms do not come cheap. They also include more boys from the valley helping with carpentry and all the girls involved as film extras, all of whom Tom now controls, since they agree to pay him £160 per extra per day and he pays the girls and boys £100 a day, which they are happy with.

'The use of the land has now shot up to £2,600 a day, plus the grasskeep and with all the extras and the horses and everything else Tom is now pulling a little over £8,750 a day. And then it rains.

'The film crew is forced to stay there, with all the horses and most of the extras, and meanwhile Tom has got a few neighbouring farmers in to drag some of these eight-wheelers out of the mud at a charge of £150 a pull and some of these blokes are beginning to claw in a few hundred pounds a day on their tractors, which is quite good, when you consider they wouldn't have been doing a lot otherwise.

'Eventually they gets back to filming and after about fifteen more days, its all done.

'Then these Americans pulls out and Tom is left with a new barn, freshly painted house, with part of the contract being that all the ground they used will be ploughed and reseeded so he gets The Bishop to do that – and Tom's quietly pocketed near on a quarter of a million, had all his grass keep paid for for a year, got jobs for everyone in the valley and he goes back to shovelling muck out the calf pens. Oh, and by the way, Tom Owens is eighty-three years old.

'As these Americans are leaving, they are beginning to look pretty sick with this business as it has cost way over what they reckoned and by now their opinion of Tom is that he is one very, very crafty old wuzzuk and what they'd really like to do is blow up his farm and house with him in it, but then before they get the chance to do this, he drops the bombshell first.

'Just as they are leaving, they say to him they hope he is satisfied with what he got and this nearly chokes them to say it, so old Tom he says, well, it wanna bad, but it wanna as good as the last lot.

'The last lot? they gasps. What last lot?

'The lot as come to make a film last year,' he says, 'as is due to come out in two weeks' time.'

'On top of his farm earnings and a bit of subsidy,' Ivor finishes off saying: 'Tom Owens clears a little over £2,500 an acre on his patch, over a couple of years, which is pretty good when you consider most people reckon £100 an acre is not bad – plus all the other bits. Oh, and I forgot to say that he ate from the film canteen every day too, which he enjoyed. In fact, he enjoyed it so much, if you ask him about the whole deal he'll tell you he saved quite a bit on shopping money. He liked their treacle tart best and having all them pretty girls fussing over him. Oh, and he even got a job as an extra one day hisself and they had to be pay him £160 for that, as well. I got a job too, and Knukky. It was good.'

Then Ivor goes on as he's got the wind under his tail now: 'And I tell you something, there's one or two in this valley as is jealous of old Tom Owens, and others as think he's an old crook, but look, the thing is, them Americans were out to crook him first: they were willing to kick an old man out just to have this place for theirselves and what is that if it is not crooked? What Tom did was pay them in their own coin. And even if there are those in the valley as is jealous, there's a lot more as think he's great because he brung a lot of money to this valley and shared it out as best he could.

'And so,' says Ivor turning to the tourist Welsh Assembly bloke: 'dunna think as because we lives out here that even the oldest of we aren't as sharp as razors, when it comes to money. These people haven't held onto their land because they're dull. And if you wants to bring business in here by all means do so. But be warned: if they thinks they can come in here and take over they'll all be sent packing with their tails between their legs, so they will, you hark my words. When push comes to shove we sticks together. We'll help them as wants to help we, but God help them who only wants to help themselves at a cost to anyone in these valleys.'

So this bloke he says: 'I understand what you say, and me, I know I am a learner but things are changing and there are new pressures on farming and you farmers have to go with them or else you will be fighting a losing battle.'

'Fair enough,' says Knukky. 'What you need is someone to come between you and the farmer because if you goes on to farms telling them to polish their tractors and wash their Landrovers and stick things in rows like the Germans, we shall be in for major complications, believe me.'

'All right,' says this bloke: 'that's true. We need someone to be a kind of go-between – two or three even – that really knows their way about, knows the landscape, knows the country people and what makes them tick, that's what we need. A man – or a woman – or even a group – that can put the town and country together and make a way forward.'

And Ivor the Wellies, he gives me a long, long look and leans forward, taps my knee and says to me:

'Burt,' he says, 'You better not be thinking of migrating just yet, it's your round.'